KING PENGUIN

THE MYSTERIES OF

Robert Irwin has taught Arabic and Middle Eastern history at the universities of Oxford, Cambridge, and London. He is the author of two novels (both in Viking and Penguin), *The Limits of Vision* and *The Arabian Nightmare*, as well as numerous specialized studies of Middle Eastern politics, art, and mysticism. He lives with his family in London.

ROBERT IRWIN

THE MYSTERIES
OF ALGIERS

KING PENGUIN
PUBLISHED BY PENGUIN BOOKS

PENGUIN BOOKS
Published by the Penguin Group
Viking Penguin, a division of Penguin Books USA Inc.,
40 West 23rd Street, New York, New York 10010 U.S.A.
Penguin Books Ltd, 27 Wrights Lane,
London W8 5TZ, England
Penguin Books Australia Ltd, Ringwood,
Victoria, Australia
Penguin Books Canada Ltd, 2801 John Street,
Markham, Ontario, Canada L3R 1B4
Penguin Books (N.Z.) Ltd, 182–190 Wairau Road,
Auckland 10, New Zealand

Penguin Books Ltd, Registered Offices:
Harmondsworth, Middlesex, England

First published in Great Britain by
Penguin Books Ltd 1988
First published in the United States of America by
Viking Penguin, a division of Penguin USA Inc. 1988
Published in Penguin Books 1989

1 3 5 7 9 10 8 6 4 2

The passage quoted on p. 5 is from Albert Camus, *The Rebel*, translated by Antony
Bower (Penguin Books, Harmondsworth, 1971) and that quoted on p. 11 is from
Albert Camus, *Selected Essays and Notebooks*, translated by Philip Thody (Penguin
Books, Harmondsworth, 1970).

LIBRARY OF CONGRESS CATALOGING IN PUBLICATION DATA
Irwin, Robert, 1946–
The Mysteries of Algiers/Robert Irwin.
p. cm.
ISBN 0 14 01.2767 4
[PR6059.R96M9 1989]
823 '.914—dc20 89–32773

Printed in the United States of America
Set in Linotron 202 Bembo

Chapter One

Necessary and inexcusable, that is how murder appeared to them. Mediocre minds, confronted by this terrible problem, can take refuge by ignoring one or other of the terms of the dilemma. They are content, in the name of formal principles, to find all direct violence inexcusable and then to sanction that diffuse form of violence which takes place on the scale of world history . . .

Mercier was pretending to read Camus. He found the pretence very hard and, every now and again, it was forgotten and he found himself engaged with the actual text. An essay could be written about pretending to read serious books. Perhaps Camus should write it? Perhaps Mercier should write to Camus about it?

A man who thinks that he is going to Fort Tiberias will find it difficult to concentrate on such stuff. Mercier had arrived off the plane from Paris on Friday at midday. He had stood blinking on the overheating tarmac and marvelled at the sharpness of everything – the air-control tower hacked out in hard-edged white against the brilliant blue sky, the stunning yellow hills in the distance and the fierce profiles of the Arab porters. Then a young woman had emerged from the shadows of baggage control and hustled him through it. He had hardly had time to assure himself that she was his appointed contact from the Section de la Documentation Extérieure et du

Contre-éspionnage before she had hurried him into the car and set off, driving at top speed towards the city. Since she was both pretty and intelligent-looking, Mercier had tried to engage her in conversation. It did not go well.

'Since Indochina I have mostly worked on diplomatic security. This sort of work is all going to be strange to me and this will be my first assignment in Algeria.'

'I know, but you were specifically asked for.'

Since she seemed disposed to say nothing more, he tried again.

'I have often thought that an educated man's first impressions of a place are likely to be filtered and shaped by what he has read. For instance, as I look through the window now I am not sure whether I am looking at the real road into Algiers, or Gide's road to Algiers.'

'That sucker of African cocks!'

She laughed. It really ought to have been an ugly laugh, but Mercier had to admit that it was not. She gave Mercier a swift glance.

'I should not take Gide as a guide to our country. Let me warn you, if you are that way inclined, it is better to go to Tangiers. Here, it has been known for the FLN to use the Arab boys as decoys, and you are liable to end up smiling the Kabyle smile. Besides, I bet you don't find that in Gide . . .'

The car had had to move out into the middle of the road to avoid a column of Arabs with their hands on their heads who were being shepherded by steel-helmeted troops on to an army lorry.

'But if you have never read Gide – '

'Let me concentrate on my driving.'

Mercier was reduced to studying the car's documentation, and from this at least he learned that his driver's name was Chantal de Serkissian. She put him off at the SDECE building in the rue de Sarras. She was about to drive off, but he clung to the car door.

'Mademoiselle, I assure you, I am not "that way inclined". Will you have dinner with me tomorrow night? Perhaps, since you know the town, you could suggest the place?'

She refused but countered with an invitation to a beach party the following day. Then he went in to see his briefing officer.

Castiglione was forty-six kilometres outside Algiers and Mercier had had to hire a car to get himself there. The beach was covered with lean brown bodies like a fauvist design for a ballet and he had found her only with difficulty. There was no opportunity for serious conversation. He had been roped into a game of football with the young men, while the girls watched and sang songs, disposed upon the beach like so many sirens. A lifeguard and two paras with sub-machine-guns watched over it all. Languid girls and muscle-flexing young men, they were all posing and telling lies with their bodies. Mercier, pale and grey, felt uncomfortable, open to their examination. In the evening, they wandered about as a gang on the boulevard. There wasn't much to see, just the Monument aux Morts and the aquarium. Outside the aquarium there was a poster advertising the forthcoming screening of Cocteau's *Orphée* at the Bardo cinema in Algiers.

'I must see that film again. Maria Casarès is a friend of mine. I have only met Cocteau once but – '

Chantal leant wearily against the wall of the aquarium.

'Another bumboy. Cocteau's attempt to raise trick photography to an art form has been applauded by all those who . . . who . . . Oh damn! I have forgotten how the rest goes.'

Chantal was reciting with her eyes shut.

'That is a quotation?' Mercier had asked.

'Not one of your Paris intellectuals. Captain Roussel said it, but I can't remember the rest of what he said.'

'This is Captain Roussel of the Fifth Compagnie Portée de la Légion?'

'Yes, him.'

'But I know him. He is one of the few people out here that I was hoping to get in touch with.'

Philippe and Mercier had worked on the survey of the Plain of Jars, been involved in counter-insurgency operations in the

Bay of Tonkin area and had fought together at Dien Bien Phu, actually shoulder to shoulder. But they had parted company after Indochina when Mercier had been seconded out to the SDECE in Paris.

Chantal opened her eyes. She was all animation and surprise.

'What a chance! We know Captain Roussel too! Daddy is giving a big dinner party tomorrow – a formal dress affair. Philippe will be there. Why don't you come too? I love hearing veterans going over their wars.'

Yet it seemed to Mercier that there was something studied in her animation, and something plotted and predatory, too, in the way in which she now took his arm.

It is one of the problems of working in intelligence that one's work gives one little to talk about at dinner parties. The dinner had been disappointing from Mercier's point of view. Philippe had embraced him on arrival, but was stiffer and more reserved than Mercier remembered. They didn't refight the Indochina campaign that evening, for there had been another guest at table, a sharp young Algiers lawyer, at least ten years their junior, Raoul somebody. Raoul and Philippe had locked horns over the conduct of the present war – or containment operation as Philippe pompously called it. In the course of the evening, Philippe had given ground and was driven to rely on claims that he was only a simple soldier who obeyed orders. But if Raoul ran rings round Philippe, it still seemed to Mercier that Raoul was the prisoner of his own cleverness.

Mercier enjoyed intellectual debate, but this just seemed like two men playing chicken and trying to force each other to the outside edge of the pavement. Come to that why didn't the soldier and the right-wing lawyer just clear a space on the table and arm wrestle? In Indochina the soldiers used to make it more exciting by holding upturned knives behind the clenched hands, so that the loser's hand would slowly but surely be impaled. Surely Chantal was bright enough to have become a little bored with the garrison population of Algiers and what passed for its intelligentsia?

Chantal went over to sit beside her father and demurely rested her head on his shoulder while he praised his daughter's shooting to the other guests. But after he had retired early to bed, she produced an exotically carved cigarette holder. The dress she was wearing – an extraordinary Schiaparelli creation, low cut and of pink silk – and the way she brandished her cigarettes, made Mercier think of an adventuress. He told her this and she looked pleased. The row between Philippe and Raoul thundered on. Mercier mocked their swagger and their uncompromisingness. He had told Chantal that beneath the formalities of political debate, what they were actually engaged in was a competitive demonstration of brute male strength – a not very subtle way of impressing women, using their inflexible logic as a method of social oppression. He had gone on to quote something from de Beauvoir's *La Deuxième Sexe* at her.

Chantal had looked impatient and tossed her head.

'Who on earth is oppressing me? But all this political talk is boring me.' She clapped her hands and an attendant came running up. 'Boy! I am going for a swim. Get me my swimming things and have Hamid put the pool lights on.'

Chantal strode off towards the changing cabins, and a little later some of the younger guests followed her into the pool. She took pity on him only as he was leaving.

'I'm sorry if I seemed rude, but it was so hot and I wanted to swim. I'm sorry about this evening, but, as you will swiftly discover, things are not what they seem. I don't know if Philippe has told you, but the office will tell you tomorrow. He's fixed it for you to do a short assignment in Algiers and then for you to come and join him at Fort Tiberias. I have work down there too. Perhaps down there, next week, we can talk about books and things . . .' she tailed off vaguely.

So now he was on Philippe's little assignment, pretending to read Camus, actually shadowing al-Hadi. There were plenty of distractions in the café – a pair of youths noisily exulting over their triumphs at the pinball machine, a repulsive small boy crawling under the tables pretending to be a dog, and a very pretty girl sitting directly opposite him. And there was the clack of dominoes, and the radio blaring out. There had just been a five-minute blast of martial music. Doubtless they were being prepared for another important announcement from Metropolitan France, from General 'Manifest Destiny' himself. The view from the windows was of the harbour and of the corniche road towards the casino. Thick brown clouds had been rolling in over the sea since midday and it was very sultry. Mercier's shirt clung to him like a wet facecloth and he felt the pressure in his head spreading to the muscles at the back of his neck. Every few minutes or so he found himself infuriated with all these distractions and equally frequently he had to pull himself up and remind himself that he was not supposed to be reading the book anyway. He wished that he had brought a less interesting book along with him. Between Camus's arguments and the diversions of the café, he was constantly distracted from his real business.

Al-Hadi sat at the bar. A brown-paper parcel was parked at the foot of the stool. Al-Hadi had been in the café for almost half an hour now, but as far as Mercier could see, he had made no contact with anyone. Unless perhaps it was the barman who supplied him with Pernod. He had not expected that al-Hadi would turn out to be a drunk. Even if he proved after all not to be a runner for the FLN, it was still the case that al-Hadi was not a city Arab, but a Sahrawi and few of the Sahrawis had a developed taste for alcohol.

But perhaps al-Hadi was only pretending to get drunk, just as Mercier was pretending to read Camus and the small boy was pretending to be a dog? And perhaps also the noisy bluster of the two youths at the pinball was designed to conceal their homosexuality? And the barman a police informer? And the pretty girl a transvestite prostitute? For sure, this bar and every bar and every place on earth was full of people pretending to be what they were not. Drunks pretending to be sober, introverts pretending to be extroverts, *petits bourgeois* pretending to be upper class, unhappily married women pretending to be happily married. Algiers, specifically, was a city of frightened people pretending not to be frightened. Disguises and pretence, then, were hardly what distinguished agents from other people. What was extraordinary about Mercier's trade was that he was supposed to tell lies in order to discover the truth. Why should we all spend our lives telling lies? Mercier was very depressed.

Al-Hadi was believed to carry information from Fort Tiberias to the FLN command cell in Algiers. Whenever Mercier thought of his forthcoming assignment to Fort Tiberias, a heavy ball of sick fear began to gather in his stomach. Mercier knew what danger was. The difference between him and Philippe was that Mercier thought about what he was doing, and that he did not think that the end of winning the war in Algeria justified the use of any and every means, no matter how foul. Algeria should be policed with honour and compassion. If, and only if, it could not be held thus, then it should be relinquished. Fort Tiberias's reputation as an interrogation centre was exceeded only by that of the Zeralda Barracks outside Algiers (and this itself may have been because fewer of those questioned at Fort Tiberias survived to complain about their experiences).

The small boy under the table, pretending to be a dog, had fixed his teeth into Mercier's trousers. Mercier shook him off impatiently. What was honour? The Arabs regarded their women as the vessels of their honour. Reputation among women, that was the only thing that counted among the men. Secret vessels of honour, the folds of their white gondourahs clenched between their teeth, gold ornaments clinking with every step, the women who walked on their roofs by night and called to one another across the narrow streets. He tried to imagine Chantal or the girl sitting opposite him resigning themselves to becoming shrouded vessels of honour. The hoarse mocking laughter, the shrill ululations of triumph . . . No, it was impossible. Then in an effort not to think about Chantal, he looked down at his book.

It is a well-known fact that we always recognize our homeland when we are about to lose it. Those whose

self-torments are too great are those whom their homeland rejects. I have no desire to be brutal . . .

This time a sports car pulling up outside the café pulled him
away from his book. A young man and his girl got out and,
with their beach robes draped negligently over their shoulders, entered the bar. Yacht club people. It was a timely dis-
traction, for as his eyes followed them to the counter, Mercier
realized that while he had been reading and alternately brooding, a row had broken out between al-Hadi and the proprietor.
Al-Hadi was shouting in Arabic. The proprietor obviously
had no idea at all what it meant. Neither did Mercier. Then
al-Hadi was showering money on the counter, many coins
and quite a few notes – more than the price of a few drinks.
Al-Hadi appeared to lose patience and, stooping low to
retrieve the brown-paper parcel from the floor, he thrust it
into the baffled proprietor's arms. Then he gathered his long
white robes around him like an affronted woman and flounced
out of the café.

There was no need for Mercier to follow. There would be
another tail waiting round the corner, waiting to see where
al-Hadi's trail led them next. Mercier waited for a couple of
minutes. Then he put the book down, apologized to the pretty
girl for moving the table out a little, and started towards the
proprietor. The flash was so brilliant, he could not see the
proprietor. His feet were somewhere not on the floor. Something seemed to be flooding his ears. He closed his eyes to
think more clearly. When he opened them again, he saw without surprise that he was covered in blood and dust was drifting
down to settle on the blood. He wondered if the blood was
his. Probably not, he thought, that girl beside me has lost
both her legs. It's probably her blood. He closed his eyes again
and waited for the sirens.

Chapter Two

This was the third rock 'n' roll session. Al-Hadi was stripped and bound with leather straps to the wooden plank, which we had tipped at an angle of 45 degrees. As for the two leads of the field telephone, one went up his nostril and the other we had fixed to the tip of his penis with Scotch tape. Crocodile clips would have been better, but we didn't have any. The current surged up again, and al-Hadi rocked and rolled. The eyes dilated and bulged as if the skull was going to spit his eyeballs out at us. We took the current back down, and I ran over my notes. Mercier's last moments must have been pretty much as I had them reconstructed on my clipboard, though there is no certainty in such things. A story created under close questioning, and in which pain has been used, not mindlessly, but as a technique for investigating the truth – it will achieve results, but they are not necessarily entirely reliable.

Anyway, we are not especially interested in Mercier's last moments. According to Colonel Joinville, the first thing we want from al-Hadi is what or who was his source of information here, deep in the Sahara, information so valuable that the FLN command cell in Algiers needed and could risk al-Hadi's irregular but frequent runs to the coast. Second, who could have tipped him off that there was a tail on him that day? Third, how did al-Hadi know that the middle man in the chain of shadows was not some low-grade trainee or gendarme in plain clothes, but Mercier, the man who had been due to take over security here? Mercier was in on the shadowing operation only to familiarize himself with al-Hadi's appearance. Half an hour or an hour on the job – that should have been all, but within half an hour of sighting al-Hadi he was dead.

The lieutenant and I are both shivering. This is not a pleasant working environment. The solitary light bulb is protected by a wire grille and its tight meshwork casts odd shadows over the buckets of water and other stuff on the floor. Packing cases are piled high against three of the walls. I have to share this room with the ordnance section. The lieutenant rarely looks at the prisoner or at the mess around us. Instead his gaze drifts upwards to a point on the wall above al-Hadi's head where Brigitte Bardot and Suzy Delair flash their saucy bottoms at us. Such pin-ups are Scotch-taped all over the fort – in the lockers, on the jeeps, even on some of the guns. I remember, in Indochina, thinking how odd it was that the Viet Minh had no pin-ups. Men and women, their partisans fought shoulder to shoulder – and I guess now that the fellagha hiding up in the mountains, hundreds of miles to the north of Fort Tiberias, have no pin-ups either. It is not the torture but the pin-ups that signify that the Legion is going to lose this war too.

But now another puzzle for Joinville – if al-Hadi knew he was going to be tailed, what suicidal impulse made him bring a bomb out with him on his ramble through the streets of Algiers? He must have known that he would be picked up afterwards – as indeed he was, ten minutes later, after a short chase. There had been five dead in the bar and twelve wounded. Also two gendarmes had to be hospitalized after injuries sustained protecting al-Hadi from the *pied-noir* mob which swiftly gathered around the arrest.

Al-Hadi looks at me. It is such a look! I can imagine the lieutenant thinking to himself, 'This is the look of complicity that passes between the torturer and the tortured. There is a bond here.' Perhaps there is such a bond. Al-Hadi understands why I must torture him and I already know why al-Hadi had to kill Mercier.

'Do not think that I do not know what you are going through,' I tell our prisoner. 'I am a man like you and I can tell you. As the current begins to ease up there will be an unpleasant tingling, bearable at first, but soon you will be out of control. You will be grateful for the gag, but I am afraid there is nothing we can do to prevent you damaging your wrists still further on the leather straps. You don't even know what damage you are doing to your body as one electric explosion after another fills your head. And, when the gag comes out . . . in the end, you must say exactly what I want you to say. As you can see, I am not in any hurry. So now, we come to your marriage. This woman of yours, this Zora, how often does she come to your bed? Or do you go to hers? Is she circumcised? Does she shave down there? Do you kiss? You know, I have never seen an Arab kiss his woman. If we bring her in, will we have a good time? What do you think, if we bring her in, will we have a good time? You are going to tell us everything. Nothing will be left to our imagination. In any case, as you can see, Schwab has no imagination.'

The interrogation was going slowly. I was deliberately taking it slowly. Schwab, the lieutenant standing beside me, was looking increasingly restive and sulky. I have explained to him that the nature of the Arab mentality is such that if we can get al-Hadi to talk about his wife and his private life, if we can break into the filthy harem of his mind, and get him to talk about it, then he will talk about anything. He will indeed be a broken man.

To Joinville, the commanding officer at Fort Tiberias, I should rather put it that I was engaged in a rare form of person to person anthropology. But I doubt if I shall have to justify the slowness of my procedures to Colonel Joinville. As far as our colonel is concerned, it is not the results achieved by torture that are valuable, but rather the torture itself. Torture is precisely the forcing engine for bringing the benighted races of the world to civilization, part of the melancholy passage from childhood to maturity for the happy-go-lucky blacks and feckless Arabs.

'Pain,' Joinville says, 'is not a penalty. It is part of civilization – indeed it is at its heart. The European peoples have had to suffer in order to attain to reason and obedience. Now it is time for the others to follow in our footsteps. Civilization is not a fun palace. It is indeed a miserable affair. Yet they have asked for it and we must respond to their request.'

Though the colonel is much admired by the men who serve under him, he is not exactly popular. For one thing he, like me, believes that the French are going to lose this war. An officers' briefing rarely goes by without him pointing out that there must be a certain nobility in the defence of a cause that is lost.

'We have enrolled in the ranks of Hector while the FLN have taken the side of Achilles. It would take a subtle man to determine who has chosen the better part.'

And again, while Joinville's ruthlessness is admired, it takes many peculiar forms.

'We burn their douars, we rape their women, we confiscate their crops, we carry out the necessary exemplary executions and we round up those who are left into what I can only call concentration camps. These wretches suffer for us. God has chosen the Algerian Arab to suffer for the sins of France, but God must hate the French very much to let our Algerians suffer so . . .'

In any event, it is clear that Joinville would sympathize with my stated intention to break into this man's head. But I have a different story for everyone.

I had been thinking that Schwab didn't like the business with the Scotch tape – that he was one of those that didn't like touching Arabs. Then it occurs to me that he may have compunctions about 'deep questioning', and that this series of interrogations may be his first. Such virgins are increasingly rare these days.

'Pissed off, lieutenant?'

'You can say that again.'

I steeled myself to give the standard pep talk.

'Not all army work is pleasant. Very little of it is. Come on – you saw the pictures. That girl will be a freak on two stumps for the rest of her life. Have you heard one word of regret for that from this creature? I've seen it before. When the ambulances come the Arabs cheer and their children pelt the stretchers with stones and the women stand on the roofs making their damn *youyou* noises. You cannot stand back and do nothing. That is not on offer. If you are alive today and still alive in two years' time when your service is up, it will be because somewhere – somewhere and sometime – I don't know when – one of our men has submitted one of theirs to deep questioning and he has discovered the cache of landmines, one of which would otherwise have blown up you and your jeep. Face it. You can't ride on the backs of your fellow officers with a fine liberal conscience. Your life here is not a gift. It has to be worked for.'

He looks obstinate.

'I do not like your way of torture.'

'This is not torture. Well of course it is, in a loose sense. There is no point in mincing words in the Legion. It is torture in the sense that pain is applied to extract precise points of information. But it is not torture in the sense that the communists practise it. They use horrible methods to break a man's spirit, to make him into a zombie who will renounce anything, denounce anything. But here we respect a man's physical and moral integrity. Am I right, lieutenant?'

He looks doubtful. And I am about to try my 'I would not ask any of my prisoners to undergo anything that I have not myself undergone' line. In my case it is more or less true. After the fall of Dien Bien Phu, I spent ten grim weeks in a special detention camp outside Lang Trang. But he breaks in –

'All right, it is probably necessary to put a little extra pressure on this man, but it is a dirty business. Could we not get it over with, in his interests and ours? Could we not go a little faster?'

'Faster?'

'You keep going over the shitty business over and over again. The bomb factory, the Bar des Ottomans, and so on, and now all this stuff about his childhood and his family, and his work, and who were his neighbours ten years ago and

17

such shit and more detailed shit. It makes my flesh creep to watch him screaming, while you try to piece together his earliest memories of childhood – as it were.'

'Know the mind of the enemy, lieutenant. Know the mind of the enemy – not just what is in it, but how what is in it got there in the first place, and what the enemy will do with what it is that is in his mind. We must know the mind of the enemy better than the enemy knows it himself. It is the only way that we can win this war.'

'Well, I can accept that I suppose – '

'You'd better!'

' – but we seem so close to a breakthrough on what we really want to know. But then you bring the current down again, and start the questioning and then when you've got him confused and he's about to make a slip, then it's back on with the current. With respect I am fucked off with it all.'

'Lieutenant, you are new to interrogation technique, aren't you?'

He nods stiffly.

'That is all right with me. I've been working with these techniques since '55. Lesson 1: If you are going to use the magneto, there is no point in shooting up to top voltage from the start and keeping it there. While the voltage is on the poor guy just tries to swallow the gag, and when the switch is off he is too dazed senseless to speak. No, you work through gradations of pressure and fear. It is a matter of finesse. Finesse.'

During all this our voices have got lower and lower, conscious of al-Hadi's baleful eyes trained on our dispute. Disturbed, I turn away from the lieutenant and put my hand on the field telephone. Al-Hadi cries out, 'If you put me through that again, I'll tell all.'

'That is what we want, isn't it, lieutenant?'

My eyes are back on the lieutenant now. He doesn't like me. He does not respect me even. Well, I am used to it. Al-Hadi has switched to Arabic and is jabbering away. The lieutenant seems to understand no Arabic. The voltage is pushed up a little way and then stops, for the corporal has poked his head around the door. He is careful not to see our detainee.

'Captain, there is a lady . . .'

'A woman, corporal. A woman. We don't interrogate ladies.'

'No, I mean . . . to see you. She insists that she has a right to be down here. She has a pass, but it's not a military one and I told her that she – '

'I assure you, captain, I am all woman.'

'Lieutenant, get Mademoiselle de Serkissian out of here.'

Schwab is already at the foot of the stair, blocking her way. Chantal waves her SDECE pass and tries to peer over Schwab's shoulder to see what is going on.

Al-Hadi switches back to French.

'Help! Madame, help me! Tell them what you see down here. They are killing me . . . Tell the newspapers.'

I lean over the prisoner and suggest that he shouts a little louder. Chantal has no ears for the prisoner. She has been engaged in a polite struggle with my lieutenant, trying to push past him, but it is not possible to sustain a polite struggle for any length of time. They smile sheepishly at one another and Chantal allows herself to be conducted upstairs. If I leave them alone for long enough she will be suggesting that Schwab should look in on her some evening to see her stamp collection. Poor fool, the proposal will not mean what he will think it means. I am not in fact displeased at this new interruption of our interrogation and I absently pat al-Hadi on the head.

'Take a rest. I'm impressed.'

Then I go upstairs to simulate the displeasure I do not feel. She and Schwab are talking animatedly in the corridor. The stamp collection for sure. Telling Schwab to take a break, I take Chantal by the arm and steer her outside.

'This is my investigation and it stays that way.'

Out in the sunlight of the parade ground she puts on her broad brimmed floppy hat and sunglasses. She looks like a masked cavalier.

'Your interrogation procedures,' she sighs. 'They are all so sordid.'

'Sordid is how you see it. The enemy doesn't think that torture is sordid. "The fires of torture lit by our imperialist oppressors are the fires that purify our revolution." '

'Shit on their purified revolution. It's sordid.'

'Oh well, interrogation's not my job usually. I'm only in on this one because it was Mercier who got killed.'

'Oh, I know, but all that translation and filing, that's so dreary too!' Her lip curls in mock petulance. 'Anyway, Mercier was my friend too . . . even if I didn't like him very much.'

'Your message?'

'Message . . .? Oh yes, the message! The security review meeting has been brought forward a week, so it's the day after tomorrow and it will take place here, not at Laghouat. There will be several unscheduled guests sitting in and a new item on the agenda.' She fishes in her handbag and produces a brown envelope. 'It's all in here, except that while you will probably recognize our military guest, the civilians – there are three of them – will only reveal their true identities in the meeting. Anyway, the colonel expects you to sort out clearances and find accommodation for these three pseudonymous gentlemen.'

'We are holding the meeting in the fort for reasons of unusual security, right?'

'Yes.'

'What about item one on the agenda?'

'It's item two now. First we have to listen to whatever the paras and these civilian gents may have for us.'

'But, Chantal, item two raises the possibility of a high-ranking traitor within Fort Tiberias itself! That's not going to impress our security-conscious guests. And it is even possible that the traitor, if there is one, may be sitting in on the discussion of item one, whatever it may be.'

She smiles uncertainly, then shrugs. Chantal, like me, works on intelligence records, but her main area of responsibility is tracking deserters. When harkis go on the run, these Muslim troops tend to take themselves and their weapons straight to the nearest FLN battalion. Of course, it is Military

Intelligence's job to work out which FLN group, if any, the deserting harkis have gone over to. When I take men out on operations in the Jebel and if we are lucky enough to flush out any of the fellagha, then most of them get killed in the fighting. Even those who are taken alive have a way of dying an hour or two later. However someone is always detailed to cut off the heads of our 'bag' and, somehow or other, these heads are got back to base. It is Chantal's job to compare these heads with photographs of enlisted men in army records.

Down in the cellar once more, Schwab hands me my roster of questions. It is a matter of the slow unfolding of revelations. It may be that tomorrow or the day after we shall have the truth. But today and for the moment all I am looking for is a convenient lie.

Chapter Three

What is she doing? Her dress is off. I have unzipped it for her, but Chantal is taking her time. She said that she was just going to remove her ear-rings. There are muffled thumps and bangs in the other room. Then the door swings open and my doubts are answered.

'Hands on your head, Philippe.'

My gun is in her hands. I know it is loaded. I do as she suggests.

'Stand right where you are.' And she sidles round me to reach the bed.

'You can turn round now – but slowly, with your hands on your head.'

She has settled herself back comfortably against the pillows. Though she still holds the gun with both hands, it shakes a little. The gun is a Tokarev T33, a Russian pistol, heavier than the MAS 35s carried by my fellow officers, but in most respects a superior weapon. I bought it from a sailor on my way out of Indochina.

'I've been doing some thinking, Philippe. No, you don't have to talk. I have been looking at your books through there.'

(I don't have many books. I don't believe in them and I don't read for pleasure. I have never owned more than a dozen books in my life. What I have out there are three dictionaries (French, Arabic and Vietnamese), Marx's *Capital*, and *Economical and Philosophical Manuscripts*, *The Thoughts of Chairman*

Mao, Ho Chi Minh's *Selected Works* and Fanon's *Black Skin, White Masks* – oh yes and Peltier's *Psychology of Persuasion*.)

'You are the logical traitor. I mean, logically you must be the traitor in our midst. All this "know the mind of the enemy" routine is a bluff. You are the enemy within.' Chantal is flushed and triumphant. 'And I have been going over your dossier. There are far too many bungles and missed catches in it. You are my man. Now bring your hands down slowly and get your trousers off, but slowly.'

Again I do as she suggests.

'What are you going to do with me?'

'Now your jacket off. Slowly.'

I seem to have some trouble getting the jacket off, but now as my arms are at last free of the sleeves, I hurl it over Chantal's head and leap after it on to the bed. I am over her and trying to get the gun. Rather than surrender it to me, she drops it over on to the floor. There is a wild scrabble as we both tumble after it. I outreach her. Chantal is breathless and giggling, but she sobers up when she sees that I have the gun. I am pretty fierce now that I have it. All the time we make love, I hold it pointed to her skull. It is a strain on the arms but worth it.

'That was great. We must try that one again.'

'It probably wouldn't work a second time.'

A lake of sweat and other fluids has formed on the sagging mattress and Chantal and I lie close together in it like the well-greased parts of a weapon in machine oil.

'I knew you kept your gun in one of the drawers – and I remembered what some thriller writer I read once said: "When in doubt what to do next, have someone with a gun in his hand come through the door." '

Chantal is by no means wholly committed to me. She likes to flirt and play around a lot. We have only been to bed about half a dozen times. She probably wouldn't have given me a chance first time round, if on the occasion of our first meeting I had not asked her what her favourite flower was. It was the white gardenia. Then, when she came round to see me, she found the bedroom door open, and the entire bed covered in

23

white gardenias. We made awkward love, rolling over and over on their crushed stalks. The second time it was her surprise. She brought a stock whip which she had borrowed from one of her farm managers. Afterwards the ceiling was covered with fleck marks which were hard to explain to visitors, and neither of us went swimming for a week. That was all in Algiers. Now that she had joined me at Fort Tiberias, she has talked about forming a 'humping club'.

I have lumberingly explained that this sector of the Sahara is not as free from watchful eyes as it looks. There are Piper Cub spotter planes all day long cruising around, looking for FLN infiltrators from Tunisia trying to come in south of the Morice Line. And there are the harkis, the bedu, and maybe a few successful ALN infiltrators. Doing it privately on the back of a camel was not going to be easy . . .

'Oh, forget it. My little joke.'

This is the first time she has come to my room in the fort. We have kept our liaison pretty quiet, for Chantal estimates that we shall have more weight on the security committee if no one realizes that we are involved with one another. It is better if we are perceived to be two independent voices in its deliberations.

I am indeed surprised that she agreed to this afternoon's assignation, for she has already begun to flirt with other officers at Fort Tiberias, and in the committee meetings we do indeed speak with two independent voices now. In these meetings she is sounding increasingly critical of my plodding methods and poor results. Too many files, too much plod and no one could understand how the files were organized apart from me.

We lie quiet for a while in bed watching the great fan slowly turning on the ceiling and drinking Martini from the bottle. Then Chantal begins to talk about item one – now item two – on tomorrow's agenda (neither she nor the colonel would say anything at all about the new item one). I lie back and contemplate Chantal talking and speculating. Chantal has what I have always privately classified as fascist good looks – unfairly, doubtless. One sees many American girls like

Chantal – strong teeth, strong jaws, big bones, large milk-giving breasts, healthy diet, assurance that comes from family love and a good income.

I try to pull her over on to me again, but she keeps going on about the damned security agenda. It was I who had put the possible existence of a traitor on the agenda and argued forcibly with the colonel that none of the officers, not even the most senior, especially the most senior, could be considered above suspicion. Colonel Joinville's eccentricity verges on madness – madness to the point that he does not even resent my suggestion that his strange ideas render him suspect. Captain Kolbetranz is one of those rare officers who has risen from the ranks, a refugee from East Germany, he could be a Soviet plant. Captain Delavigne is an intellectual. God knows what goes on in the minds of those who read *Le Monde*. Captain Yvetot is an excessively conventional and conservative officer. He may well be secretly and implacably opposed to the nuclear test about to take place at Reganne and to de Gaulle's new *force de frappe*. Major Lacan is a ghost of a man. He has left his soul in Dien Bien Phu. It is enough to run through the long list of possible suspects to see why France is going to lose this war.

'You suspect even me, don't you?' says Chantal.

'No, there are limits even to my suspicious nature.' But I take care to put the slightest note of hesitation in my reply, for I am careful always to keep her a little off balance. And if she is only having a game with me, it is also true that at this stage I am by no means wholly besotted with her. My natural cast of mind is to have two minds – on anything. I can see that Chantal is a magnificent creature, but at the same instant that I marvel at her body I find it revolts me. The big breasts, the flesh round the hips, superfluous flesh everywhere, the big eyes which out of the context of her carefully made-up face might be mistaken for jelly fish, smells that allure and repel. I have seen so much flesh in other contexts, electrocuted, charred, drowned, dismembered and smelling, that my response to any human body cannot be unambivalent. It must be the same for all of us serving in Algeria.

Temperamentally and politically too there was a great divide between Chantal and myself. It is enough now to remark that Chantal's politics are the politics of the shoulder-blades. So she herself has described it to me. The shiver that travels up the spine, between the shoulder-blades, and tingles at the nape of her neck and brings tears to her eyes, this shiver is her political master. The manifestations of the political shiver are rare and not announced in advance, but they are crucial. The singing of the 'Marseillaise' in a night-club, the Spahis cantering by on full-dress parade, a child, miraculously still alive, dragged from the rubble of an FLN bomb outrage, suchlike stuff. My view of politics is more logical.

And there is her class. I am not of her class. Who is? In Algeria, only members of 'the hundred families'. The de Serkissians own vineyards, olive groves, tobacco plantations, a bauxite mine and a casino. And despite that frivolous champagne and Jaguars look, she is an intellectual and a reader of books. I am not fond of all that. It's the negation of action. It is after all the intellectuals, the academics and the journalists who are paralysing the military offensive now. The French are going to surrender Algeria after losing a series of debates in a coffee bar. And a lot of men on both sides have got killed, while the intellectuals maundered on. Killed for nothing. I am serious about this.

In Chantal's favour it has to be conceded that the books she likes best are about or by men of action – Saint-Exupéry's *Voyage through the Night*, Junger's *Storm of Steel*, Ouida's *Under Two Flags*. Most endearingly of all, she is devoted to *The Three Musketeers*. She knows all their adventures by heart and she has told me that on the day of her first communion she took a secret vow before the altar to live her life exactly as D'Artagnan would have lived it – if D'Artagnan had been a woman living in French Algeria.

I lie silent for a while thinking of the case that could be put to the colonel that the traitor has only just arrived at Fort Tiberias and that Chantal is that traitor. She has had access to most desert operation files for over a year now. She met

Mercier. The family estates were vulnerable to an FLN protection racket . . .

We continue idly discussing the shortlist of suspects, though really shortlist is a misnomer. A full-blown traitor in the army, as opposed to some liberal intellectual officer with a queasy conscience, a full-blown military traitor is so rare in this war that internal security procedures have become very sloppy here at the fort, and at Laghouat and Tizi-Ouzo. Almost every officer knew or could have known about al-Hadi's trip to Algiers and the tail that was being put on him. Most of them knew about the planned swoop on the Bani Fadl, and again could have known about the July pipeline patrol arrangements. Most disturbing of all from a security point of view, almost every man, commissioned or other ranks, in Fort Tiberias has a pretty good idea what was going on thirty miles to the south at Reganne and how the nuclear test could be disrupted by the FLN. Even if fears of a full-blown traitor are judged to be without foundation, still desertions from the Legion are a common enough occurrence, and escaped legionnaires often like to make a new start in civilian life by selling their story to the papers. I at first assumed that the three civilians and the para major who were going to be present tomorrow were to do with arrangements at Reganne, but the way in which Chantal and the colonel do not discuss the matter now makes me doubt this.

When we have been through the list, she leans back again. She is struggling not to show too much excitement. 'Philippe, I'm just beginning to realize . . . It's been coming to me all afternoon. I think I know who the traitor is. But I'm not sure . . .'

'I'm not even sure that there is a traitor. Who do you think it is?'

'Oh, I'm not sure yet. And besides it's going to be my coup. I will perhaps suggest the name at tomorrow's meeting. You go back to your archives, and that Arab you've got on the board. I shall be very interested to hear what you get out of him.'

I go to the window and look down through the slats of the shutters at the Legion at drill below. The sex is OK, but how long can I keep up these games with Chantal?

Chantal is looking thoughtful.

'That board with the leather straps. Does it have to stay down in that dingy cell? Couldn't you think of some reason to have it brought up here?'

Chapter Four

We are three-quarters of the way through my lecture on insurgency technique. I used to be nervous about lecturing. A surprising number of soldiers who have seen action are. These days I reckon that if my shirt-tail isn't hanging out and if my flies are done up, than at least the lecture has reached the minimum standard. The lecture is a waste of time. Only experience teaches us about the enemy. The platoon is squeezed together on what must be old school benches.

'Men! Mao as we have seen described the guerrilla as moving among the people like a fish in the water, quiet as a goldfish in his pool. But this applies only to the first stage of guerrilla warfare. In the second phase our goldfish acquires teeth and becomes a shark cruising around among the other more innocuous fish. The aim now is to detach these innocuous fish, the "oppressed" from the "oppressor", and the guerrilla's trick is to get the "oppressor" to do most of his work for him. General Giap proved himself a master at this strategy.'

I do not have to think about what I am saying. Instead I am reflecting that it is given to few people to think when they wake up in the morning, 'Today I am going to murder a man,' but that was my first thought this morning. I have yet to commit the murder. I have this lecture to get through first and then some work on those blasted files.

'So now I want to turn to the tactics of outrage and how the terrorist and the guerrilla turn reprisals against terrorism to their advantage. A bomb is thrown. The authority –

military or civil – must take reprisals. They can't find the actual culprits, or it may be that they do have them in their net but they can't distinguish the terrorist in their net from all the other fish. So they practise mass reprisals. Now we should note here that from the "oppressor's" point of view – and, for the sake of argument, let us here classify ourselves as oppressors – this strategy is not as senseless as it seems. For often the original programme was ordered by a particular sector of the liberation movement, without authorization from the command cell. In any case the liberation leadership have certain responsibilities towards the people they are supposed to be liberating. So the bombing campaign may be called off. Corporate responsibility and mass reprisals can be made to work on behalf of the occupying power – in the short term. Look at Massu's successful operation in the Algiers kasbah a couple of years back.

'But more generally, and in the long run, mass reprisals and so forth only play into the hands of the insurgents, for they alienate a previously friendly or at least neutral populace. They make more visible to the masses the naked oppression of the occupying power. These ideas I am telling you about do not originate with the FLN, or with General Giap. They go back to Trotsky. It is not helpful or accurate to regard the perpetrator of a terrorist outrage as a criminal psychopath – any more than it is to so regard the torturer. The terrorist is an able strategist. We must respect him and understand him. Know the mind of the enemy, gentlemen.'

The lecture is not arousing much interest. True it is a very hot afternoon, but all afternoons are hot down here, and if I had been talking to a platoon of conscripts or even of paras, some of the ideas I had been discussing would have aroused argument and some of the deliberately provocative terminology I had used would have drawn criticism. More than half the French army in Algeria are barely more than schoolboys, and most of them have a vague idea that they are here to fight 'international communism', but beyond knowing that international communism is evil they don't know what it is. A few months before they got shipped out here, their parents were worrying if they went out for long bicycle rides on their own.

But my legionnaires are different. A few of the old lags in this room, mostly the older ones, know their Trotsky pretty well. They fought for Trotsky – or for Stalin – in the Spanish Civil War and when the war was lost, they signed up and came here. Another, slightly younger, group came face to face with the real menace of international communism on the Russian Front. They know what it is about. So we have a lot of Waffen ss in this platoon too. Then we got a lot of refugees from Eastern Europe in the late forties. Even the criminal recruits prove to be surprisingly politicized, but they are not going to argue it out here in this classroom.

I have a brief fantasy of a couple of the hard-bitten old Stalinist thugs in this room turning up at a dinner party at the de Serkissians', bristling and sweating in the unfamiliar monkey suits. I pride myself on my ability to think two things simultaneously and, while the lecture is delivered by automatic pilot, I start to think back on the last of the de Serkissian dinners at which I was present. Mercier was there too . . .

Now, suddenly, it occurs to me that the men may be more interested in learning what was said at the dinner party than in me going over the whys and wherefores of our defeat in Indochina. They should know what the civilians think of us. They should be reminded of what life can be like outside the Legion. I will paint the scene for them. I will rub their noses in it. Toughen their spirits up a bit. That sits well with the philosophy of the Legion. So now the lecture abruptly changes course.

'It is vital to know the mind of the enemy. It is also useful to know what your friends are thinking of you. I should like now to describe a dinner party which I had the honour to attend in Algiers last week . . .'

The lights were strung out along the Bay of Algiers. We dined out of doors beside the swimming pool. But as Maurice, Chantal's father, was swift to point out, this was not a barbecue. ('Beastly American custom. Probably copied from the Red Indians.')

Instead Maurice sat at the head of the table, looking on his guests and his napery with equal pride, and houseboys wearing fezzes and white gloves brought the food out from the kitchens. With the coming of autumn, Maurice's mind had turned to thoughts of hunting. But the Challe offensive is still going on, and every day there are reports of skirmishes, sometimes small battles with the fellagha in the Aures. The hunting season started a month ago, but only that week had Maurice wangled a permit to do some shooting in a restricted military zone. A couple of his companions from the *chasse*, thickset heavy-browed men, sat further down the table. Pierre Lagaillarde, the ex-para briefly over from the Paris Assembly, was the guest of honour. Lagaillarde had brought with him one of his political allies and protégés, Raoul Demeulze, the brightest of the young Algiers lawyers. Chantal and I had met Raoul before. Indeed it was clear that Raoul and Chantal had become very well acquainted of late. Raoul liked to pose as wit and *flâneur* of the boulevards and she seemed to find this pose attractive. Mercier was at the far end of the table, ill at ease to be seated so far from Chantal or myself. (This dinner was on Tuesday night. Mercier was to die on Thursday. I was already pretty sure by Tuesday that Mercier was going to die. Only I still did not know when or how.) Raoul sat opposite me and Chantal next to him.

As I describe Chantal to the men in the platoon I know for certain that I have them with me and, in my mind's eye, they enter Maurice's garden one by one and file behind us at the table and each one leans over the woman's shoulder to get a better look at her breasts. Now of course I am not going to tell the men what I knew about Mercier, nor what I felt about Chantal and Raoul. I am not going to tell them anything about my thoughts and feelings. Nor will I tell them how halfway through our argument about music in the barracks, I noticed that Raoul's flies were open and how Chantal's hand rested tenderly on that place. But I will tell them what was said at my end of the table, and I make sure that they can picture the scene, the cut glass and the candelabra, and I tell them what we ate – *moules marinières*, casseroled pheasant, oranges in

chocolate and salad and cheese – and what we drank – Musca-
det, Côtes du Rhône and brandy. And I am careful to point
out to the men that of course we did not have to fight for it
as they do in the Legion canteen.

Maurice and his pals will be hunting wild boar and partridge
and just possibly lynx. In past years I have taken legionnaires
through the area they will be hunting in. My men were on
search and sweep exercises against the FLN.

Maurice and his pals wanted to compare notes. Flushed and
jocular, they were keen for me to acknowledge that we are all
one brotherhood of men with guns – as if their weedy potting
of birds really compared with our man-hunts against the FLN.

'Don't suppose you have left any for our beaters to flush
out?'

'Your fellagha is a wily bird. You can practically walk over
one without seeing him.'

'Come on now, Captain. Admit, for all the seriousness of
things, there is still an element of sport, of fun even in a man-
hunt . . .'

'The trouble with the sort of man-hunts I take my men on
is that from minute to minute one can never be sure who is
hunting whom,' I replied.

It was at this point that Raoul decided to join our conversation.

'It seems to me that there is something, how shall I put it –
well it seems to me that the pleasure can be as great for the
hunted as the hunter. At the risk of seeming absurd, yes, I will
venture to suggest that there is something in being sought
after that is pleasurable, and that pleasure has something of
sex in it. Yes indeed, but I can see that you do consider this
absurd.'

Maurice certainly looks very grim, but Raoul plunges on
regardless.

'Gentlemen, I urge you to consider . . .'

(This affected manner of speech is something that Raoul has
picked up in his practice as advocate in Algiers.)

'. . . no, to reflect back on your childhood. Those games of
hide and seek in the dark, the panting and feeling for limbs,

at times a sense of orgiastic release. And when, in those enchanting games, you were finally discovered was there not a flush of pleasure that was at its roots a thing of sex? For myself, I believe it was.'

(My platoon finds Raoul rather hard to take. Only Corporal Buchalik is guffawing.)

But the de Serkissians were becoming used to Raoul and his conversational provocations. Even so, I wondered if Raoul might not have gone too far this time. I hoped that Maurice would tell Raoul to shut up. But Maurice was distracted from immediate response by one of the guards. From our table we had a view of the blackly gleaming sea in the Bay of Algiers. Maurice clearly felt that he owned the panorama and he boasted that, though he had been advised to have the north wall of the estate raised and wired, he had refused, for the sake of the view. A life directed by fear was not worth living, he said. However a couple of Corsican retainers with antiquated Lebel rifles patrolled the edges of the grounds and from time to time in the course of the evening one of these guards would come in from the shadows and take a glass of wine from his master's hands. The lights of the bay were distant, the villas of Maurice's neighbours gave no light. They were boarded up, their swimming pools drained.

When Maurice's response came, it was more melancholy than angry.

'Everything sexual these days. The young are supposed to live for nothing else. It's fashionable now, I know, to bad-mouth Pétain, and certainly there were excesses and terrible mistakes were made, but I can't help feeling that something really rather fine perished with Vichy. And what have we now? That scruffy Johnny Halliday and this beastly rock 'n' roll one hears everywhere these days, in bars, on the beaches . . .'

'Even in the barracks,' Raoul interrupted.

I could see from the glint in Raoul's eyes that he knew what rock 'n' roll was likely to mean to me, and that he was going to make me sweat for it this evening, if he could.

'Oddly enough,' he continued, 'one of the commonest

complaints we lawyers hear from Arabs who have been lucky enough to be released from military detention is about the incessant rock 'n' roll in the barracks! Would you believe it!'

He looks at me. I shake my head.

'I mean you would think that they had other things to complain about. But they were absolutely vehement about its horrors, though a bit confused. They said para and legionnaire officers were especially keen on rock 'n' roll. Well, Philippe, can you answer for your fellow officers?'

'We are,' I said, 'a rather unmusical lot at Fort Tiberias.'

Lagaillarde was enjoying the joke. Maurice looked bored and mystified. (The platoon I am addressing look miserable.) Raoul pressed on.

'Let us take our average Arab – let us call him Mustafa – someone whom we are trying to persuade of the glories of *Algérie française* and the grandeur of French culture, but then Mustafa says, "This French culture you tell me that I should be so grateful for . . . Is it such a great thing? I walk past the barracks of the soldiers and I listen and what do I hear but the sounds of rock 'n' roll. All shrieking and writhing. It all sounds very decadent to me. What I ask myself is this rock 'n' roll? Is this part of the great French culture?" '

But before Raoul can take his prosecution any further, Maurice cuts in.

'The army has gone soft and that is a fact.'

I have heard it all before from Maurice and his grand *colon* friends. Jews and Masons in the army. The army failed France in 1940. Then we sold out in Indochina and now we are preparing to sell out to the FLN. De Gaulle was the man who betrayed France in 1940, set a bad precedent according to Maurice. Gave other soldiers the impression that rebellion and indiscipline can pay off. Since then every soldier carries a draft of his inaugural speech as president in his knapsack. The army has degenerated into a gang of politicians and *képi-bleu* social workers, doing more to help the Arabs than to protect people's farms. Why aren't the de Serkissian estates being given a proper guard? If you won't defend us, you might at least give us the weapons to do it ourselves. The officers, Jews and bumboys to a man – if men is what they are – have lost their nerve . . .' and so on and so on.

(It is pretty certain that in the year that is to come some members of the platoon I am talking to now will die, in effect defending this fat cat and the profitability of his estates. I do not point this out to the men. Corporal Buchalik sits in the front row. I can see his eyes lit up with hatred. Whether it is for me, or for my hosts of last week, I do not know.)

As Maurice's tirade began to run down, Raoul actually dared to interrupt.

'Hand on your heart, Philippe, can you swear that you are prepared to die to defend all this?'

Raoul's arm sweeps out to encompass the gleaming white tablecloth, the candelabra, Maurice's guests and servants.

(In the lecture room now my arm does the same, summoning up the invisible table, guests and servants to appear before the bored old lags of Fort Tiberias.

'Can you see it, men? Do you see it clearly? It is for Maurice de Serkissian and his pals that we fight and die in the desert. I shall tell you how I replied . . .')

'Sir,' I said, addressing Maurice but hoping that Chantal will hear me, 'I am prepared to kill for it and that is what counts. As I see it, the army is the last bastion against decadence in the West – even against de Gaulle and the clever intellectuals and lawyers around him. The army is doing its duty. It is the intellectuals, the word players, who are selling us out. We are doing our job, I swear . . .'

Raoul was charming.

'Oh, but so brutally, so clumsily. We have deprived the Arab of his dignity, and of the most fundamental aspect of that dignity, his right to choose. How can one possibly defend the methods the army are using to suppress these freedoms?'

Raoul smiled at us. He knew that we knew that he had defended the army's methods many times in the courts and in the press. But it was one of Raoul's specialities, one of his daring little outrages, to pick up the case for the Arab, and play with it for an hour to pass the time and to hone up his debating skills. And now he will defend the FLN and their bomb outrages, smirking cockily at the social risk he is taking. I had argued with Raoul before. He put on opinions like a lady trying on a frock. The one thing he didn't want to do was to be caught out wearing the same frock as any of the other ladies. He fascinated me. I had to admire him. It was impossible to win against a man like that. At best when I thought I had him cornered, Raoul would throw up his hands.

'But of course, I agree with you. I was just playing devil's advocate for a moment.'

And there would be the unspoken implication in his voice: 'That was the conclusion I was leading you on to all the time with my sophisticated debater's skills.' Just when one thought one had victory in one's grasp, one found oneself with one's nose in his hands, more profoundly humiliated than ever. (I try to explain this to my men, but they look hurt and ashamed. It seems I have failed them and, at the dinner table, became a lost leader.)

That night Raoul defended the logic of the FLN's tactics, and sneered at the heavy-handedness of our army.

'The true battle of Algiers is not going to be won by charging around the kasbah letting off rounds of small-arms fire – refreshing though it is to see such energy, such rude high spirits in our young troops. No, the true battle is going to be won in the mind of the Algerian and it's wise words not bullets that we need. Now our Algerian, let's call him Mustafa, I can imagine him saying, "That's all very fine. You say you offer me a chance to become a Frenchman, etc., the next thing I know the paras are upon me, tearing down the walls of my shanty hut, feeling up my women . . ." '

I interrupted.

'As for complaints about the way the security forces treat the fatmas, the army could not treat those women worse than their own fathers and husbands treat them . . .'

My remark started Mercier off on how all women are oppressed. Even Frenchwomen are subtly oppressed. Eventually the boredom of it drove Chantal away from the table and into the swimming pool . . .

I use my hands to give my men some impression of what

37

Chantal looked like in a swimsuit, but I do not trouble to relay Mercier's account of de Beauvoir's limp liberal ideas about womanhood to the men. It would not interest them. It does not interest me. I shall stop with Raoul's attack on our operations in the kasbah. Raoul's rhetoric fascinates my poor soldiers. Their brows are furrowed in concentration. They cannot realize, as everyone at the table at the time realized – even Maurice who was somewhat slow in such matters – that Raoul was only playing with words and ideas, and I lack the skill to make my men really understand the situation.

As I finish, I note with satisfaction how the overheated lecture hall seems to throb with a concentrated hatred, but I see also no hatred on the faces of a few of the men, but only a dream of longing and envy.

'Platoon dismissed!'

Chapter Five

I hurry back to the intelligence office and immerse myself in my beloved files. Many of the files are routine reports, mostly compiled by my predecessor about purely Saharan matters. They deal with the seasonal movements of the tribes and local tribal rivalries. They are really of more value to the anthropologist than they are to counter-intelligence. The greater part of the more recent files, however, are my work and they are highly classified. They deal with disaffection among the tribesmen, with pro-colonial informers and collaborators, with FLN fund-raisers and propaganda officers, with FLN routes for the transmission of men, weapons and information from Tunisia into the Algerian Sahara, with the FLN regiments mustered on the other side of the Morice Line. Above all they purport to trace the chains of communication between the bedouin and the fellagha in the desert and the commanding FLN wilayas in the big cities of the coast.

Now, as on many previous occasions, I lose myself in rapt contemplation of my work – the cross-referenced files and the charts which map out the chains of command in the FLN and counter-intelligence. The FLN wilaya divides into sectors, the sectors into subsectors, subsectors into districts, districts into subdistricts, subdistricts into groups, groups into cells. Or one can look at it another way; a cell – three men form a cell – once formed recruits new members. It may expand to twice its size before it splits. When it splits, two cells are formed and the combination of these two cells in turn creates a group. A sufficient accumulation of groups in turn will create a sub-district. There is a beautiful organic geometry about the revolutionary cell system. It generates the FLN structure of command which is pyramidal in shape and this FLN pyramid is matched and mirrored by the French pyramid of surveillance and counter-intelligence. Pyramids, lattice grids and cells, but there is nothing frozen about this geometry. It is ceaselessly in movement, generating new structures and sloughing off old ones. The twin geometries of revolution and counter-revolution generate discipline and violence. And these two pyramids twist in upon one another, as informers and double agents bind the two systems together and as the two systems seek to mirror each other's techniques and advantages.

I see it all in my mind's eye. However, it must now be confessed that the delineation of the FLN chain of command as I have created it on paper here in the intelligence office in Fort Tiberias is far from perfect. My FLN pyramid lacks its apex; everywhere in the structure there are crucial steps that are missing and pathways which seem to lead upwards but actually go nowhere. I have FLN agents listed as double agents for the French and pro-French double agents queried as FLN triple agents. Every intelligence profile is docketed, but almost half the cross-references on the dockets refer to files that seem to have been mislaid. Here confusion has made his unobtrusive masterpiece. Over the past four years I have rendered the revolution many services, but I am certain that this botched and bungled intelligence compilation is my greatest contribution.

At regular intervals I send my materials and accompanying analysis to the main archives of the Deuxième Bureau in Algiers, Oran and Paris and they have been unquestioningly fed into the system. Until recently that is. Of late there have been queries and criticisms of my results. I have had some successes of course. My masters have been careful to provide some successes to sustain my position, but not enough. Many men have been tortured and died under torture to sustain my imposture, but not enough. Still the drift of my critics, and

...hey are still few, seems to be that I am an incompetent plod- ... cannot detect any hint of the suspicion of treason. But ... much longer will this last?

...hantal is one of those who look down on me as a failure ... my job. It is implicit in her patronizing flirtation with me. ... the meetings of the security committee she is in fact my sternest critic. In bed, I fancy that it is not the intelligence officer she spreads her legs for, but the legionnaire. Even when I stand before Chantal stark naked, she sees an irregular-shaped aura around me. This aura consists of a white *képi*, a blue cloak and red epaulettes. I am sure it is so. And I am perhaps not so very different. This afternoon it was not the body of Chantal that I made love to, but the class enemy that I raped. As I rape Chantal, I sodomize her landowning father and put my prick up the arse of capitalist bourgeois society. I find deceit to have aphrodisiac effects and betrayal to be the greatest of the sexual perversions.

The incident with the gun this afternoon was alarming. No – there was a moment of stark terror. In an instant I might have given myself away, but that instant was long enough to persuade me that no one planning to arrest a senior agent of the FLN would do so dressed only in silk underwear and stockings. Another futile game of the bored silly idle rich girl. Silks, perfumes, perversions – one can read about the worthlessness of capitalist society – it is another matter to have direct experience of such things in bed. Action is the thing. As Marx says, 'Philosophers have only interpreted the world; the point however is to change it.' That is right. You don't understand anything by reading about it. The only way to understand the world is to make it yours by acting upon it, changing it, handling it. I have handled Chantal enough and I understand her pretty well. 'Know the mind of the enemy.'

I gave the lieutenant a hard time this morning. The truth is that I disapproved of what we were doing even more than he did. Para torture techniques are brutal and degrading – take that Boupasha woman who had a broken bottle thrust up her cunt, the one that the middle-class intellectual, de Beauvoir, is making such a fuss about. All that revolting stuff done to extract particular points of information, often misleading information at that. No, I cannot approve of such things. No, torture can be justifiable only when it is used to bring about personal and moral changes in the individual being interrogated. Torture is an instrument in the re-education of mankind. Take my own case. I might have read books and gone on specialist courses, but I would never have understood the essential truth of Marxism without passing through the fires of torture. My enlightenment was born in pain and hardship. I guess that Chantal thinks her boyfriend is some good-looking ox graduated out of Saint-Cyr, but the truth is that she is being violated by a Vietcong peasant, for my spiritual rebirth, the birth of the me that I am, was in the re-education centre in the little village of Lang Trang on the Gulf of Tonkin, forty miles from Hanoi.

Looking out of the window now, a Hungarian doing *la pelote* under the supervision of Schwab provides a centre of interest. Schwab is making him run and crawl round the armoured cars with a sack of stones on his back. They are watched by a queue that is forming outside the dispensary. Delavigne is supervising the putting out of the screen and chairs for the evening's film show. I can't see round the corner, but I know that McKellar will be watering the colonel's garden. A sentry with a sten marches back and forth in front of the steel gates. Two more pace the walls above, watching and waiting for the cloud of dust on the horizon, waiting for the wild screams and popping guns of the nomad horde. The nomads will never come. We are fifty years too late for all that. The only men outside the walls are the sharp-shooter team on the range and I can hear that the command to fire at will has been given, so, soon, they will be coming in again. Captain Delavigne will do the evening kit inspection and then there will be *la soupe*. I think that I can see the boredom rising in shimmering hot waves from the courtyard. Without moving from my place in this room, I can list what everyone in the fort is doing now and will be doing in an hour's time and will be doing this time tomorrow, moving at the direction of the rosters, to the sound of bugles. I can count it all off on my fingers like a rosary. I was young when I elected to take my commission in the Legion. I thought that I was opting for endless movement and adventure. I did not anticipate the deep monastic peace of the military life. This fort is like a beautifully functioning timepiece. Only there is this dirt – this traitor – in the works . . .

I am intrigued by Chantal's revelation that she is confident she knows who the traitor is. I wonder which poor bastard she is going to put the finger on. I don't think she can be on to me yet. If she is, I think I can talk my way out of it, for a time at least. She is widely regarded as a society girl who rather fancied being something to do with spies and intelligence, so daddy wangled her a job. It's not true, but I can use it. She will be certain that I am not the type to be the traitor. She likes my uniform, my tales of bedouin life, my romantic nonsense with the gardenias. But I don't think she thinks I am bright enough or tough enough for the sort of operation I have in fact been running. Raoul has a mind she can respect, she once told me. The clear implication was that she didn't respect mine. I am looking forward to tomorrow's meeting. I would like to know who the three civilians are and what the para colonel is doing with them. If I do make a run for it, I don't want to go to my masters empty-handed. But I shouldn't like al-Hadi to be interrogated by anyone but me. We have not needed to speak. He knows that I have been handling the interrogation as gently as I can. At times, I think, he has even managed to exaggerate the agony for Schwab's benefit. He has courage, but that courage cannot be sustained forever.

It is time to tie up this loose end.

Al-Hadi strains eagerly under his bonds.

'You are getting me out?'

'I am getting you out, sidi.'

'Alhamdulillah.'

I fix the electrodes to his skull, bring the magneto up to maximum voltage and keep it there an instant. Then I hastily disconnect the beastly thing and hurry up into the sunlight. It is hard. Of course it is hard. At least there was a reason for al-Hadi to die. Too many people have died in this war for no reason. I might try 'heart failure while under questioning' at the security panel meeting tomorrow. It will probably go down on the registers as 'killed while attempting to escape'.

Chapter Six

'Have you ever thought of suicide, Philippe?' The colonel's question seems to have been prompted by his prolonged contemplation of the sands and now he reluctantly turns away from those sands to let his eyes gaze into mine. The whites are large and brilliant. They seem to belong to some sacred animal – perhaps a panther chained to the pillar of an Egyptian temple.

'Never, my colonel. That is, not since Dien Bien Phu. In the last days at Dien Bien Phu I thought about it every day.'

'Ah, yes. Tell me once more about what you saw at Dien Bien Phu.' And he turns back to gazing on the sands as I make another attempt to describe what I saw and felt during those fifty-five days in the spring of 1954. I tell him about the continuous rumbling barrage of the artillery on the hills around us which went through the bones as vibration even when one could not hear it. It never stopped in all those fifty-five days. I describe the weird labyrinth of waterlogged subterranean trenches whose walls in the last days were infested by long white maggots which burrowed over from the impromptu mass graveyard close by the airfield. In those dark passages one might encounter a Meo tribesman in traditional warrior gear or one of the Rats of Nam Yum in a uniform looted from a dead paratrooper, or one of the Ouled Nail madames from the army's mobile field brothel. All of these our subterranean friends had been trapped in the enemy's closing of the noose round our fort. Little hollows had been scooped out from the sides of the main passages and served as wards for the wounded, as store rooms and as wayside chapels.

Colonel Joinville listens attentively. It is just these details that he wants to hear. He does not want the standard précis of the siege itself, for after all, though he was not at Dien Bien Phu, he is, like so many of us here, an old Indochina hand himself. He was with De Lattre de Tassigny on the Red River Delta Campaign. Then he came out here and, as he describes it, at the age of fifty-four he fell in love for the first time. He fell in love with the Sahara. As he said to me a few weeks ago, 'I should like to make love to all this, these fierce blues and yellows, this horizon line and these dunes whose crests seem to have beem sculpted with an invisible knife. To make love to it all . . . I should not say that it was impossible . . . only I have not discovered the way yet . . .'

But now it is I who am talking. I describe the Legion's last pitiful attempt to celebrate Camerone Day with Vinogle wine concentrate. I recall Mercier leaning against the mud wall with a stethoscope to his ear listening to the sound of the little yellow men burrowing their way towards us. And there were the human bombs, suicide squads who came over the wires, arms stretched out towards us smiling and nervously attempting to conceal the explosives which they had strapped to their chests. And those last sordid days when we fought among ourselves for soap and razor blades. Half our commanding officers seemed to have had nervous breakdowns or committed suicide already. Naturally I thought of it too. Only I should have liked to have found a razor blade . . .

And here Colonel Jean-Marie Joinville stops me.

'But you have not thought of suicide since?'

'Not since. No.'

'It is not a bad thing to think of. Surely it is impossible that such atrocious suffering should have no meaning. If there is one thing that I am certain of it is that the meaning of human existence is closely bound up with the transference of suffering. I should like to take some of your pain from you.'

I make a sort of shrugging gesture which he may interpret as meaning that he is welcome to it. The colonel has said that, when he dies, he would like to be buried in these beloved sands of his. I should like to bury him in them.

The photographer – attached to the Services des Renseignements photographiques militaires – is waiting for us at the foot of the stairs. I know him. I have seen him working with Chantal in the records section. Together Chantal and he pore over the thousands of passport-sized photos, checking and breaking down the month's body count and labelling the heads on the table.

After conferring with the photographer and Captain Delavigne, Joinville hands his *képi*, white wool cape and swagger stick to Corporal Buchalik and hurries off to change. That cloak always makes me laugh. The men love it – and him of course. A real aristocrat, just like his old commander, De Lattre de Tassigny. It was an aristocrat, General Henri de Navarre who sent me to Dien Bien Phu and another, Colonel Christian de Castries, who actually presided over the bloody shambles. And now here in Algeria, they are everywhere, men like our former commander-in-chief, Raoul Salan, mandarins and military Jesuits. In his white cloak Joinville likes to appear among his men as Crusader and mystic. Yet I think it absurd, for in fact the colonel is short, close-cropped, muscle-bound and overweight (though even the paunch is muscle-bound). In fact he looks very like me.

In any case, today Captain Delavigne, who is responsible for liaison with the Algiers Ministry of Information, is determined that we are to present a different image. No *képi*, no *fourrageur* epaulettes, no Croix de guerre. The word from Algiers is that the public want to see men of action, relaxed, utterly informal but tough. They want to see an image of future victory. The fashion this year is for camouflage-striped combat fatigues and green berets. That is what we are seeing in the glossies. The 'Lizard' forage cap is an acceptable alternative to the beret and since Colonel Bigeard redesigned our uniforms, the trouser leg is nicely tailored and ever so slightly flared. Bigeard is another old Indochina hand. We all came out here. Salan the mandarin, Massu the victor of the Battle of Algiers, Trinquier the counter-insurgency expert, Argoud the tough-talking hero of the paras. We are all here in Africa, keen to apply the lessons we learned from Ho Chi Minh and General Giap. Only the lessons I have learned are different from the lessons they have learned.

When the colonel reappears, we all pile in after him into the committee room. A corner is selected by the photographer and while he fiddles about with his flash, a map is spread across the table. Cigarettes are distributed in the corners of mouths and heads are arranged over the map. I find myself standing next to Captain Rocroy, but the colonel calls me out –

'I don't want you in this picture, Philippe. I don't want the faces of intelligence people in this picture. So not you and not Chantal.'

He takes my place in the huddle of officers and self-consciously rolls his sleeves up. The tattooed number appears. After covering the retreat to Dunkirk, Joinville joined the Maquis, was captured and sent to Matthausen, escaped from Matthausen, joined the Free French in North Africa, fought against Vichy in Syria and finally pioneered guerrilla operations in the jungles of the Indochina Delta before finding peace of a sort in the desert. That tattooed number on his arm is his reply to insinuations that he might be a colonialist oppressor and a crypto-fascist.

It is going to make a good photo. The striped bars of sunlight from the shutters spread over the men in their camouflage kit making them look like a pack of beasts posed over their kill in the jungle. Short hair, scars, hard jaw lines, the pipe hovering over the map and pointing to some decisive spot, the heads bowed in concentrated unanimity. It seems incredible that this army will lose this war, but it will. I was in a similar photo taken in this command bunker at Dien Bien Phu. I appear just behind Bigeard, who was presiding over the morning's briefing. We looked relaxed, but formidable. The reporter who took it went out on one of the last planes to get off the airstrip. I think the picture appeared in *Life* with the caption 'French Para Colonels make plans for crushing offensive against the Reds'. Here, too, in Fort Tiberias, at this very table, in a few years' time commissars of the People's

Army will be holding their briefing session. But now the cameraman's task is done and they all break away from their studiedly relaxed tableau. I spoil it for Delavigne by telling him, 'I prefer the more formal type of military picture. You know – where the back row are standing, the senior officers are on chairs and the front row are cross-legged in front of them and we have a few dead fellagha splayed out in front of us as trophies.'

Captain Delavigne gives me a dirty look. We spread ourselves round the tables in the committee room. We are a 'fine body of fellows'. My fellow officers would rather die than allow the honour of the Legion to be sullied. *Legio patria nostra*. On the other hand, they would not lift a finger to save the honour of an Arab woman. They are the black heart of white Africa. The colonel and Chantal go off to fetch the guests who will be sitting in on our conference.

Chantal reappears with a bundle of files. Then Joinville enters accompanied by Major Quénault of the Eighth Foreign Legion Parachute Regiment and our three civilian guests. I am startled to see Raoul Demeulze among them. Raoul smiles briefly in my direction. I had not known that he was in the fort. I recognize one of the others as Potier, a big shot in the Oran Chamber of Commerce, but the third man I have never seen before. Potier wears the Knights of Vercingetorix golden-eyed tie-pin, and now I notice that though none of us is wearing military decorations, Joinville also displays the Vercingetorix tie-pin.

There is always an elegant carriage clock placed beside the blotter at the colonel's place, so that he may pace out the day's agenda. Today the colonel carries in an armful of objects which he carefully places beside the carriage clock – a small samovar, a scorpion in a bottle and a sand rose. The colonel explains that he has brought along these objects for the purpose of demonstrating something –

'All will be revealed at the end of the meeting, gentlemen.' And he smiles gently. The colonel is famous for such eye-catching, mystificatory gestures.

'You may smoke.' Then the pained look of one who has

been drawn into politics only by his duty as a Christian gentleman comes over Joinville's face –

'If you will turn to item one on the agenda –'

Surely the matter has been decided in advance? Important issues on the agenda usually are. Joinville will have taken soundings with the majors. But we will have to go through the forms of consultation on item one, before turning to the problem of the possible traitor in Fort Tiberias. Then we have matters arising from the testing of de Gaulle's first H-bomb at Reganne some hundreds of miles to the south of us. We will be responsible for policing the necessary evacuation of tribesmen in the region. Then there is a run of items concerning desertions and the disciplining of other ranks. Al-Hadi's death has been scribbled on as a late addition to the agenda.

'Our guests have a tight schedule. They have to be in Constantine by evening and cannot be with us long. Not all of you will have met them, though Major Quénault of our own Legion is I am sure familiar to us all – by reputation at least.'

Major Quénault grins wolfishly at us. A real thug, but a good man to have on your side in a brawl. The colonel continues –

'I do not think that there is any need even to name the civilian participants at our meeting. It is enough to say that they represent a broad spectrum of interests in Algiers, Constantine and Oran. The fewer who know that we have been talking to them the better. It therefore seemed desirable that they confer with us here in the Security Panel rather than addressing the officers' corps as a whole. For the same reason they will remain in this room until the moment their transport is ready to take them on to Constantine. I must say that in my conversations with them, I have become conscious that what they have to say is of the utmost importance for all our futures. Gentlemen, the Turks are at the gates of Constantinople!'

And at that moment Joinville does indeed resemble a Byzantine scholar who has been roused from deep contemplation of the Neoplatonic Triads by the roar of Turkish artillery beyond the walls. He mutely gestures to Raoul who takes the floor.

'Thank you. I won't waste your time. I know, Colonel, that you can answer for every man assembled here. We all have the best interests of France at heart. But what are those interests? I have now to ask you all in this room what, in your opinion, would the Legion's attitude be if there were to be a breakdown in civil order in Algiers – having regard particularly to the possibility of civilian casualties among the *pied-noir* population? I think that here we are envisaging the possibility of widespread demonstrations in the coming months. In such circumstances the future of white Algeria might hang on a knife edge.'

'Here at Fort Tiberias, this is where Western civilization makes its stand,' murmurs Joinville. 'I only wish it were better worth defending.'

Raoul acknowledges this with a quick smile and continues –

'More generally, I must ask would the army as a whole view with favour a new direction in the administration of metropolitan France? I do not think that anyone can be unaware of the widespread unease that is being caused by what some have termed "de Gaulle's sell-out in Algeria". We may deplore it, but we do not gain anything from ignoring the fact. There is talk in some quarters of the need for a demonstration in strength by responsible parties. Major Quénault has with him a list of para colonels which he will show you if required. The officers on that list have expressed concern about the dangers to public order and the possibility of civilian casualties in the sort of situation that we are envisaging. The gendarmerie won't act to clear the streets unless they have their cover guaranteed by the army. It is not possible to envisage the use of conscripts against Frenchmen in the cities. So now, naturally, we have come down here to discover what the attitude of the Legion will be.'

Raoul sits down. The brilliant white eyes of the colonel swivel round the darkened room. Everyone is alert and they have been listening intently. Raoul's speech was uncharacteristically circumspect, but we all know what he is talking about – insurrection, *coup d'état*, demonstrations by *pied-noir* militias and youth groups, designed to draw out the army into a proclamation that it cannot fire on the civilian population. This proclamation would in turn only be the prelude to a *coup* against de Gaulle and his ministers in mainland France. Our Fifth Compagnie Portée de la Legion may have a crucial role to play in all this. The words were turgid, mealy-mouthed even, but my fellow officers are sharing an unspoken vision with Raoul – of proclamations posted on the walls, pamphlets fluttering down from office blocks, barricades going up, tanks cruising down the streets. Yes, and then the heady days of successful revolution, the women hugging the troops and climbing on to the tanks with garlands of flowers, the indiscriminate gestures of affection and solidarity, the days of hope.

A traitor among the traitors, I sit listening to these men talking in pompous and measured terms of betraying their country, doomed muddlers having to consort with student agitators and over-excited grocers. It seems to me that the ghosts of Dien Bien Phu whisper from the shadows of the room calling on them to avenge the shame brought upon French arms in Indochina. I see here the slow step of the Legion towards disaster. They think that this decision will cleanse them of shame and indecision. But they have no understanding of the material bases of change or of the necessity for a revolutionary proletariat, so their putsch is really kitsch. Those who do not move in the direction in which the historical process is moving are condemned to impotence. I am not without compassion for them, but it will be as if their lives had never been.

Joinville too has his forebodings.

'Too many Hungarians in this company,' he mutters enigmatically.

Looking round the room, I can see that I am surrounded by friends. Been through good times and rough times with them. Shared quite a few beers. I am glad that I have had the courage to betray them. Some would say that with Rocroy in particular I have a bond, a thing created by words, but too strong for words. Rocroy has become for me in Algeria what Mercier was in Vietnam. Out in the Jebel hunting the fellagha, Rocroy and I have talked not only about families, fatigues and women, but ultimate things. We have talked until it might seem that we have truly reached the bottom of things (not the sort of talk one has with a woman), but yet there is always a false bottom to my mind. Rocroy and I share a smile across the table now. What I do not share with Rocroy is my knowledge of him as one of those engaged in maintaining through violence the expropriation and oppression of the miserable people to whom this land rightfully belongs. The round-ups, the tortures, the rapes – a few beers and some disarming confidences aren't going to change that.

For sure, some people would say that I have been brain-washed by the Viet Minh, but look at these men, the prisoners of their class and social circumstances! What is this freedom? Who is not conditioned? Life brainwashes everyone. My masters at the re-education centre at Lang Trang on the Gulf of Tonkin simply took out what my parents, the *lycée* and Saint-Cyr put in. In my opinion the result has been a considerable gain in objectivity.

Chantal is the only one to speak plainly. She speaks of giving the Reds and so-called liberal intellectuals a bloody nose. As she speaks Joinville cringes into his seat at the vulgarity of this plain talking. (The Joinvilles are old money, while the de Serkissians are of course new money.) Cutting her short, Joinville winds up our circumspect little plotters' debate –

'No final answer can be given at this meeting. It seems to me that we are always marching to the sound of an invisible drum. It is distant in the wilderness, but always audible if we but pause to really listen. It is not for me to say who plays that drum, but we must all consult our consciences and that is not a thing which is done in haste. Are there any more questions?'

Rocroy whispers to Delavigne that, yes, he would like to know when we are going to get on to the sand rose, scorpion and samovar, but Joinville does not hear this –

'In that case we proceed to item two on the agenda.'

Well it is time now for me to present my report on the security – or rather lack of security – of communications between the fort and Algiers. My report is at least as dull as anything that has gone before. Privately I exult at being able to ladle all this rubbish out, but I take care to keep my voice as dull as my message. It is all in the most general terms. My report calls for a heightened awareness of security needs. Alarmism would be out of place and I emphasize the need for more time and cross-checking.

As I speak there is a lot of reaching for cigarettes and a lot of chair-scraping. I have taken pains to be known as a dull, plodding speaker. Colonel Joinville picks up the sand rose and begins to meditate on its prismatic surfaces.

I press on. Clearly opportunities have been missed and there have been some disturbing failures in recent counter-insurgency operations. The possibility of a double agent, even at the highest level within our ranks, cannot be categorically dismissed. A review will be necessary. It will be time-consuming. I have no clear recommendations. I merely remind those present of already existing security procedures. I would, of course, welcome comments or detailed questions from other members of the Security Panel or from our distinguished visitors.

'I do not like long drawn-out security reviews and, in this case, I do not think one will be necessary,' says Joinville without looking up from the sand rose which revolves in his hands. 'Chantal, you have something to say I believe?'

Everyone sits up. Chantal has one of those voices which carry from one end of the Galeries Lafayette to the other.

'I too share Captain Roussel's unease and like him I have been going over the archives here and in Algiers, in the hope of discovering the source of the leaks that we all know are taking place. It is indeed a slow process of elimination and narrowing down. In my researches I found that again and again I was being let down by our intelligence records. I was not the first to have found this to be the case. I have formulated slowly, reluctantly and very tentatively the notion that it might not be that the defects of the filing system constituted an obstacle to the solution of the problem . . . rather they were a pointer to the answer to the problem.'

Listening to her, I feel a little queasy. Is it possible that when I thought that I was playing with her, she was playing with me?

She continues –

'I have to say that I can draw no conclusions from all this. What I would recommend is that a fresh eye undertakes an overall investigation of the intelligence archives at Fort Tiberias. It is certainly possible that Captain Roussel and I are too close to the material for us to be able to resolve several puzzling features that I have noticed in them. I think it would also be helpful if all those involved in the collation of intelligence archives prepared reports on their work for . . .'

The bitch! The bitch! She has not actually said it, but everyone understands perfectly what it is she has not actually said. On the one hand, I think surely I can talk myself out of this. On the other hand, I think that Chantal has started a process which is slow but whose conclusion is inevitable. Events at the Security Panel move too slowly. It is time to give them a push. Action is always the answer.

'My colonel, I have an answer for all this.'

Joinville looks up surprised from his contemplation of the sand rose. I let him see my Tokarev. Then I fire it. At this short range the shot sends him and the chair flying backwards. The sand rose shatters. Next, I shoot the big-shot tradesman Potier, simply because he is sitting next to me and I am in a panic that he will try to pull my gun away from me. After that it is impossible to be sure what I or anyone else is doing. People are diving for cover. I think my third shot, aimed at Chantal, went over her back. People are screaming. Someone else in the room, Rocroy possibly, has a gun and a shot ricochets off the ceiling. The siren on the courtyard wall has gone off and there is shouting outside too. The door swings open. There is only one trooper there. The other must have gone for help. I take the remaining one easily before he can get his rifle up to fire.

I start running down the corridor. Once round the corner I find Captain Desineux and six legionnaires coming in the opposite direction.

'Captain Desineux, those civilians . . . there is an FLN suicide squad in the room . . . the colonel's been shot. Have a guard put on the corridor. And I want men on the roof. And others on the wall opposite watching the windows.'

He finds it hard to take in, but he nods and I run on. Out in the courtyard, I see that I am not going to make it through the main gate. It is firmly bolted and a guard is already on alert there. I might try bluffing my way out through the gate, but I can't see that it will work. I should like at least to return to the archive room and wreak some final damage there, but paper burns disappointingly slowly. Whether I leave here in a jeep or a coffin, I should like to have done as much damage as possible. So where now? What now? Think. Think.

Chapter Seven

Along the corridor to the laundry, halfway along the corridor I stop, look and see if anyone is coming either way. Then I slide against one of the walls and put my feet on the opposite one and push and wriggle. The corridor is four foot wide. With my back against one wall and my feet against the other I am levering myself up the passage towards the ceiling. There's a space up there, eight feet up on the left-hand wall, I noticed some time ago – had no idea what use it would be. This ledge is narrow and goes up to the ceiling. I suppose that it was created by irregular boxing in of the laundry pipes. It is two foot wide, four foot long and about three foot high. It is not going to be comfortable. Indeed it resembles the detention cells we use for other ranks. I am going to spend the night here. While legionnaires tramp below I have time to think. It is all I have.

Now what the hell do I do? I listen to the legionnaires passing below me. Their snippets of conversation do not help. They have not been told much of anything really. They don't know what has happened to the colonel or to me. We have not been seen. The gates of the fort are closed. All leave is cancelled. Most of the reconnaissance patrols have been cancelled too.

I stretch out on the ledge and think. It is my curse that I always think several things at once. So I think how am I ever going to come off this ledge and get out of here. But I also go over the events at the security meeting and I think about

Chantal. There are never less than two chains of thought running simultaneously.

In the last three days I have tortured a man and then murdered him. I have killed three others. The colonel I sort of respected and liked and murdered. But murder is not murder when it is committed by an agent of the people. It is an execution. I have also systematically betrayed the woman I was sleeping with. But I consider myself superior to a woman like Chantal. I can appreciate her and her values. In a way I admire them I suppose, but I am also opposed to them.

Many a schoolboy would see nothing wrong in Chantal's oath to carry the values of D'Artagnan on into the twentieth century – quite the contrary. But this requires a little thought. What are D'Artagnan's values? He is a royalist. Chantal is a royalist. In Chantal's eyes there has been no legitimate government in France since 21 October 1791. D'Artagnan is an old-fashioned Catholic. Chantal is an old-fashioned Catholic. He is a traditionalist. Chantal is a traditionalist. They are both fervent patriots. D'Artagnan believed in taking justice into his own hands, for did he not supervise the execution of Milady de Winter? Chantal and her friends see nothing wrong in that too. The sword, the axe and the horse are their symbols. Their blood and their faith have given them the right to rule over the Arabs.

In the dark shadow world of Chantal and D'Artagnan, we stand on the edge of a forest which seems to stretch into infinity and we are filled with unassuageable yearnings. Deep in the forest we dimly glimpse the candlelit windows of a chapel. Smoke from a peasant's cottage straggles across the face of the moon. There is the premonitory sound of a huntsman's horn, and then another and another, and we see the horsemen flickering between the trees on the fringes of the forest, cavaliers in scarlet capes fringed with gold. Steel helmets glint gold under the torchlight, silver under the moonshine. The white banner with the golden lilies of France has been unfurled. The oriflamme has been presented to the virginal bride who stands before the altar in the forest chapel. What are we yearning for? Sacred mysteries? Or old simplicities?

So Chantal, toiling over badly cyclostyled records in a jerry-built office block in dusty Algiers, dreams of a marriage of the blood and the soil. But for myself, I am for the sullen peasants who watch these cavaliers ride by. When surly Jacques stands his ground and refuses to doff his cap to the fine huntsmen, I am shoulder to shoulder with Jacques.

To get out of here, I might move to the edge of the ledge. Then, when one of the troopers comes down the corridor, I might drop on him, overpower him without a sound, drag him into the laundry room, put on his uniform. Then with the *képi* pulled deep over my face, I would march across the parade square and talk my way through the gate. That's ludicrous. It is not so very easy to overpower a professional soldier without a sound and why should a trooper have his *képi* on at such an unmilitary angle and why on earth would he be going out for a walk in the desert? Everyone in the fort knows me. The gates are closed and I am not going to get through them that way.

I have no time for Mercier either and all that liberal values and slowly-slowly stuff. That cow de Beauvoir in her comfortable armchair in Paris going on and on about the cancer of torture in French Algeria . . . I don't even respect that stuff in the way I do what the true enemy stands for. Objectively what liberals do is shore up the oppressing power, commit little kindnesses which only delay the necessary revolution, the salutary bloodletting. They are panders smearing cosmetics on the face of Moloch. Of course if one thinks about the Algerian tragedy objectively, there are two sides to it. I can see the other side's case. Marxists are trained to think objectively. But seeing two sides is not the same as impotent dithering. I believe in action. Action to secure the rights of the oppressed!

I might drop lightly down, steal into the laundry room, wrap a sheet round myself, pretend I was an Arab . . . ludicrous, ludicrous. All these flights, deaths and concealments, this desperate pass that I am in, it seems so extraordinary that I could ever have reached it. It was not of my seeking. It was in the beginning a matter of cautious contacts made with people who knew people who knew FLN section heads, of anonymous meetings and then small testing assignments. There has been no dramatic moment, only a slow escalation of the risks involved, until this morning when I prepared to go to the security committee and I thought that nothing would happen, but at the same time I thought that I should take my gun to the committee.

I could wait up here until I saw the chance of taking a hostage. It would have to be Chantal. Then I could talk them into surrendering a jeep and opening the gates to me. That is of course totally preposterous. A film director can risk having a preposterous scene like that in his production, but I cannot risk the implausible, because in my case if things don't work out I die. If Chantal with my pistol to her head says, 'No, I'm not moving' (and she is a woman of courage), what would I do then? Blow her brains out, or say, 'Oh well forget it.' Even if I did manage to propel her along in front of me, their marksmen would almost certainly take the risk of killing her to get at me. They just cannot let me escape. And how if we got a jeep am I going to drive holding a pistol to Chantal's head? Well, I could force her to drive, I suppose. But the jeep is going to be spotted from the air pretty fast.

There's all that Camus crap. If I was a hero in one of those existentialist novels, I would be thinking now about blowing my brains out. Dinner-table stuff for the intellectuals. Not for me. People just go on about how they are thinking of committing suicide to make themselves seem interesting. It doesn't to me. Willy-wet-legs. Suicide is one of the curious indulgences of the bourgeois.

I should have tried to get out earlier. Talked the gates open before anyone had quite realized what was happening. Damn, damn, damn. If only it was yesterday and I knew then what I know now.

Maybe, if I did try to make a run for it, they would make it easy for me to get away? In the hope of seeing where I led them? Well I certainly wouldn't count on that. Besides, I don't want to lead them to my comrades.

Cautiously and quietly I keep shifting my position on the

ledge. I am uncomfortably aware of my body. It is I suppose the last time that I shall contemplate my body whole, all my fingernails there, all my teeth, still perfect hearing for a few more minutes or hours. I am still in my right mind and still potent. I notice that my hands are clutched over my balls as if in self-protection. It is a little bizarre, but perhaps I should masturbate now? It will surely be my last orgasm. No, my bladder is full and, though the rest of my body is hot and stiff, my penis is limp and cold. Fear takes away desire, makes a man impotent. Now I can consider Chantal without the coloration of sexual desire. Look at her objectively, and I wonder how anyone so beautiful can be committed to a cause that is so evil? It is hard to get away from the notion that a beautiful face is the outward expression of a beautiful soul, a healthy body the appropriate sheath for a healthy mind. It is hard to get away from that idea, but I should. In any moment in history the oppressing class has most of the beautiful women. I wonder what Chantal thinks of me now? Strange for a professional hunter, now to be the hunted. I really ought to know all the tricks. But the right one for the present moment does not occur to me.

I might get down from here. Go along to the barrack room of third platoon. Address the men. Appeal to the old Spanish Civil War lags. Organize a mutiny and a mass desertion. Claim that we are acting to support de Gaulle and the civil authority against a projected colonels' putsch in Algiers. My men will follow me anywhere. Bunk. They won't. They hardly know me. I have hardly interested myself in their welfare. I leave all that to the NCOs. They don't particularly like me. I am the officer that busies himself with all that dirty work down in cell 2. It is hard for me to contemplate with detachment what my men would do to the officer who has been betraying their comrades to the FLN.

I fired four shots at the security meeting. It is an eight-round magazine. Of course if it comes to it, I might have to blow my brains out. But there are a lot of other people's brains I'd like to blow out first. If I do shoot myself, there will be nothing grand about it. I don't want to be on the end of a rock 'n' roll session in cell 2. And it is crucial that what I know about the command structure of the FLN should not pass into the hands of the enemy. Death then would be necessary to preserve the revolution's secrets. Indeed it is objectively necessary that I get out of here and get what I know to the comrades in Algiers. First, the stuff about barricades week; FLN bomb squads can make good use of that. Second, the date of Operation Sunshade and details about its preliminaries. So far I have not even managed to get to my masters the information that Sunshade (code for the testing of the first French H-bomb in the desert) will take place at the beginning of next year. That is why the tribes are being cleared around Reganne. Third, Tughril in Algiers must be told how I have been blown and persuaded to do something about Chantal.

Could the FLN organize a rescue operation to get me out? Not on. They don't know what is going on and I have no way of contacting them.

I detest and adore the woman, that body, those hips like a cavalry officer's and that mind like a sewer. Simultaneously angel and pig, she rises before my vision as the flying pig. She is committed to *Action Française* of course. Daddy's estates are in hock to the Jews and the Masons. De Gaulle is a crypto-communist preparing to sell us out. In her bedroom in Algiers she has a lithograph of Marshal Pétain standing on a storm-tossed hillside. The military cape on his shoulders and the tricolor above him billow in the wind of history. Chantal said that we should couple beneath him to get his blessings on our union. In her next breath, she said Pétain was the only man to have offered France a chance of moral regeneration in this century.

And now that Pétain is dead? Order, discipline, purity, Chantal and her friends estimate that the old values can be restored, but a few heads will have to be broken first. The old values, the simple values, as little words who can quarrel with them? Chantal worships health, strength and beauty. We all worship them, don't we? Chantal will never sleep with a man who wears a surgical truss. A man who wears a surgical truss, though he may have many admirable qualities and go on to do great things in life, will never sleep with Chantal. Neither will a Jew, an Arab nor any of those made joylessly ugly by poverty and disease. Reflecting back on yesterday afternoon, I see now that she must have known already who I was and that at the same time she made love to the soldier's healthy body she was sizing up the atheist Marxist for his coffin. The business with the gun was a test and warning, a life-or-death tease. I thought I was playing with her. Now that I find that she has been playing with me, I know . . . What do I know? I don't know anything.

Maybe I should hole up here for a couple of days, three even, until they assume I must have got away somehow, so the heat is off. Then make a run for it? That is not on. I can't stay up here that long. I should be weak from hunger when I finally sprinted out into the desert. Besides I am bursting to pee now. It is fear which fills my bladder and stops me from sleeping. I could really use a sleep. An effect of shock I suppose.

This constant pressure in my bladder, it was like that at the political education centre Lang Trang. Everything they gave me to drink just went straight through me. Horrible sores developed on my legs. The sores attracted bugs. If I had my hands free I used to try and catch the bugs and eat them. They never allowed me to sleep. Lights shone day and night and my eyelids were peeled back and clipped so that they never closed. They made me beg to be given permission to drink urine. I thought myself particularly lucky if it was my own that I was allowed to drink. A small thing, but in such circumstances a small boon can give great happiness. It was a brief happiness, for the urine was too salty to satisfy thirst. I have described to Rocroy and to Mercier the things I went through at that camp. What I never told them is how I feel about it. I look back on Lang Trang with nostalgia and on my educators with respect. Of course they showed me the truths of Marxism. But it is not just that. The generals and politicians who sent us to Dien Bien Phu in such a hurry, once Dien Bien Phu was lost and that strategy seen to be not so smart, what hurry did they take to get us captives out of the hands of the Viet

Minh? They didn't really care. We were inconvenient bargaining counters in the hands of the enemy. Objectively viewed, my interrogators and teachers at Lang Trang were all cruel men, but they did care intensely about me and, in their rough way, they looked after all of us when we had been abandoned by our own generals.

Something simple. Wait till night. I know the routine of the guard on the walls. Wait till the guard has passed, then over the wall and drop on to the dark desert below. Ha! ha! Just having my little joke. It is a forty-foot drop from the walls. A lot of people, even some of the *pieds noirs* on the coast who should know better, think the Sahara is all softly rolling sand dunes. Well the Legion never builds a fort on a softly rolling sand dune. It's scrub and hard stone for about half a mile around at least. I'd break my leg.

Really bursting for that pee. Got it. Got it! I wait up here until the next trooper comes along. Then I urinate on his head. Then when they come for me I feign insanity. My God! By now, I'm not sure it would be entirely feigned. The objection is of course that they would sweat that nonsense out of me fast enough in a few sessions of rock 'n' roll, breast stroke and sodium pentothal. I'm hungry. It would be pleasant to think about a hot meal, but I keep thinking that the next thing that is likely to enter my stomach will be a long rubber tube.

Every solution I have come up with is ridiculous. Absolutely ridiculous. Stuff from the adventures of the Three Musketeers or some other juvenile wet dream. But I am going to have to make a run for it soon and it will be by using one of these absolutely ridiculous schemes. The question is, which?

Chapter Eight

I come off my ledge. There's an officer's toilet at the top of the stairs. I have a pee. I am so nervous that some of it goes over my trousers. I count my ammunition.

It's evening when I come out on to the parade ground. A few men are standing around smoking. I try not to look at them. I lean against a shadowed doorway. I still don't know what to do, but I am waiting for inspiration to come – or anything reasonably close to inspiration. I see Corporal Buchalik fiddling around with one of the jeeps. I put my hands in my pockets and stroll over. I adopt a faintly bullying voice.

'Is everything all right with that jeep, Corporal?'

'Just the clutch is a bit stiff. I thought I might – My God! Captain Roussel! I thought you were – '

'No, I'm fine, as you can see. The security exercise is over now. Have you got the keys? I'm requisitioning this jeep.'

'Yes, but – '

'Hand them over, Corporal. I need the jeep now.'

I get in without waiting. He passes me the keys but he is bursting with doubts and questions.

'We were told you'd been shot – and the colonel. You'll need to see the major before you take the jeep out. No one is going through the gates until further notice. Can you – '

'The exercise is over, Corporal.' I have the ignition on now. 'You and your men will get your briefing on the whole operation tomorrow morning. I'm fine and the colonel's fine.'

'Here! Hold on a minute! I saw the colonel's body, it was – Captain, wait.'

That was a mistake that last touch. The jeep lurches across the courtyard with Corporal Buchalik running after it. At the gate, there is more argy-bargy.

'Sergeant Hughes, something's come up. I want the gate opened on the double. Once I'm through it, see that it stays closed and report to Major Levy for further orders.'

The sergeant starts to unbar the gate, but he is dubious from the first. Then Buchalik comes running up. Buchalik is so vehement and excited that he starts by yelling at Hughes in Polish. Hughes is getting terribly confused. It is clear that he is having second thoughts. He is not going to swing the gates open for my jeep.

'If we could just sort this out with Major Levy, sir. We seem to have got our wires crossed here.'

Sighing heavily, I get out of the jeep and go over to Sergeant Hughes. I thrust a piece of paper into his hands – it is the agenda for the Security Panel meeting. Then, while he is puzzling over it, I shoot him. Buchalik is off like a hare in the direction of the guardroom. I don't bother with him. But I pull one of the large gates open myself. It is ages since I have had to drive myself and the gears do not come easily to me. The thing lurches forward and lightly prangs the edge of the other gate. Then I'm back in the jeep and out into the desert.

Stones hiss through the air, thrown up by the tyres. As I say for half a mile round the fort it is rutted gravel. We call this sort of gravelly stuff reg. The jeep jolts and thumps from rut to rut, and the teeth rattle in the head, but one can travel fast on this sort of ground. I am heading north, I think. I have left the jeep's lights off. In a few minutes I am driving into something closer to most people's conception of real desert. Hard-sand deep ruts radiate out from the fort crossing and criss-crossing – the tracks made by lorries. If possible in desert driving one tries to follow an older track, but if the ruts get too deep there is a risk of the central ridge damaging one's sump. So a new track is created and then another. In the jeep's mirror I can see arc lights switched on now on the walls of the fort, but they cannot reach so far and I continue to drive without lights. There seems to be no attempt at pursuit. I suppose that they will use spotter planes in the morning. There is no hurry for them. They will be radioing to Laghouat now. Corporal Buchalik seemed to think that I had been one of the victims in the Security Panel shootings. What the hell is going on back there?

I am heading north, towards the Mediterranean. It is, of course, possible to navigate by the stars. Find the Big Dipper and use it to locate the Pole Star. It is possible, but travelling fast and turbulently all stars look alike to me. Every time I think I have a fix on the bloody thing, the jeep bucks and thuds over more ruts. So, I just rely on a general sense of direction. Going north, but what for? I am not deceiving myself. In the morning they will come after me and find me. I am as good as a dead man already. All that I have gained and what is left of my life is a night's driving in the desert. Captain Philippe Roussel, he dead man, he zombie.

All goes well for the next two hours. After an hour, the jeep runs out of petrol, but there is more in a jerry can in the back. Then the rutted ground begins to give way to something else – the feel of the ground tells me that I am entering the region of the sands – pushing in on the fringes of the Grande Erg Orientale.

It is eerie driving in the pitch darkness, among the billowing, rising, undulating, twisting dunes, unable to see them, but knowing that they are there. Feeling the jeep lurch, tip and scurf along. I cling to the wheel and pray for the dawn, but we never reach it. Cresting what may be our four hundredth ridge, when the crest abruptly begins to crumble, I slam my foot hard on the accelerator, but it is too late. The wheels flail impotently in the sand. One shouldn't of course, but after a few cautious attempts to ease the vehicle out of the accumulated drift, I abandon all attempts at caution and put my foot hard down on the accelerator, digging the wheels deeper and deeper into the sand. Then I rest my head against the wheel and wait for the dawn.

When I awake, the sun is dancing fire on my face. It is

almost at the zenith and I have lost the best time of the day for travelling. In circumstances like these, when one's vehicle has conked out, one should in no circumstances abandon it, if one hopes to be rescued. I prepare to abandon the jeep. I unscrew the compass from the gearbox and squeeze the cumbersome thing into one of my pockets. Then I feel under the seat for water flasks. Sod Buchalik! There should be filled water flasks in all our vehicles at all times, but there aren't in this one. However, there is still the water for refilling the radiator. I take a long drink from the jerry can. It tastes disgusting and I can feel the rust on my teeth, but the rust is reassuring. It means that I'm not drinking that poisonous anti-rust stuff. I get most of a litre inside me, but that's it. I pour the rest of the water over my body.

Standing on what is left of the crest of dune, I half-heartedly shovel sand on the jeep, but I soon give up and start walking away heading north. It will soon be winter, but at midday it is, I guess about 100 degrees Farenheit. I have no real aim, but to walk away from that jeep, what remains visible of it. I shall be the master of my death. Their chances of spotting me from the air are rather slight. Even for someone who wants to be rescued, it is difficult to attract the attention of a spotter plane. Those Piper Cubs only really have sideways visibility as far as the ground is concerned. And even if I were spotted, where could a plane land among these vast rolling dunes? Twice in the course of the day I hear a faint droning in the air, and I throw myself to the ground and cover myself in the scorching sand. Nothing happens. Sounds travel for miles in this region but the planes never become visible.

La belle France, whole and indivisible from Dunkirk to Tamanrasset. France is a country whose two halves are joined by the Mediterranean. It is truly wonderful to me as I walk over and round these rolling and curving dunes, bleached of all colour by the noonday sun, that I am taking a walk in Metropolitan France. Over there to the left, one might see the *mairie*, a *tabac*, some cafés and a few old men playing *pétanque* during the lunch hour – only there is a very large sand dune in the way. And just ahead where I am walking now there is doubtless a vineyard, and a team of labourers clearing out a ditch. Oh! But there is an only slightly smaller sand dune in the way! Everywhere I look, everywhere I turn, there is glorious, beautiful, prosperous, bustling France. One cannot see it, because of all the sand that is in the way, but it is there. Our legislators and map drawers tell us it is there, so it must be so. I should get a grip on myself.

No, really the dunes are very beautiful. One has to climb to the ridge of one of the larger ones really to appreciate their beauty. That means climbing a hundred metres or more, before one can have any true notion of the scale of their beauty. I am in the region of the barchan dunes. The barchan dunes are crescent-shaped, curving away from the wind. They stretch in every direction as far as the eye can see, rippling and overlapping. A fanciful person might see patterns, even things and faces, in the chance arrangements of the sands, but I am not that sort of person. No, the devil of it is that I am trying to follow the compass needle due north, but the gentle pressure of the dunes, the gradual curving first one way and then another makes this impossible. One can't keep cresting dune after dune cutting a direct way north. The windward side of a barchan dune is not too bad. It is a gradual slope of fairly tight-packed sand, but to go north, I first have to climb the leeward side and that is steep, and gives with every footstep. Worse, the leeward slope is liable to sudden slippage. One might be buried alive in these boiling sands. But to follow the dunes around the foot of their slopes is also tedious and one can walk for half a kilometre east or west, finding one barchan linked to another and no easy way through, and the unverifiable suspicion grows that one has been driven by insensible curves actually southwards.

Ah, but then what does it matter? I have to keep reminding myself that I am a dead man already. Every step I take is pure gain. Without water, I guess that I have an absolute maximum of four days to live, and I should bear in mind the fact that towards the end I will be so delirious that I won't know whether I am alive or dead. But there is the possibility of death by heat exhaustion, particularly if I keep walking in the sun.

It could come suddenly, perhaps tomorrow. This heat I am used to. It is tiring to walk in, but otherwise it does not bother me. I revel in the austere purity of my world. Austere, limitless, infinite. I am exactly the man I wish to be in exactly the place I wish to be. I shall certainly die, but it is no less certain that my cause will triumph. It is only a matter of understanding the laws of history, for it is certain there are such laws. Of course the Marxist laws of historical development cannot predict the behaviour of an individual from moment to moment, no more than a geologist can determine the movement of an individual grain of sand, but the pattern of these dunes, the overall movement of the individual grains of sand in their near infinite numbers is predictable given a knowledge of the prevailing direction of the winds. It is like that with history – the direction is determinable, once one has understood the labour theory of value. And having understood what direction it is that history is travelling in, one would be a fool not to travel in it oneself. It is not because the proletariat is the suffering class that we fight for it, but because it is ultimately the triumphant class. Who knowingly would enroll as a sucker on the losing side, that of the bourgeoisie? So even now I am not dismayed. I may be on the run, but that is at the level of the individual grain of sand. On the grander scale it is international capitalism that is on the run.

Towards evening, the winds begin to rise. It gets cool. The sun sets in the south. I stare at my compass unbelievingly. Then as I slowly work out what has happened I start growling at the thing. Those jeeps have a lot of steel in their bodywork and have quite a substantial magnetic field. This compass was adjusted for that jeep's magnetic field. The bloody thing really is of no use at all. Now I think about it more clearly, I realize that it never has been. It is just a useless weight to carry about. I smash its glass face, cutting myself in the process. I drink my blood. Then I drink the diminutive amount of spirit on which the compass needle floated, and I throw the bloody thing away. The winds die away and it becomes hot and humid again for an hour so, but at least the sand is now cool enough to stretch out on. I do so and fall almost instantly into a dream-laden doze. My dreams are racked by the body's pains. And sleep becomes shallower and shallower as the temperature begins to fall again. In the end I am lying there, my eyes closed, but fully awake, shaking with cold. I stagger up and urinate into my cupped hands. Not much there, but I drink it. It doesn't do any good, I know, but it moistens the mouth, and it brings back memories of my time in the detention camp on the Gulf of Tonkin. Then I start walking in the pre-dawn. My face is blistered, but my teeth are chattering. At least in the early morning the sand is cold and hard to walk on. It will take two or three hours to warm up.

Halfway through the day, a meaningless and unbidden memory comes to me. It is the summer of '53 and I am sprawled in a cane chair on the back lawn of the family farmhouse in Normandy. The evening dew falls early in those parts. The sun is going and the air seems to be turning green as I stare at the ivy-covered wall beyond the vegetable garden and the orchards beyond the wall. I can smell the glass of Pernod in my hand. It is all there. I know exactly what the sounds are that I was listening to then – wood pigeons in the orchards, a barking dog further up the road and the rattle of crockery in the kitchen behind me. That was the summer of '53. A week later I took ship for Indochina and Dien Bien Phu. Then the memory in all its unbidden vividness is gone, and I find myself slithering down another sand dune with only the memory of a memory in my head. I continue walking, though I perceive that the walk is really more of a stagger. The mind drifts from one thing to another. As one crests a great dune one can see for miles, but then as one descends again one can see very little. Up or down there is really very little to see. It is really rather dull dying, when one has to walk so slowly towards it.

Towards the end of the day I see people, Arabs with their camels, strung out along the ridge of a sand dune. It is an amazing chance. Why should anyone be travelling in the Grande Erg Orientale? As soon as I see them I sit down. Why should I tire myself out walking over to them? Curiosity will surely bring them to me. And it does. There are four men, two boys and ten camels.

When they are close to me, I produce noises which I hope sound like 'Please help me.' It is difficult to speak, for not only are my lips cracked and bleeding, but my tongue seems to have swollen to fill up all my mouth, but I continue.

'I am a deserter from the Legion. Take me to the fellagha. I wish to join the FLN. I will see that you are paid.'

They are perplexed and suspicious. These desert Arabs are a primitive lot with a primitive attitude to the land they occupy. As Marx says, 'Among nomadic pastoral tribes the earth, like all other conditions of nature, appears in its elementary boundlessness.' They belong to a pre-feudal mode of production. When the revolution comes these nomadic anachronisms will be swept away. Their lawlessness purged, they will be forced to settle. I have no sentiment to spare for the noble bedouin.

For a while they argue noisily among themselves. Since I spoke to them in French, they assume I know no Arabic. I pick up bits of it. They might be intercepted by Legion helicopters before reaching the fellagha . . . I might be an infiltrator . . . someone put out on the sands to trap them . . . In any case the fellagha are not in the direction they are going. They turn back to me.

'We are peaceful bedu. We want no trouble. French a good thing. The Legion a good thing. We are loyal citizens of General de Ghool – '

'We do not know you, we have not seen you,' one of them cuts in.

'Yes, you can see me,' I protest.

'We have not seen you.'

'Some water please.' I point at the flask hanging on the edge of Hamid's camel. The flask is thrown at my feet.

'You take the water. We do not give it you.' (I understand that this means that they will not take me under their protection.)

They return to talking among themselves. There is a rather silly argument about whether I am likely to be carrying sugar or cigarettes on my person. One of them, a real idiot, seems to believe that I am a rich American tourist who has somehow got lost in the desert. The fucking idiot! There haven't been any tourists down here since the war started. Hamid, their leader, vetoes a proposal to slit my throat and see what I am carrying on me. I learn with a sinking heart that they are on their way to Fort Tiberias, where they hope to persuade the *képis bleus* to sell them some kerosene and some medicines. Hamid offers to load me on to a camel and save my life by taking me back to Fort Tiberias. I produce my gun and point it at them. I would like them to come my way. North. It is no use. They just edge away. And with no formal farewells they ride off in what must be the direction of Fort Tiberias. I watch them flicker away in the haze on the horizon.

I sometimes wonder about nomads, whether they can read minds, whether in this case they could read my contempt for their primitive way of life from small inflexions in my voice. Desert Arabs are supposed to be experts in detection. From a little heap of camel dung they can tell you the sex, age and state of health of the beast, which tribe it belonged to, when and on what pasture it last ate and which direction it was travelling in. Yes, it's impressive but it is an anachronistic skill. They and their medieval crafts have been artificially preserved under the protection of the Legion and in the interests of capitalistic tourism. When we go, they go too. The irritating thing is I am pretty sure from my own dossiers that Hamid is a link man for the FLN with the tribes – and one of al-Hadi's contacts, what's more. It is unfortunate that I have never had any direct dealings with him. It's bloody ironical.

I find myself thinking again of that lush time in Normandy. It was nothing to do with me. It was experienced by another man, the one who occupied my body then. As for myself, I was born in Indochina. Perhaps I would like to be that other man safe in his walled garden. I should have got out of the army in '53. There wouldn't have been any problem for a Saint-Cyr graduate in getting a job. At the very least I could have got work as something like an international salesman for a Grenoble-based pharmaceuticals firm. The odd thing is that even now I still think (and I hope that I am thinking lucidly) that it would have taken more courage to become that salesman than to follow the course I have actually pursued. When I think of the difficulties and aggravations of business correspondence and meetings, of the concomitant responsibilities that come with the inevitable marriage and children and loans from the bank to buy a house, a pit of fear forms in my stomach, just from thinking about it. There is the courage one needs to bullshit and sell a new product one really knows nothing about, the courage needed to fire an incompetent subordinate, the courage needed to attend the deathbed of an aged parent and perhaps also the courage needed to watch one's oldest son drifting into surly unemployment and then hopeless alcoholism. When I think of the immense courage needed to face the futility of a lifetime's bourgeois domesticity. I quail. Army life on the other hand has a pleasing simplicity, and as for the risks taken by operating as a communist traitor within that army, well, they are only risks of a certain sort.

There are many such thoughts as I continue to meander over the sands. The emptiness and abstraction of the desert encourages such generalizings and musings. As evening comes on, the featureless white sands of noonday are shaped in reds, purples and blues. I look out on it from what feels like a skull of caked salt. Yesterday it was difficult to see for the salt sweat streaming down into my eyes. Today there is less sweat and it is ominously pure. Tomorrow, I guess the cramps will set in. A lot of the time now my attention is devoted to simply moving my arms and legs in the right way, and negotiating my passage over the next small stretch of sand, but still odd thoughts and memories come unbidden.

Those sodding Arabs – I should have started shooting them the moment they turned their backs on me. Have I been lying, killing and torturing so that men like that may be free? Sod them. Fuck them. Up the revolution, down with Arabs! One thing I do hope for his sake alone is that Saint-Exupéry's goddamn Little Prince doesn't turn up in my part of the desert. The way I feel now I would put a pistol shot through his brains as soon as look at the little fellow. What was it like to kill Joinville? Like nothing really. It's like the torturing of al-Hadi, it's so long since I killed my first man or tortured my first man, that I really can't remember what it was like. One gets used to anything, and it's no use the Little Prince turning up now and telling me in shocked tones that nothing can justify murder and torture. It just isn't true. That's just a pious catchphrase. For myself, I believe that one must live absolutely according to one's beliefs and judge by one's own values or else abandon them.

Anyway did I really kill the colonel? My enemies hardly seem alive to me. The officers at Fort Tiberias are men who have been constructed according to the rules, doing what they have been told is their duty and looking down the line all the time to look and see if they all are doing their duty in the same way that their neighbours are. Chantal on the other hand is an evil woman, but she is at least alive. I remember when she first arrived at Fort Tiberias on a tour of duty, Joinville, who like most of his fellow officers is suspicious of pushy emancipated women, called her into his office to give her a lecture on how she should comport herself. Chantal listened to it all and gave him the sweetest of her smiles. She told him that she had no time for pushy emancipated women either.

'I too believe that women are inherently inferior to men, Colonel. It is just that I haven't found a man to be inferior to yet.'

She made the colonel very nervous. When I think of her account of that meeting I sit down and start laughing. I spread myself out on the sands and laugh like anything.

Chapter Nine

This morning – is it the second or third? I forget – I find it difficult to stand at all. But I do and recommence shuffling. The heat drops a little. There is an unpleasant vitality in the air. My skin starts to prickle and I look down and see that beads of sweat have begun to pop out of the pores of my body. I am astonished. I could not have guessed that I had any moisture left inside me. The brilliant white of noonday has mysteriously dulled to yellow. Wraith-like coils of sand begin to whip around my ankles. There is a rumbling and a crackling at my back. Although I know what it is that is coming up behind me, nevertheless I turn to face it. Thick billowing brown clouds of sand are rolling towards me and, at the heart of the dust storm, electric rods of lightning intermittently travel between heaven and earth. I turn away and keep walking. The sand begins to sting at my face. It is not at all pleasant. One might be flayed alive in such a sand storm. Once I saw all the paint on a jeep stripped off in a storm like this. I tie the greasy mechanic's rag round my eyes and keep on walking.

A blind man walking among the columns of fire in the desert, surely I am the seal of prophecy, the culmination of both Marx and Muhammad? Though I hear the lightning crackle to the left and right of me, I have no fear, for, in all respects that matter, I am a dead man already. A spectre is haunting the Algerian desert. It is the spectre of communism. I am carrying the contagion of revolution towards the Mediterranean. At the salons, at the race meetings, at the opera, I shall be there with my parcel of bombs, the vengeance of the poor.

'Life is a desert and woman is the camel that helps us cross it,' as the bedouin proverb has it. On reflection, now, I should like to live a little longer and be revenged. That flush of triumph on Chantal's face as she rose to denounce me. The grand coup, the surprise gesture in the middle of the committee meeting, wonderfully vulgar like all her acts and beliefs. Vulgarity is the hallmark of all fascists – think of the fat little men covered in medals, orating from overblown pseudo-classical rostra, raving on about blood and fire. Fascism is not a political doctrine in the way that anarchism is, nor a scientific perception of the world which is Marxism. Fascism is a style and a vulgar one to boot. Gleaming jackboots covered in the saliva of alsatians. The curves of a black-leather boot covered in spittle, that is very much to Chantal's taste. The curve of the whip, the curl of the lip, the moistly gleaming eye, the moistly gleaming boot.

Surely I shall live to be revenged, for, as Marx says, 'Mankind only sets itself such tasks as it can solve.' I should not like to die without taking Chantal with me. Marx also says, 'If you have loved without evoking love in return, then your love is impotent and a misfortune.' Not that I have loved of course. I shall return from the desert, sun-scorched and sand-blasted, to lie with her once more, a final time. She will be gloating about my presumed slow death in the desert when I step out from behind the door . . . Of course, there will be nothing personal in my revenge. It will be like putting down a rabid dog. The white foam runs down her jaws on to her gleaming black boots. Chantal's vulgarity is contagious, communicated in embraces and easily caught in crowds. I shall make her regret what she has done to me. I will have her kneeling with tears in her eyes, confessing her errors before I send her to the People's Justice.

I can walk on forever. I have undertaken the thousand-year march of history. The further I walk the better. This is a demonstration of the labour theory of value. The more labour I put into this stumbling trek across the desert, the more valuable it becomes. Only Marxism gives man his full value. With part of my mind, I know that I am delirious. The other half however does not. It is an infernal dialectic. The contradictions do not trouble me, for they are fruitful contradictions. I am the master of the sands. The winds are directed according to my will. The man who recognizes the world he has made is free. The man who has understood the laws of history is God, the only God there is. The revolution in the kasbah awaits my coming, me, the star-crossed navigator on the tides of history, the furnaceman of revolution. History moves too slowly. I shall give it a push.

I welcome the opportunity to experience the hunger and hardship of the oppressed. Hunger and hardship of the oppressed. Hunger and hardship of the oppressed. I throw myself down to kiss the scorching sands. There is a black fist in my brain.

As the black fist withdraws I return to consciousness and heave sickly on an empty stomach. I am blind. Blind! Then after a while I remember the rag tied round my eyes and remove it. I lie where I am looking at the dune that towers before me. There is no possibility of climbing it. It is better now just to lie here and think about things. Though the sun is only a glowing brown in the dust-laden sky, the sand storm has passed, the atmosphere is less heavy and it is possible to be lucid once more.

I have been in a delirium, that is clear to me now. It is disturbing to find out just how much too little water and too much sun can alter a man's thoughts. It takes very little to bring a psychotic delirium to the top. The matter is all the more complicated for me in that desire for revenge, death, murder, torture and the arbitrary act – yes, even delusions of grandeur – may be necessary to the revolutionary. Looking at the matter dispassionately, I am pleased to acknowledge that only his objective role in the historical process distinguishes the acts of a revolutionary from those of the psychopath. Nevertheless, the distinction is there and it is crucial.

After an hour an Arab appears over the crest of the dune. Then, after some minutes, other Arabs appear beside him. I lie there at the foot of the dune wondering what they are doing at the top of it. Then they start to step and slip sideways down the ridge, approaching me warily like crabs. Only when he is directly above me do I identify their leader as Hamid.

He speaks.

'Peace. We have been to Fort Tiberias. What we found there, we did not like. Shall I tell you what we found there? We found the body of al-Hadi with no shroud, buried like garbage in an unmarked pit outside the fort. Why did you not say that you were a friend of al-Hadis?'

I just lie there looking up at him. There is something about this that makes no sense. Yes, surely they cannot have been to Fort Tiberias and back in this time? Or have I been walking in the desert for longer than I think? Or have I been walking in circles? Who has told them that I was al-Hadi's friend? In any case I can say nothing. It just is not possible for me to speak.

'We will take you to the fellagha and you will help us be revenged against the killers of al-Hadi. But it will be dangerous. Do you have a weapon?'

It is unnecessary for me to answer as Hamid kneels over me to take the Tokarev from its holster. He examines the weapon from all angles, seeming to marvel at its craftsmanship. Then, apparently satisfied, he points the pistol at my legs and there is an explosion.

Chapter Ten

'Quiet now. You will wake the children.' In my agony I hear or dream I hear a voice saying this. Then the pain is gone.

When I open my eyes, all I can see is the white ceiling, but most of the time, I keep them clenched tight shut, for as the stuff in the needle wears off, the pain gathers in intensity. But then the needle allows me to drift again and I can look back calmly on the pain when the bloody trouser leg was being cut away from the flesh and that is like a meditation on my own crucifixion. Out of the corner of an eye I glimpse small hands like black butterflies resting on my arm and trying to shift it ever so slightly, so that a new vein can be found for the needle.

The next time I open my eyes I find myself looking up at a face. It is a fascinating face, fascinating because it is so familiar. I close my eyes and try to remember but I keep drifting. God, my puerile ravings in the desert. Of course, I was delirious even at the times when I thought I was lucid. But I am alarmed to find such juvenile fantasies of omnipotence lurking about in the shallows of the mind. I must have been babbling for days. I imagine that I am in a military hospital. Suppose when I am seen to be recovering consciousness, the nurse hands me over to the torturers? It is better to keep the eyes shut. Still I squint up through slitted lids.

The ministering angel hovers above me once more armed with the blessed needle. She is dark complexioned, with big brown eyes and brilliant teeth. Then it comes to me easily where I have seen that face before. It was five weeks ago. It was my last meeting with al-Hadi, before his final mission to Algiers and arrest. I warned al-Hadi that they were on to him. I did not tell him that it was I who had put them on to him. It was my decision to throw this fish to French Military Intelligence, but it was with the approval of Tughril, who monitors my operations on behalf of the command cell of the Algiers FLN. The message came back, 'The revolutionary troika can carry no passengers.' I think Tughril liked sacrifices for their own sake. As far as I was concerned, I needed a small coup to keep my employers in Military Intelligence happy. The sacrifice of al-Hadi was objectively necessary.

We met at Laghouat. Al-Hadi ben Shaykhoun was, in his very small way, as diversified in his enterprises as Maurice de Serkissian. We met at his 'hotel'. It was actually a lodging house, almost a brothel, patronized by the dancing girls of the Ouled Nail when rooms elsewhere were full. The Ouled Nail women came from the south to towns like Bou Saada and Laghouat. They came to earn their dowries by dancing in public and engaging in prostitution. Then they went back to their tribes again, their dowries carried as jewellery and pierced coins about their bodies.

The manner of my meeting with al-Hadi had been carefully arranged beforehand. I went first not to al-Hadi's hotel but to a neighbouring house of ill fame where Shirina was performing. She stood and swayed in a long flounced dress. With every movement the coined turban and belt jingled. Then two women seated in the corner struck up on their tambourines and Shirina began the Dance of the Daggers. She sidled round the room, turning all the time to face the audience seated against the walls. There were a couple of Kabyles who dribbled tobacco on to the floor and half a dozen legionnaires, one of whom I recognized as McKellar from my own company. With every step she took she slapped the ground with her bare feet and thrust her hips out. Her arms snaked this way and that, before returning

81

to her breasts to thrust them out at her audience, but the fiercely spiked bracelets warned the men to attempt nothing. Her eyes, brilliant in the midst of the dark kohl, invited the men to delight, but the haughty set of her barbarous face refused them. In short it was the usual tatty bogus oriental stuff the Ouled Nail offered to sex-starved soldiers and tired commercial travellers. She ended up rocking on her heels squeezing her breasts and thrusting them at me. I indicated that I was interested and, as had been previously arranged, we left the room together and she took me across the street and handed me over to al-Hadi. There were other Ouled Nail women leaning over the stairwell, but still there was a domestic atmosphere to the place conferred by some respectable long-term lodgers, and still more by al-Hadi's children. He had three children, the oldest of them was four and one of the dancers had a child too.

Al-Hadi and I ate and talked in the living room – in unpleasant proximity to a child's plastic potty. One of al-Hadi's alsatians padded in and slavered lovingly on his master's knee. Al-Hadi was very Western in his tastes and proud of them. Few Arabs cared to keep dogs in their houses. Al-Hadi was a hard drinker but a good Moslem in his own eyes at least. 'God pardons the man who performs even one-hundredth of his obligations to Him,' and 'The man who has given as much as a quarter dirhem to the poor will never face the fires of Hell.' I doubted whether al-Hadi had given much more, but such pious consolations were often on al-Hadi's lips. His wife, Zora, brought us lagers. When she had also brought us couscous and hot peppers, he bawled her out of the room. We let the plates go cold, while al-Hadi proudly showed me how he kept his explosives hidden behind a stretch of tiling that ran round the wall.

'What do you think, Sidi?' he asked anxiously. All that was in my head was the question, what had possessed him to put a floral frieze of bathroom tiling in the living room? But I kept that to myself.

'Very good, al-Hadi,' I said.

When Zora returned a little later, I think to see if we needed more lagers, he just shouted at her, 'Go away, cow! Cow! Cow!' and she stood for a while regarding him with tender brown eyes, before retreating into the kitchen.

And now . . .

And now I am sure that it is Zora who is shooting my veins with the analgesic stuff. Her face is bent close over me and its coarse pock-marked skin, presumably the legacy of childhood smallpox, occupies most of my field of vision and the ends of her long oily black hair rest on my chest. There is something reptilian in her face, not unattractive, but suggesting some sort of ancient pre-human wisdom and a resignation to the ways of the world, yet Zora is still young, at least ten years younger than her husband had been. So Zora is my nurse. I close my eyes again and wait for the pain-killing drug to circulate. It is unlikely that I am in a hospital. This must be their bedroom. I should guess that I am in the bed of the late al-Hadi. I should like to drift off for a while . . . for a minute . . . or a day . . .

When I come to again she is not in the bedroom. With some pain I can move my head to gaze at a wall tapestry on which stags in a forest are picked out in a rich mess of magentas, vermilions and yellowy browns. There are a few pieces of heavy European furniture. The large wardrobe is open, and I can see that al-Hadi possessed two Western-style suits, as well as an accumulation of Arab robes. On the chest of drawers there are a plastic jug and cups and a clutter of cosmetics, both Western and Eastern, lipstick, henna wash, powder puff, mastic paste and antimony. Apart from the tapestry of the stags, there is a tourist poster of Annecy pinned to the wall.

When she returns she has a child under her arm which she puts down to crawl on the floor, before busying herself with the needle.

'What is in the syringe?'

'Morphine. I have been giving you morphine to stop you screaming. The other guests must not know that you are here.' I marvel at Zora's hoarse throaty voice.

'One of the Arabs shot at me.'

'They found you in the desert. You were hit in the leg.'

'They rescue me and then they try to kill me?'

'It was an accident. Hamid is a simple desert Arab. He had never seen a pistol before.'

'That's absurd!'

'No, he had never handled a gun before. He and his brothers smuggled you into Laghouat. They took great risks. You should be grateful to them.'

'You know who I am?'

'I know you. You are the soldier who worked with my man. You work with him for the FLN.'

'Good. Now it is very important that I contact the FLN now and get a message to Tughril.'

'Do not worry. Tughril will get the message. He has been sent for.'

'When will Tughril come?'

Silence. Considering her reply.

'Soon. I am pleased to have you here. It is not so good without a man in the house and you can tell me how my man died. He admired you very much.'

'It is time for that shot.'

Catching the look of longing with which I regard the syringe, she smiles.

'This morphine is difficult to get hold of. The chemists will not sell drugs they think may be used to treat the fellagha. It is good that I have friends. I do things for them and they do things for me. But we must be careful with our supply.' After two failures to find a vein and a finally successful though bruising shot in the arm, for Zora is certainly no professional nurse, she pulls away.

'Is that better for you? You like it better than me I think.' It is a sneer not a complaint.

Standing beside the bed, she does a shimmying little wriggle to emphasize how awkwardly the pendulous breasts and buttocks are contained within the blue dress of cheap synthetic silk. Her step, as she marches out of the room, is unmistakably jaunty, taunting. I think she hates me.

Objectively I approve of that. She, her late husband and I – and the Arabs in the desert and the oppressed women of Algeria – we are all on the same side. Even so, it is good for people like Zora to hate people like me. For though I am on her side, it is still good for her to hate the man, the European, the Saint-Cyr graduate, the colonialist officer. I approve of that hatred. Objectively it is a good thing. Class envy is one of the greatest forces for good in the world. Hatred is the engine of change. It is good to hate the rich, the powerful and the successful, and though I have thrown in my lot with the oppressed, still I am forever contaminated by my former association with the oppressing class. I accept that and I understand and approve of Zora's ambivalent attitude towards me. At least I think I do.

The pain is not back, indeed the sensations conferred by the needle are so pleasant . . . I think back to Hanoi. Mercier and I had decided to visit an opium den – at least it was not a proper den, but just a parlour above a night-club casino where one could retire to smoke opium. I was a bit drunk and I found it difficult to focus on the heating of the pellets of opium over a flame and the ritual of the preparation of the pipes. Instead I struggled to read a page of *La Meilleur du Reader's Digest* and found that difficult too. I would rather have been dancing downstairs. But we were young then and there was this feeling that we ought to have tried everything before we went into combat. It was before Dien Bien Phu. We drank green tea and waited for our ten-piastre pipes to take effect. I kept thinking of the Cochinois girl I should have been dancing with. I drifted in and out of darkness, but I had the impression that the opium was doing nothing. Still it would be something to tell one's girl about when one got back to France. When my head cleared, Mercier seemed to have been talking for some time.

Mercier was reading Marx and Malraux that year. I smile to think of it now. That was Mercier's intellectual dabbling. It went nowhere, except towards more books. You can't understand Marxism by reading, you have to live it. Anyway at that time I had no interest in the stuff, but over our third pipe, Mercier took it upon himself to explain in a rather incoherent way what Marx meant by 'religion is the opium of the people'.

'What you have to realize,' he said, 'is that in the nineteenth century, opium was conceived of not as a soporific, but as a stimulant. The workers in the factories of Paris used to take it to get them through their working day. Closely read, Marx's statement "Religious suffering is at the same time an expression of real suffering and a protest against real suffering. Religion is the sigh of the oppressed creature, the sentiment of a heartless world, and the soul of soulless conditions. Religion is the opium of the people . . ." should not be taken as an outright condemnation either of opium or of religion. It is certainly possible to be a good Catholic and a Marxist.' The Chinaman at the door kept nodding his head all the time Mercier talked, but I don't know if he knew French or not.

Then Mercier told me about the mist-soaked valley of Dien Bien Phu, the air drops and the heavy guns being gathered together on the hills above it. Then there was, I remember, a Eurasian who entered the parlour with a concertina. This character made a start at an orientalized rendering of 'La Carmagnole', before the Chinaman forced him to stop. But the Eurasian needed to raise a little more money for his pipe, so he crawled round the room, reading people's fortunes in their palms. Looking at my palm and then up at my face he told me, 'You have two months to live.' Sod him. He obviously didn't like my face. Mercier and I and some of the others took opium away with us that evening. We agreed that it might be useful if we went into battle. When Mercier had talked of that remote valley and the early morning mists, I could imagine it so perfectly in the opium parlour. A week later we were actually there and the mist rose from the valley floor and the enemy's barrage began.

Zora is back again, making faces as she removes the bedpan.

'I have to go out now. But do not worry. The dog will protect you.'

'Where are you going?' I am full of suspicion.

'I am going to the hammam. It is the ladies' afternoon in the hammam.' She finds her purse and slips it in the handbag. 'Ah, you would like it there. You cannot imagine how much a man would like it in the hammam. Soft bodies moving through the steam, we are so many women without men, we are waiting for them like houris in paradise. But the men do not come and we sigh and are lonely.'

There is no mistaking the way Zora is baiting me. She does a slinky wriggle to get the white gondourah wrapped over her blue dress. Then she slips out of the door. Why is this game of verbal seduction practised on a sick man? I am not interested in her, how could I be? All I want is for my body to stop aching. I do not really think that she desires me either. Beneath the sexual teasing, she is, I sense, frightened of me, and the way she thrusts that needle in suggests hatred rather than desire. So I am curious as to what her game is.

I lie here looking at the high window, calculating what I would see if I could make my way to it. I remember al-Hadi's house as being in the southern part, the native quarter of Laghouat. If the bedroom faces in the direction I think it does, then if I were at the window, I would look north towards the military hospital and the public gardens on three sides and the tennis courts. Laghouat is on the edge of the Sahara, an oasis town being eaten up by military installations. In my mind I drift down its white streets and the hours pass. Flies buzz over what I guess to be a turd in the child's potty. From time to time the alsatian pads from end to end of the room. Zora has been gone a long time.

But I do not think that she has gone to the hammam. I imagine that I hear her pacing on the roof above me, her anklets clinking. I think that she is pacing round and round. I think that she is plotting something. I turn on the bed, thinking how I might seduce this woman or be seduced by her, but it is an abstract desire for seduction, for the drug makes me impotent. It is only in the head. There is such a thing as the physiognomy of the oppressed. I have only to compare Zora's

87

skinny pock-marked body with my memories of Chantal. Zora inhabits a world of secret shames. Women scuttle out of the women's quarters and mutter their mysteries to one another holding the edge of their gondourahs over their mouths, conferring anxiously over their laundry at the public fountain.

But in fact I know this woman Zora very well. When I was interrogating al-Hadi and there were others in the interrogation chamber, then the electrodes had to be switched on. But I did not wish al-Hadi to give more away of fellagha operations than was strictly necessary. On the other hand at the same time I had to keep my fellow torturer, Lieutenant Schwab, amused. So the trick of it was to probe into al-Hadi's sex life. Al-Hadi didn't like it but I think that he understood what I was doing. It was really rather eerie listening to the man describe his greatest sexual joys, screaming and sobbing as he spoke. So it was that we discovered every detail of this woman Zora's performance in bed. We investigated everything from the first bloody penetration of the frightened child bride and the cries of joy which greeted the display of bloody sheets, on through the years of systematic abuse of that skinny work-worn body. I explained to the lieutenant that it was the ultimate betrayal. Once an Arab's honour has been broken, like an egg it can never be put together again.

Where are my clothes? Perhaps they do not matter. There is something very comforting in lying here, though there are odd aches and pains, blisters and scabs, quite apart from the bullet in the leg and what I guess to be a fractured fibula. There is something very comforting in being invalided out of the struggle. The wound is my ticket out of it. But hours pass and my impatience grows waiting for the return of Zora and the morphine. At times I could swear I hear Zora's voice in the next room.

She comes in smiling as though someone has just told her a joke.

'When will Tughril come?'

'Ah it may be several days yet . . . It is not yet safe for him to come. Tell me again how my husband died . . . or . . . or

88

you may not get your shot, bad man.' She smiles to show she does not mean it, but I think she does.

'I admired your husband very much. His death was a tragic loss to the cause, but there is no nobler way to die than as a martyr for revolutionary socialism.'

'What went wrong?'

'He took too many risks.'

'Bad man, you could have secured his release, now don't say no.'

'Zora, it wasn't as simple as that.'

'Or protected him?'

'He wasn't my responsibility.'

She comes to lie on the bed beside me the needle poised over my shoulder like a talon. The thoughtful melancholy eyes are concentrated on my face.

'Don't be so vague. You can tell me. How did he die? Was it a bullet or did they strangle him?'

'I can't say. I wasn't there when they killed him.'

'But you should have been there. He was your man. You should have protected him.' Now at last she gives me my shot. Then she moves away towards the clutter on the chest of drawers and she cleans her teeth. This she does by rubbing them with soot. Then, pulling up her skirt, she sits cross-legged on a tartan rug spread out on the floor beside the bed and combs her hair. Then she curls up fully dressed and goes to sleep.

The following morning I raise a niggling suspicion that has been at the back of my mind for some time.

'There is someone beyond the door. There may be someone in the next room spying on us.'

'There is no one in the next room. Perhaps it is the children. You mean my little babies.'

I would like to investigate. Indeed I would like to get up and see if it is possible to stand on my good leg, but she presses herself against me, forcing me back against the pillow. Then she disengages herself.

Later Zora brings one of her children in, the four-year-old.

'Good child, this is a great friend of your father's.'

'When will Daddy be back?'

It seemed to me almost as though the child's pathetic question had been rehearsed.

'It is hard managing without him. You must look after your poor mother.' Then Zora sends him toddling out. She smiles. It is that secretive smile that irritates me.

'Keep those bloody children out. I want some more morphine. I need it.'

She is grinning madly as she swishes out the syringe and fills it with morphine solution. With my eyes I follow the needle circling over me, then it jabs down. Zora's ministrations are not kind and both my arms are now covered with scratches and bruises.

'Shshsh now. Go to sleep. You are safe here. You will wake the children.'

I drift off thinking about Zora's children. There should be medals for mothers of the revolution. The determinants of the mode of production apply as much to human beings as to factory commodities. The Arab prick is a powerful revolutionary tool. Four million Arabs at the beginning of the century. Almost 10 million now, and, from now on, the population will double every twenty years. The white man in Africa is being fucked out of existence . . .

In the morning when I wake up anxious for the needle, I find her as usual lying on the floor beside me. Looking round the room and at its French furniture and tapestry, I cannot approve. Some of my fellow officers would sneer at its bad taste for snobbish reasons. It's not that, but what I see in this ill-conceived clutter is clear evidence of al-Hadi's and Zora's determination to belong to the bourgeoisie. After all that this woman has gone through and all that the revolution should have taught her, all she wants to be is a big bourgeoise and hoard expensive furniture and clothes.

'Zora! Zora! Wake up, please! I need another shot.'

She is slow to stir and lies on the floor looking lazily up at me. There is a faint sleepy smile.

'Zora! The needle, I need the needle. I am beginning to hurt again.'

The four-year-old has come stumbling into the room, rubbing his eyes sleepily, woken by continued shouts. 'Zora! The morphine! Zora, it is time!' The alsatian in the corner is up and growling, but Zora just lies there smiling to herself.

Now I find that when the shots wear off, everything aches. My whole body is a cold grey ache. But yet it can be easily solved with the needle. Still she is not moving. Christ! I can get it myself though. Surely I can get across to the chest of drawers over there? I have been in bed long enough. I roll myself over to the edge of the mattress and painfully get my legs to hang over the edge. Now at last, when she sees what I am trying to do, she does stir herself. She is up on her feet and pushing me back on to the mattress. She is desperate to keep me in the bed. She is a skinny, slender little creature, but I am very weak and our struggle is prolonged.

As she presses herself against me, it comes into her mind to try to hold me back with something else. All the while pushing against me, with considerable difficulty she manages to get herself out of that hideous blue dress.

'Stay in bed, you bad man.'

She comes down upon me and her long tongue like a lizard's explores my mouth.

'Come on now, you darling. Why won't you tell me how my husband died?'

The child and the dog look on as we attempt love. Morphine is strange stuff. It brings on lust, but it all turns out to be in the head. And when the drug has worn off as now, I find I have the shakes. She lies on top of me and I catch a pleased, almost admiring expression in her eyes, but I sense that what she is admiring is not me but the shakes and the cold sweat that I have. After a while we cease to struggle and with a sigh she gives up.

'All right I get you the needle. Have another needle now, darling bad man.'

As the needle goes in the relief is tremendous. I can lie back and think coherently once more. I wish I knew why I am here, what part Zora has for me in her world of mysteries, but with the good stuff coursing through my veins once more, I can relax about it a bit. Faintly smiling, Zora comes back to lie on the bed beside me. She whistles the dog over to her and lies back contentedly allowing the dog to tongue-wash her toes.

The next time, a few hours later, it is not so easy.

'Bad man, you must beg for your shot.'

I can't allow myself to remain at the mercy of this woman much longer. That is clear.

'When is Tughril coming?'

She shrugged.

'Who is Tughril? I know no Tughril. He is not coming.' She slips away from the the bed, before I can grab her by the throat.

'What is your game, Zora?'

'I know of no games. I am not having any games.'

'I warn you, you are making a big mistake treating me like this. Give me my shot and stop playing all these silly games. Then I'll tell you how to get in touch with the nearest fellagha command cell. Now the needle, please.'

'Captain Roussel, you are not just a bad man, you are full of folly. They told me you killed my man. Now you tell me how you killed my man and you get your shot.'

'Who has told you this?'

There is a secretive little smile, but no reply.

'It is absurd!'

'No, you killed him. I know this.'

I lie back thinking. Why should she or I be shielded from the truth?'

'Yes. It was a necessary sacrifice for the revolution. He could not have escaped. He might have talked. I killed him as quickly as I could.'

'Ah bad man, what if he had talked? What then? Tell me now, you made him give up his life to save yours. What makes your soul so much bigger than his? And you killed him for nothing anyway. They found you out. That clever woman found you out. And now you lie on our bed, where I and my man used to lie and you have been happy for me to be waiting on you and nursing you. I do not think you are a man at all. You are a djinn, a very evil djinn.

'I am thinking that there is no more morphine for you any more. Imagine that. So now what are you going to tell me that is going to make me change my attitude? I cannot imagine. I am taking the morphine away from this room now. I think I shall go to my sister's house for a while. When I come back I shall have you on your knees telling me about how my man died.'

Now I lie coldly sweating on to the already damp mattress. My whole body seems to crawl, as if thousands of tiny maggots were active under the skin. I suppose I will tell her whatever she wants to know. Nothing is worth this. If there is something, I can't think too clearly about it. My head feels as though blunt pieces of wood are being slowly hammered up the nasal shafts into the porridgy brain. I throw myself on to the floor and . . . this is where Zora finds me screaming two hours later.

She looks perturbed to find me in such a state. She looks so distracted that I snatch at the opportunity. From the floor I lunge for the needle. The syringe drops to the ground and there is broken glass all around us. But I am on my feet and determined to make a break for it – or take control of the flat, or kill this Zora bitch. I don't know what exactly. But the wounded leg can hardly bear any weight at all. And the alsatian comes out of its corner snarling and then barking furiously. I hold on to Zora and use her as a shield against the raging dog. Zora wriggles and in her struggles kicks over the child's potty. The floor is slippery with shit and urine and brittle with broken glass and stained with blood from our bare feet. The dog keeps circling, trying to get at me behind Zora, barking all the time. Zora screams at me and the dog and it takes both my hands to keep her with me. So I wonder how I am going to get the door open and myself out of the bedroom without having the dog at my throat? I cannot stay upright much longer.

But now the door flies open and a black and brown shape hurls itself upon us. Zora and I crash to the ground and I find myself having to use the woman against two alsatians. And there is a second person in the room. It is one of the Ouled Nail dancers from downstairs, and Zora's four-year-old follows in after her. It is the end. The two women get the alsatians off and me back into bed, but not before one of the dogs has got its teeth deep into my bad leg and the claws of the other have raked an arm that was already covered with needle scratches. I lie there trying to get them to find me another shot, but the two women cluck and squawk away at one another in harsh Arabic. They are arguing about whether it is time, whether 'the gentleman' should be fetched.

'He is ready now.'

'He is really desperate,' the other woman agrees.

'We will have to buy another needle.'

Chapter Eleven

About an hour later I get the shot that I need and I can drift off. When I come round again, there is Raoul seated in a chair some distance from the bed and resting a pistol on his knee. There is a smell of disinfectant in the room, but no sign of Zora. Raoul seems faintly amused by the whole situation. I marvel at his elegance, the lightweight cotton three-piece suit in white and, beside the chair, the panama straw hat.

'I expect you are wondering what you are doing here?'

'Yes.'

'Wonder away.'

Then, about ten minutes later, he ventures, 'I don't think that we have decided what to do with you yet. Chantal and Schwab aren't here yet. Not everyone finds it as easy to leave Fort Tiberias as you did, but I expect they will be here tomorrow. Meanwhile, it seems that Madame al-Hadi can't cope any longer. So here I am to baby-sit for the lady.' Then he yells to the next room, 'Madame! Madame, get me a lager if you please.'

Zora comes trotting in with a can of beer. There is no lager for me. Raoul tells Zora to take al-Hadi's clothes out of the wardrobe and get rid of them. There is no reason why they should make escape easy for me. He has her find a key to the bedroom door too.

'But somehow I think that a naked drug addict with a bad leg is not going to get far in a sober little town like Laghouat.' Raoul reaches for his hat to fan himself.

'Well, we haven't decided what to do with you yet. But it is reasonable to suppose that, one way or another, you can be of use to us. (If you don't respond this is going to be very dull for me.) Chantal believes that you work for the other side from conviction but also that you became a convinced Marxist in one of those detention centres in Indochina. As we see it, you were brainwashed. She says that if you could be brainwashed one way, you can be brainwashed the other. It is a possibility. We might try that.'

I say nothing, just stare up at the ceiling. Let him tire himself out with talking.

'Christ Jesu! It's going to be dull, if you are not even going to talk. Chantal is quite impressed with your performance, both before the committee meeting and afterwards. She respects that kind of derring-do and ruthlessness. Mind you, it won't necessarily stop her castrating you with a blunt stone knife tomorrow.' Raoul laughs easily. 'And if we should decide to re-educate you, I should warn you it will not be a gentle process.

'Oh for Christ's sake you might say something! Look I have something to propose – a sort of wager. Let's debate Marxism. If I can persuade you that Marxism is fundamentally mistaken and evil, and we are convinced of the genuineness of your conversion, then Chantal and I will be delighted to have you in the struggle fighting shoulder to shoulder with us.'

I snort but Raoul continues, 'If on the other hand, you can persuade me that Marxism is right, I hand you the gun and you can walk free. Not only that but I will join the Party and follow you to the ends of the earth. Yes, that's perfectly serious. I am right-wing, some would say an extreme right-winger, but that does not make me a fool with a closed mind. I know that there are millions in the world who have gone over to communism, and without the brainwashing that you endured. There must be something in it. I should genuinely like to know what it is that they saw in it. I am curious. Educate me.'

'Leave off, Demeulze. This is not serious.'

'Oh but it is, life and death serious. An English bishop,

I think it was, once said, "Things are as they are and the consequences of them will be what they will be. Why then should we wish to be deceived?" ' Raoul throws the pistol up in the air and catches it, before continuing. 'I am like that. If you are right and I am wrong, then I will throw up everything for communism. There is no point in living in bad faith.'

'Piss off.'

'Come on. It is worth making the effort. I may be a fascist – I am sure that you have me tagged as that, but I am not one of those blood and soil fascists (and between the two of us Chantal is a sweet thing, but her politics are a bit irrational). No, I believe in reason. Indeed I believe that it is precisely their power of reasoning that has given Europeans hegemony over most of the world.'

'That's naïve irrational rubbish. It is money that has given international capital hegemony over most of the world.'

'Ah, so now we are talking! Go on. Go on, whether it is reason or money that has given France power over Algeria, why should I not support that French presence?'

'Because it is going to lose. It is stupid to back losers. Colonialism is the last gasp of the crisis of capitalism.'

'What crisis of capitalism? I see no crisis of capitalism. What's wrong with capitalism?' Raoul simulates a clownish bewilderment.

'So far capitalism has been able to stave off the escalating crisis of boom and slump that Marx predicted for it by finding new cheap markets in the colonies, but when the capitalists cease to control those markets, then comes the crisis of the capitalists and the triumph of the proletariat. What is wrong with capitalism is that it is based on a value system that is both false and inequitable. Take any commodity, it is the labour not the capital that creates the value, so it should be the labourer not the capitalist that gets the reward.'

'I don't see the moral force in that – but anyway how do we know that it is labour that gives a commodity value? What about . . . what about demand? Supply? Investment? The value given to a commodity by utility or rarity? And surely the capitalist deserves some reward for his cleverness and the risks he has taken?'

I ease myself up on one elbow and we smile at one another. We both know that I have very little chance of jumping him with his gun. It rests on his lap. I have to pray that I can get him so involved in the debate that the gun falls to the floor or something. And so the debate gets going. Sometimes Zora comes in with another lager for Raoul. I get water and a shot of morphine. It is over a grain a shot now.

At one point Raoul tries to draw Zora into the argument.

'What gets me is the squalor and drabness of Marxism. It is ugly thinking and ugly looking. Look at him, madame, as he lies on your bed, with his straggly half-grown beard and his hard fanatical eyes, and think of his belief in the ends justifying the means so that it is all right for him to torture and then murder your husband. Madame, can you find it in your heart to find that sort of creature attractive?' And Raoul makes a preposterous rhetorical flourish. A baiting gesture, I think. He intends to make me go for the gun.

Zora finds Raoul's French hard to follow. She pauses a moment and looks down on me with brooding eyes. Then, without saying a word, she puts the tray down and scuttles out.

Back to the labour theory of value. Raoul continues, 'No capitalist would deny that part of the cost of a finished commodity lies in the cost of labour and that the capitalist's profits come at least in part from the difference between what he has to pay his labourers and what he has to sell his goods for. But why should this blinding insight make us all Marxists?'

I don't believe that Raoul can be converted. It is only the irritability of the drugged that makes me argue. Raoul can't afford to abandon his old ideas. We all have a vested interest in the ideas we have grown up with.

Lunch comes in on a tray. I drift in and out of the argument. It's hard to listen to Raoul all the time when one is as heavily tanked up with morphine as I am. I guess that Raoul sees himself as some latter-day Socrates firing off his tricksy questions and me as some dimwit disciple stumbling after him round the Acropolis being led by the Socratic questions by the nose until the dumb pupil comes to the truth that the great philosopher was taking him to all the time. But Socrates didn't carry a gun. And I, the disciple he has chosen, facing a MAS 35, lie naked on a filthy bed, naked except for an awkwardly lumpy bandage round one knee, and am further handicapped by what seems very close to an overdose of morphine. I am thirsty all the time – and painfully constipated.

'And what is this abstract notion of value? Surely labour only has a price, the price an employer is prepared to pay for it?' Raoul seems to be obsessed by hammering these silly arguments home. Perhaps I should try to jump him now? I must make the attempt some time. But Raoul continues, 'I mean here I am arguing with you and pointing a gun at you.' (Blast! He has picked the gun up again.) 'It is labour – at least it feels like labour to me. Tell me what value my labour has and where it fits in with the Marxist scheme of things?'

Oh, it rambles on with both of us repeating ourselves and contradicting ourselves. We cover trade cycles and economic crisis, the role of the agrarian sector in a communist regime, the possibility that Marxist prophecies might be self-fulfilling, the arbitrariness or not of class-based analysis of society, the impossibility of gradualism and much else, but always we keep coming back to the god–damn labour theory of value.

'Roussel, I hope you won't take offence if I tell you that all I have heard from you seems to me . . . a little strange. Well, it is worse than that. It reminds me of a man I met on the boulevard Gaspigny a few weeks ago. He tried to sell me some drawings, diagrams really, lots of circles with faces and squiggles in them. He wore one of those broad-brimmed gypsyish hats and at first indeed I had the impression that I had been accosted by an artist, but when I looked into the shadow under the hat, I made another guess, a guess which was to be confirmed by what he went on to tell me. He told me that he had devised a system, based on mental hygienics, which allowed him to see into

99

the future. Even as we talked, there were invisible forces moving down the boulevard Gaspigny. They were invisible to everyone except him. He knew what was happening because he could see the radio waves in the street. Everything that happened in the world was based on radio waves. Everything in the world could be explained by reference to these radio waves. But because of his special knowledge there were people after him. The Director of Renault Cars was trying to have him killed. You have the picture? He had presence that man, with his big hat and long white beard. His craziness carried a certain conviction. For about half an hour after our meeting, I found myself looking over my shoulder for invisible radio waves or the no less invisible agents of Renault Cars. Absurd. Later it came to me that Marxism is like that – a contagious form of mass insanity, all hidden forces and great conspiracies, immensely elaborate, everything explained within the system – it's a total delusional system. Don't take offence now.'

Yes, I can picture the old man – one of Algiers's dispossessed, part of the drifting lumpenproletariat of poor whites – and I can imagine Raoul with his head cocked attentively, but smiling a smile that is almost a sneer.

'Did you buy the old man's drawings?'

Raoul impatiently waves the question away.

'Well, we'll call it a day, but I am enjoying our chats. You are the first real communist I have found to talk to. True I have met a few young ones in Paris, where a sort of Marxism is fashionable, but it seemed to me that for a certain type of young man it was something to talk about at parties and a way of getting up girls' skirts.' Raoul smiles as he polishes his glasses. 'But, for you and me, it is life and death serious.'

Then he stands up and makes for the door, but I still want the answer to my question.

'Did you buy the old man's drawings?'

Raoul laughs delightedly.

'No. Of course not. I made the old man up for the sake of the argument. You are so naïve, Philippe.'

He waves his hat at me at he leaves. Then bursting with an afterthought he sticks his head round the door again.

'I think that your commitment to communism is beginning to crumble. I have lit a long fuse, but, in the long run, you will come over to us.'

Then he is gone and the key turns in the lock. I am shaking with exhaustion and I ache all over. It's hard for me to focus properly on all that labour theory of value stuff, not because it is difficult – Raoul is just wilfully making difficulties – but because it is so boring. I have always preferred praxis and action. All that crap I was thinking in the desert about how it takes more courage to commit yourself to a dull but useful job and share your life with a wife and children, well I do think that at times, but I also think that it is crap. No pharmaceutical salesman from Grenoble could have put himself through what I have been through for the sake of the cause. To end up wounded, drugged and threatened by a young fascist maniac with a gun. I could make it to the window, but I know there is nothing to see, so I just lie here.

As I lie here, I hear a muffled cry from the next room. For a moment it crosses my mind that somehow Tughril has found out my whereabouts and the comrades have come to liberate me. Then I hear a rhythmic panting and I realize that Raoul has taken Zora and that he is probably having her on the living-room floor. Looking at it objectively I can see that I lost most of the arguments today. That doesn't necessarily mean that Raoul is right. Clever people can always twist things to suit themselves. Raoul is cleverer than me, OK, but so what? There are cleverer people yet on my side. People who could carve Raoul's arguments into little bits and have them for breakfast. It is my misfortune that none of these people are in this room at this moment. Still, no matter how clever, logical and well informed Raoul may be, he is not going to win me over. The moaning in the other room has stopped at last.

In the morning our investigations into the labour theory of value start all over again.

'The running dog of the fascist warmongers and captains of industry is back again,' says Raoul as he settles back into the chair. 'I wish, I really wish you could convert me. I love the language of communism. I love its running dogs and paper tigers and kulaks, captains of industry and imperialist lackeys. But now tell me again what you think the labour theory of value is and make it concise and clear this time. Chantal will be here by lunchtime and we shall have to bring our little disputation to a hasty and possibly brutal close.'

Wearily I go over some of yesterday's ground again, but Raoul says, 'I have thought of further objections to this labour value. Suppose an employer hires two men to make carriage clocks. They both spend the same amount of labour, that is time, making their carriage clocks, but one makes his of gold while the other makes his of zinc. Are you going to tell me that the two clocks are or should be of equal value?'

'Piss off, Demeulze. The truth is you are not worth converting. The cause does not need you. You nickety-pick at these intellectual problems and . . . and your intellectual niggles will, if you are lucky, save you from having to confront the *bidonville* that has grown up on the outskirts of Laghouat and on the outskirts of every town in Algeria. Your cleverness preserves you from seeing this shanty town where the dispossessed huddle in shacks of cardboard and corrugated iron and collect their water from gutters which run with faeces. People like you are not worth arguing with.'

His good humour abruptly vanishes.

'I want an answer, Roussel. Give me an answer about the two carriage clocks, one of gold and one of zinc, and make it a good one or I will blow the fingers of your right hand off.'

I groan.

'I am not saying that the gold clock will sell for the same as a zinc clock. You can't honestly think that Marxists believe that. Of course a gold clock will sell for more, but there we are talking about gold's price, not its value . . .'

'But this mystical "value" is like the madman's invisible radio waves . . .'

'No it is not. If the price of an object were the same as its value where would profit be? How can there be profits in the exchange of varying commodities – carriage clocks, penknives, saucepans and so on – unless they have something in common? What they have in common is value. There is nothing mystical or moral in this, it is common-sense economics. I am not a more moral man than you are – '

Raoul laughs.

' – and you will not become a more moral man by becoming a Marxist – any more than understanding that the world is round not flat makes one want to help old ladies across the street.'

'I understand that, but you are telling me that it is man's labour which gives an object value . . . Well, suppose Demeulze and Co. has an industrial robot which makes gold carriage clocks, what is the value of a gold carriage clock now?'

Raoul brandishes the pistol as if it were a blackboard pointer in the classroom. Momentarily it occurs to me to wonder if the non-existent old man in the boulevard Gaspigny was so very mad after all.

'Demeulze, forgive me, I need another shot, if we are to continue with this.'

'Madame! Madame al-Hadi!' he bellows. He hasn't even troubled to learn her proper name which is Madame al-Shaykhoun. 'Get me a drink and our friend needs some more treatment.'

She nods but before she can leave the room, I call to her, 'Believe me, Zora, I took no pleasure in killing your husband. It was a mercy killing. Even suppose it had been possible to arrange his escape, what would it have been who returned home to you? A man who has been systematically tortured for any length of time isn't really a man at all. But he did die for a cause, and if you let men like this . . . this gentleman in the suit . . . do you think he has *droit de seigneur*? Your husband's sacrifice will all have been in vain . . . So he forced you . . . There is no need to feel shame. It is one of their tricks to transfer shame, but the true shame is that of the imperialist and the rapist.'

'We all have our own ideas about how the oppressed peoples of Africa can best be helped,' says Raoul smiling.

The slinky creature flashes a cheeky grin back at him and self-consciously waggles out of the room. Raoul continues to smile amiably at the closing door before he turns back to me.

'Look at you, you are a mess. And I don't just mean how you look at this moment. I mean look at your life. You are a born loser, someone who is bound to attach himself to lost causes. Your rotten destiny sent you to Dien Bien Phu. You have been severely tortured once in your life already. This afternoon when Chantal arrives you will be tortured again. You remember Lieutenant Schwab? I can see that you do. You worked with him on al-Hadi. Chantal has succeeded in recruiting him to our cause and they must both be on their way here by now. Think about it. You get yourself in these situations. Subconsciously you are a masochist – that's what Marxism is for you, your own special brand of masochism.'

Zora comes in with a lager in one hand and the needle in the other. The four-year-old comes after her trying to catch hold of the edge of her dress. She is waiting for Raoul to acknowledge her presence before giving him his beer. I make a final effort.

'Listen, Demeulze. As it happens Marxist economic theory is right, but even if it were not . . . even if it were not, it would still be worth pretending that it was, just to do something about that *bidonville* outside Laghouat.'

A look of faint concern crosses Raoul's face.

'I don't understand.'

'You never will!' And with that I heave myself out of bed and snatch up the four-year-old. I hold him up before me. I hold him by the throat.

'Give me the gun, Raoul, or I will break this child's neck.'

'Ah no! Not little Rashid!' cries Zora.

Raoul has not shifted his position. He is perfectly relaxed, his head thrown back, his lidded eyes seem only mildly amused.

'You are talking to the wrong man, Roussel. Kill the child and let's get back to our argument.'

But if Raoul is untroubled, this is not true of Zora. She plunges the hypodermic into Raoul's ear to the full length of the needle. As he sits there making the most extraordinary gargling noises I throw the child away from me and snatch the gun from his shaking hand.

Chapter Twelve

'What happened to the clothes Raoul told you to get rid of?'

'I gave them to Selima to sell.' Selima is the Ouled Nail dancer who rents a room downstairs.

'Go and see if she still has them. I will look after your children while you are gone.'

She exchanges a panicky look with Rashid before hurrying off. While she is gone I prise the tiles off part of the living-room wall and take out the package of explosive compounds that al-Hadi had stored there. The blasting caps are stored separately further along the wall.

I have left Raoul sitting screaming with the needle in his ear. I do not imagine that he will live. In Tonkin I heard of a man who died from a hat-pin thrust through the ear, but I'm not interested in what happens to Raoul. It was always certain that I would outwit him. I did not survive the death march from Dien Bien Phu to Lang Trang only to fall victim to a piece of shit like that, for I carry an unfinished story within me, my destiny. No man has to drift impotently in the face of his future. Every man has within him the capacity to imitate, on an individual basis, the success of Stalin's Five Year Plans.

Zora comes back with a large bundle of al-Hadi's clothes. I put on an ill-fitting suit. Al-Hadi was a thinner man than me. I have a job jamming the pistol into the waistband under the jacket. Then I go into the bedroom and kneel over Raoul to rifle his pockets. I find his wallet. Then I go back out to Zora.

'Morphine?'

She shows me what she has. A tiny packet, one shot's worth, two at most.

'Syringe?'

She shakes her head and points to the needle in Raoul's ear. In his writhings Raoul has snapped off the needle from the rest of the hypodermic.

'You don't have another needle?'

She shakes her head. I feel scratchy, very tight. If I start feeling worse, I won't be able to think clearly enough to think what to do. Using the pistol I usher Zora into the bedroom where Raoul lies moaning and I lock the door. Then, bag of explosives in hand, I issue out into the streets of Laghouat. It is the end of the day. It takes me a while to find from memory the town's only pharmacy, in the shadow of the Cathedral of the Bishop of the Sahara. When I get there, I see that the man is shutting up shop. I shout and try to run across the square. I do not care to think what this is doing to my leg. He pauses reluctantly at his operations with the shutters.

'Sir, I need some morphine.'

'Do you indeed? Didn't those fools at the hospital tell you when I close?'

I stare at him silently.

'Oh, very well. Where's your prescription?'

I continue to stare at him silently. I think that I am standing stock still, until I see that he is staring at my hands which are shaking horrifically and the shakes go up to the shoulders. My whole body is riven by shudders.

'Oh I see one of those . . . Ah, the pity . . . Eh, well I can't do anything . . . You are a veteran, I guess?'

His eyes are indeed filled with pity. A short man, he is even shorter than me. He has rheumy eyes and a nose like a distended raspberry.

'A veteran, yes,' I mutter.

Yes that is what I am.

'And when you were hospitalized with that leg . . .' He has his keys out, but he is not doing anything with them.

I pick up the cue he has supplied me with.

107

'Yes, yes . . . We were on ops in the Kabyle.'

I talk very fast and it seems to me that I am talking as fast as my hands are shaking.

'Our officers were wonderful fellows, but the op went wrong . . . I don't know . . . A bunch of fellagha had been spotted trying to leave over some high ground. We were dropped by helicopter, but things started to go wrong when my section was landed on the wrong hill and we couldn't find the rest of the platoon. I was sent off up the hill to see if I could see any sign of them over the crest, but I ran into a bunch of fellagha instead and bought it in the leg. That was it for me. I just lay there in the dark watching my blood oozing through the bit of shirt I'd tied round the wound, and feeling colder and colder as the blood oozed out, like it was being forced out of my body by a slow pump. I didn't dare shout for fear of bringing the guns of the fellagha on to me again – or worse the fellagha themselves. That happened to three of my mates the previous summer in the Aures. I can tell you about that. For some reason they had wandered off from the platoon's line of march. By the time we found them again they had all had their eyes gouged out. Two of them were dead from shock, the third was still breathing and they'd all had their severed cocks stuffed into their mouths. Our lieutenant shot the third man.'

The chemist has turned away, revolted by my words, but I clamp my hand to his shoulder.

'So, to go back to me in the Kabylie, you can imagine the sorts of things that I was thinking. It was hours before the captain found me. He was a terrific guy. Stayed by me till dawn. I couldn't be lifted off the plateau until then. The pain was pretty awful and the ride in the chopper was none too smooth. They gave me morphine for it in hospital. They did it for the best, but I find that I have grown to like the taste. The leg's never healed properly, as you can see, sir, and when they discovered that I had become addicted they tried to sweat it out of me a couple of times, before giving up. I was invalided out. I have nothing to go back to France for. I can pay you for the morphine, sir. To tell you the truth, I can't do without it.'

'Come inside.'

While he fishes about among his powders he tells me not to keep calling him sir. His name is Eugene. He hunts around for a new box of hypodermics and I chatter madly. I tell him how I envy him his shop and his work and what a fascinating study pharmacy must be. Slowly a thought strikes him. One can see the presence of it spreading over his face.

'I'll give you a shot now. But of course you will soon be needing another. Why don't you come to my house and I'll give you another later in the evening and we can discuss what can be done for you. There are treatments, not here in Laghouat, but . . .'

(I wonder if he is queer, but he goes on . . .)

'Oh and of course there will be dinner. My wife serves excellent food, though maybe not as excellent as the armagnac.'

'That will be fine. You are very kind. Thank you . . . er, Eugene.'

'And that leg of yours looks as though it needs attention, I'll look at it of course, but we could drive in to the military hospital tomorrow. It will be no trouble. I have to go there anyway.'

We set off in his 2 CV. The house is on the fringe of town and backs on to the oasis groves. Incongruously there are a couple of pigs lying in the rapidly lengthening shade of the palm trees. They are the chemist's pigs. He also keeps bees. It is a while yet before the sun sets, but already his wife is busying herself putting the makeshift shutters up – a night-time precaution against prowling FLN snipers, although it is a couple of years since there has been any of that sort of thing in Laghouat. Still the fear lingers on. The wife turns to regard the 2CV crunching over the gravel. In the dying light of the sun her face is like a yellow skull.

As the wife comes to shake my hand and be introduced, the chemist (I must learn to call him Eugene) explains somewhat apologetically. 'It is all right for the soldiers – forgive me –

they sometimes get leave. But we civilians, we are constantly on duty. We always have to be on guard. Over there, look. Our neighbours are putting up their shutters too.'

Eugene waves to the neighbours, but I am keen not to be seen by them and make haste to follow his wife, Yvonne, into the house.

'We are very modest here, you see.'

I ease myself into a chair with some difficulty.

'Leg troubling you? You must let me look at it – after dinner, when you will be wanting another shot anyway.'

Eugene's wife has a long death-white bony face. There are liver spots on her pale hands. But she has a sunnier disposition than was first suggested by that skull-like face and as she bustles about the table she teases out of Eugene Laghouat's pitiful modicum of gossip. At last we are all ready and seated.

'The Arabs have a proverb, "A stranger is the friend of every other stranger." Eat your fill, my strange friend,' says Eugene.

It's cassoulet. Their daughters are away staying with an aunt in Constantine. As I say, the wife is nicer than she looks and we are relaxed and merry at table. Once more I set to, telling Eugene how much I envy him his shop, and then I go on to explain how I had a job all set up as a pharmaceuticals salesman in Grenoble. But then my call-up papers came, the job was given to someone else and by the time my battalion was ready to be shipped out to Oran, my fiancée had written to me telling me that she was going to marry that someone else.

It is all amazing drivel. Now that I have this picture of me as a pharmaceuticals salesman in Grenoble clearer in my mind, I know for sure what drivel this daily beauty of the humdrum is. If I had become a pharmaceuticals salesman in Grenoble . . . I find it hard to imagine quite how evil I would have become, the million little evils and petty lies of my everyday bourgeois existence, all contributing to the single great evil of capitalism. Thinking of myself with neat little moustache and suitcase full of pharmaceutical samples, I have difficulty in choking back my laughter. Yvonne looks at me curiously.

'You look rather old to be a conscript.'

'Ah, but that was in '55, madame, and much has happened to me since then. When I got my wound and was invalided out, I stayed on here. There was nothing for me to go back to in France.'

Eugene looks concerned.

'We'll talk about this later. But you must watch yourself. This morphine business can add years to your life – in your case I think it already has.'

'Well anyway, I'm glad you came out as a conscript,' says Yvonne. 'That's better than the Legion. The legionnaires round here are like gypsies, thieving and stealing . . . They treat this place like a foreign land under occupation.'

They talk about how the war has changed the place. Eugene remembers growing up in Laghouat, that was before even the Hôtel Transatlantique was built. In those days there was less of a racial feeling in the town and as a boy he used to play in the streets with the Arabs and Jews. You don't see much of that these days. Yvonne's upbringing was rather different. She was not born in Laghouat, but came here from the coast. She starts to reminisce about her girlhood and her first ball at the Governor's Residence in Algiers. There is perhaps a hint of snobbery in these carefully hoarded memories, a yearning for something other than the provincial existence that she finally settled for. Still, Yvonne laughs unaffectedly at that young girl's gaucheness and timidity and her dreams of being swept off her feet by an officer in the Spahis.

'I thought it would go on forever, the dances and the afternoon calls . . .'

When I say that the wife is nice, and for that matter Eugene too, this does not mean that I like them. I do not like nice people. Nor does it necessarily mean that I will spare them. As I sit here chewing on the pork, I am wondering will it be desirable or necessary to kill this old couple?

The family photograph album comes out and is passed across the table. I love looking at old photos. Here is the youth, Eugene, playing cards with his father in a flowery garden and here is Yvonne picnicking with some officers on an outing to the Hoggar and there are lots of photos of the one year they took their daughters to mainland France to show them to their grandmother a little before she died. I am reminded of other photos – of the one taken of Chantal's mother sitting with a spaniel on her lap and shading her eyes against the glare of the sun. That was only a few days before the Philippeville massacre. And the one of Mercier and Jomard standing arm in arm on the edge of the metal airstrip at Dien Bien Phu. Jomard did not survive the attempt to break out of Fortress Isabelle. In my eyes and in retrospect the people staring at the lens seem actually to be facing some sort of firing squad, and so they are for, in time, they will all be dead and when we open an album of photographs we are contemplating the dead – the buried dead and the walking dead.

I would like to pump them for news of Fort Tiberias. I should like to know if the incident in the fort is public knowledge in Laghouat, but this is risky. If there is a hunt on for a renegade legionnaire officer I do not want them to reconsider me in this light. Besides it rapidly becomes apparent that the couple have no great interest in political and military affairs.

'Eh, how do we know what is going on, from reading the newspapers I ask you? Lies, censorship and simple misinformation. It is stupid to try and follow current affairs.'

'Politics is very boring,' Yvonne agrees with a sigh.

Eugene comes out with a cassoulet–rich fart.

Yvonne winces. I smile. Eugene catches my hastily vanishing smile.

'Angels flying overhead,' says Yvonne.

Why is it that all parties and all political thinkers despise the petit bourgeois? I share the common prejudice. However the conversation must be kept going, so I tell them how I, too, have never had any time for politics.

'Only the show–offs and the immature get involved in politics. And make a lot of noise, but left-wing, right-wing, communist, fascist, how much difference is there between them really? Noisy egotists, they make a lot of noise about their theories and doctrines, but when they come to power, they all do the same things in the end.'

Yvonne and Eugene are happy to consent to this comfortable rubbish and Eugene starts telling me how much more interesting bees are than politicians.

After fruit, Yvonne takes the plates into the kitchen. She refuses my offer of assistance with the washing up. Eugene pours us two out some armagnac. It is plain that he wants us to have a heart to heart.

'Don't take offence now, Philippe, but (correct me if I am wrong) I sense in you an over-fastidious soul . . . I saw you looking at my wife . . . Yes, I saw that smile . . . Well, let me be frank. If one can't fart in front of one's wife, one is not really intimate with her. It does not seem to me that one is properly married . . .'

He breaks off for Yvonne has come in to wish us goodnight. Eugene says that we will sit up a little longer and that he will see to my bedding. He listens to her going up the stairs, before speaking again.

'She is a good sort that little wife of mine. We are content . . . or we were before this war started . . . Eh, they look down on us in France. I know or at least I can imagine. All right, I don't read Camus or Robbe-Grillet and the wife can't afford to dress from *Vogue*. I raise pigs and keep bees. Is that such a bad thing? Eh . . . Now how have I offended my fellow countrymen that I must lose my home, my garden, my pigsties, say goodbye to the church in which I worshipped and the school where I learned my letters and my daughters are learning theirs? What evil have we done that we must forfeit our livelihoods and our memories? We are to become the refugees and pensionaries of the very men who sold us out. That big man, the General, showing his medals to the cameras, talking about "Frenchmen", he is not talking about us, but only about himself. It's all mad.'

Why is he telling me all this? Does he think that I have the ear of the General? He looks as though he is about to cry, but then he pulls himself together.

'Eh well, time to look at that leg.' He motions me to follow him and we go into what seems to be a small study. He wants me to take my trousers off, but I say, 'The shot first.'

I thrust my bared arm at him, a tangled mess of scratches and lumps. The needle is expertly inserted. This must be the end of the masquerade, but since the morphine is now slowly pumping through my veins, I am relaxed about it. I produce the pistol from my waistband. It is awkward stepping out of the trousers while covering the man with the gun, but I manage it.

'I want a proper dressing on this.'

From time to time as he works on the leg he looks up at me with dubious eyes, but he says nothing. Guessing doubtless how this must end, he takes his time and makes a good job of the new clean dressing. When he has finished, I shoot him in the skull. To see the side of a skull fly apart under the force of the bullet — or rather not see it, it is so fast — is something extraordinary. 'Might is the midwife of every old society pregnant with a new one. It is in itself an economic power.' Marx's watchword is mine.

Now I mount the stairs hoping to find the wife still in bed, but I meet her halfway down the stairs and I set about clubbing her down the steps, beating her about the head and not stopping until she lies lifeless in the hallway. I stand there a while catching my breath and listening to hear if the sound of the gun has attracted the attention of the neighbours. Once more I find myself wishing that my Tokarev had a silencer, but if it did then the muzzle velocity would be slower. In my experience, there is no such thing as the perfect weapon. Then I try to carry the woman back upstairs in my arms, but I cannot bear her weight so I drag her up in fits and jerks and heave her on to the bed. Then I pull her nightgown up and set to work with my tapes and detonation cords. When I have finished, I consider booby-trapping the husband's corpse too, but one will be enough for the effect. Besides, the plastique is used up. I would not dare carry such unstable stuff around any longer. All I have is some chloride and that is not so easy to use in these booby-traps.

I have often lectured on the subject but I haven't actually

handled explosives of any sort since training. I am pleased with myself. In itself nitroglycerine is no joke to handle and once the nitrocellulose is added it is even more dodgy, but it is precisely this instability, which sets the operator such problems, which also gives the stuff such a hair-fine response when the trap is actually triggered off. What I have set up is an adaptation of the wire-trip device, in which the cord tied to Yvonne's legs pulls the firing pin which sets off the blasting cap and then the main charge. The *frisson* created by this sort of outrage, it's so much more effective than an ordinary tactical strike against a railway siding or something. In the next few months a few more *pieds noirs* here in Laghouat will probably decide to pull up roots and migrate back to France. Why the death of this old couple should be so shocking, I don't know. Oh yes, I do. They are Europeans. But if forty villagers in the highlands of the Kabyle are killed in a pacificatory bombing raid, that is different. That is done by people in uniform, it is backed by state structures and the people are Arabs, not fully people. It is all quite different. But I don't have to justify myself to myself.

I can do nothing more tonight. At night the roadblocks and patrols are pretty intense – not to mention the ironic risk of being ambushed by the FLN. Part of the effect I shall be creating comes from the supposition that I have killed innocent people. Of course they weren't innocent. Of course not. Their style of life battens on the poor and feeds off the Arabs. It would cost an Arab a year's work to buy some of Eugene's medicines. He gave me dinner, yes and thanks for that I suppose, but he wouldn't have given an Arab or a Berber dinner. And he has a standard of living forty times higher than the natives. And when I was torturing Arabs on behalf of *Algérie francaişe*, did this man try to stop me? Did he as much as write a letter to the newspapers? He knew perfectly well what I and others were doing. The cells in our barracks came to resemble abattoirs. We slopped around in Arab blood, all so that the 'innocent' pharmacist might keep his beehives and pig-sties. In the context of a country in revolution, this innocence is a form of evil.

By now Chantal and that lieutenant must have arrived at Laghouat. Will Raoul still be alive to speak to them? Will Zora stay there to risk Chantal's rage? What will Chantal's next move be? Ah, but it is hopeless guessing. And it is no use being idle. Now I have got my breath back, I start to search the living room. It does not take me long to find what I am looking for – a camera and a box of flash bulbs kept in the corner cupboard. Then I go upstairs and take pictures of Yvonne's body displayed on the bed with her legs drawn up at an awkward angle and her head propped up on the bloody pillow. Then I go down to find Eugene and arrange his body in all sorts of grotesque angles for my pictures. Technically this is interesting work – aesthetically too, for photography furnishes atrocity with its aesthetics. This war of ours in Algeria has been fought in black and white and when I dream of this war it is always in grainy black and white images. There is no brilliant blue sky, no yellow sand, no multi-coloured Arab robes, only the two-colour chiaroscuro of the soldiers, politicians and journalists.

Photography produces quirky and visually enhancing effects. When some little bourgeois in Grenoble opens his newspaper over the coffee and croissants and finds my snap of Yvonne with her head clubbed in, he will not see what I have seen; in some respects it will be more horrible. I have noticed before that blood in the camera's register does not look like blood and the blood on the pillow behind Yvonne's head will probably more closely resemble shit spattered round a lavatory bowl and, though civilians in France are rarely allowed to see these photographs (it would be bad for their morale), a head that has been clubbed in does not seem to contain brains, but rather some strange black fibrous matter. So anyway this good citizen at his breakfast table will contemplate my picture of Yvonne. He will be revolted, yes, but he will also feel guilty that he is impotent to do anything about it and, thoroughly demoralized, in time he will harden his heart to the plight of the *pieds noirs* in Algeria. He has already hardened his heart to the plight of the millions who starve in Africa and Asia. When the flash bulbs are used up, I fire off the rest of the film into the darkness. Then I put the roll of film in my bag.

I lie on the sofa downstairs, thinking, plotting and dozing, until just before dawn. Then I don one of the chemist's suits and bury al-Hadi's blood-bespattered suit outside the back door. I drive the 2CV into Laghouat and use the dead man's keys to open his shop. I take what looks like a year's supply of morphine and some needles, also the small change from the till. Then I drive north. Half a mile outside Bou Hara I abandon the car in a grove of cork trees and walk into town. At the bus station I find a bus that is leaving for Algiers in half an hour. There are a couple of poor whites on the bus and me. Otherwise the bus is filled with Arabs and there are even children standing in the aisles. Jasmine water is sprinkled on the passengers by the driver just before we leave. It will be a five-hour journey. Two hours into the journey there is an inspection of papers. A conscript and his officer move slowly up the aisle carefully examining papers and irritably crushing the children against the seats. As they come close, I brandish Raoul's *carte d'identité*. Even this gesture was unnecessary. They are not interested in the Europeans, only in the Arabs. I relax back into my seat and contemplate the gentle melancholy of the Algerians. They look like sheep preparing to be slaughtered. Not that sheep do, of course. I admire the view and think. These dopey passive Arabs content to be on their way to market . . . Actually I believe that stupidity is also a form of evil . . . a culpable refusal to see the truth.

To see so many stupid people around me, it is depressing perhaps. But I am on the loose once more and free to act. They will never be able to keep up with me. I have scarcely begun.

Chapter Thirteen

I was sitting beside an autumn bonfire when I saw a woman dressed as Harlequin pacing about on the opposite side of the fire. She walked with a mannish stride, but despite the mask, I was certain that she was a woman. She was offering everyone fruit. In the orange sunset light, I at first mistook the apples for oranges. Later she sat down beside me and introduced me to her younger sister. That was the *fête de village* when I was ten, I think. That would be in 1935? I don't know why this picture should suddenly have come unbidden to me.

There is leisure for thinking on the bus, too much for my tastes. I should prefer to be moving and acting . . . Still, it is desirable that I should satisfy myself that there was nothing personal or pathological in my killing of Yvonne and Eugene. I apply the discipline of self-criticism and examine my motives. At length I am satisfied. It is true that I have a generalized hatred of old people, but this is the product of what I consider to be a political perception. Yes, old people shamble about in front of me in the street getting in my way – and there across the aisle in the bus at this very moment there is an aged Berber who has been irritating me immensely by smiling at nothing whatsoever and by grunting at irregular but frequent intervals. He is old, impoverished and a member of an oppressed nation; in those circumstances his smile is peculiarly fatuous. But no, there is nothing personal in my detestation of the old. The mutual hatred of young and old is half of politics. Simply, old people are an obstacle to revolutionary change, a dead weight on the future.

I am not a fool. Of course I shall be old myself one day. I hope that I shall have the courage to hate myself then. As long as we have not learned to hate old age, poverty and sickness, the world will never change. Revolution works towards Harlequin and the apples which glow like little suns.

But I am not going to spend four or five hours just thinking about old people. At the same time, my mind is active on other matters. Suppose this bus is being followed? I can see no consistent tail but that proves nothing. Suppose there is a tail, a shadow on the bus itself? It could be that daft old Berber. Suppose Chantal, or for that matter the SDECE, if they still believe I am alive deduce my destination and the means available to me to reach it? So that when the bus pulls up at the terminus, there is a reception committee waiting, waiting and patiently slapping their cudgels lightly against their palms? Suppose that when I do alight at Algiers and start to try to make contact I find that the cell I need to make contact with has been broken up? Or suppose that when I do make contact with Tughril, I discover that he has been turned by the SDECE, or worse I never discover that he has?

It is good to be properly cautious, and in my trade it is desirable to examine all possible eventualities, but I do not intend to go potty doing so. I am careful also to have more positive thoughts, so I think to myself how good it is that I who have worked as a loner for so long will be now able to jettison solitude and deception and walk shoulder to shoulder with my comrades. How bad it has been, these years of playing soldier and spy. It is not good for a man to be alienated from the product of his labour, nor is it healthy to be an individualist. Men should work together, to spur each other on by example and to offer each other solidarity. I am tired of playing my hand against every other man's. I want to come in. It is time for some human warmth.

Algiers the white!

The coach terminus is in Mustapha Inférieure, not far from the place Raymond Poincaré. The first need is to find a *pissoir* where I can shoot up some more morphine – a tricky business if I am to do it fast and not to drop the bag or the needle. Posted on the side of the *pissoir* is the latest round-up of faces of wanted men. My face is not yet among them. Now, how many years have I spent in this country? Nearly eight I think and never before have I had to take public transport. It takes me some time before I can work out which tram it is I need to cross town by. Waiting at a tram stop is something new for me. I am conscious of myself standing here as shabby, limping, down at heel. The once close-cropped hair now sticks out like the spines of a sea urchin, and I have a straggly beard. Well, I rejoice that I am not such a dull dog as I seem, with my little bags of morphine and chloride explosive.

There is a man at the table of the café opposite who seems to be watching me. It takes me time to assure myself that this is in fact not so. He is admiring the red-haired Jewess who stands beside me in the queue. I should say that his gaze was concentrated on the seams of her stockings. It is the hour of the anisette and the tables in front of the café opposite are almost full. Happy hour, as the disgusting Americans call it, but few of these citizens look happy. They sit there saying little, but watching each other. There is an old white-bearded man moving among the tables trying to sell the clients what may be drawings. His chosen victims look up at the old man, while clients at tables further away watch their predicament with amusement and these clients are in turn being watched by a couple of women leaning over a balcony on the opposite side of the street. And down in the street a gaggle of veiled fatmas stare up at the balcony with eyes that glitter with envy or with malice. Eye crosses eye. Suddenly and incongruously I find myself thinking of Yvonne and Eugene and Eugene's fart.

At the rival café, a few buildings along, the attention of the drinkers is rather focused on the passers-by and some men watch the women clicking by on their high heels, but other men are watching the eyes of their fellows to see what women their eyes are following. A waiter stands by alert for further orders, but I do not think that his eyes are only for the customers, for at frequent intervals his eyes sweep over the floor of the café and the pavement outside, looking for suspicious and abandoned packages. By now, this is such a conditioned part of his life that he is probably not even aware that he is doing it. A man walks by in too much of a hurry, even at this distance he is visibly sweating. All eyes turn to watch him instead. Idleness, sexual desire and now fear direct the eyes of this city. A city in fear, I like it, for fear is my element, I have lived with fear, inside fear, ever since the morning of 11 March 1954 when the guns opened fire on Fortress Gabrielle in the valley of Dien Bien Phu. To see the rest of these shits living in fear, why it makes my heart beat a little faster!

The tram takes me almost to the door of the Hydra Sports Club on the edge of the Marengo Gardens. I purchase a temporary membership ticket, but, no, I do not want to swim. Make contact with Tughril, report to Tughril, yes that will be the end of my mission, but this is not a simple matter. Even I do not know who Tughril is or how to contact him directly. 'Tughril' is certainly not the real name of this cell leader. However, one possible contact may be here at the club working as a lifeguard. I know the man was used by al-Hadi as a channel for getting messages to Tughril, but even this man who works here as a lifeguard, I do not know his real name only his nickname, so I will have to ask one of the boys for 'Nounourse'. I pause watching the dance of the lights, threads of gold on the water before calling a boy over. It takes a sort of courage for a man to ask for a 'Teddybear', but fortunately there is no smile. The boy realizes who it is I want.

The boy walks to the side of the pool. It is as if he is summoning a monster up from its depths. The vast shape breaks from the water and heaves itself up on to the tiles and advances with deliberate tread towards me. Nounourse is almost a giant, heavily muscled, bearded and smiling with the genial ferocity of a Barbary pirate. The genial smile however vanishes when he realizes that I am not a customer who has to be smiled at, but a comrade. I mutter an identification code and ask to be put in touch with Tughril. We arrange to meet in the Marengo Gardens in half an hour's time when he can get off work. Then with the grin sliced like a wound on his face once more he goes back to teaching the white children how to swim. That grin reminds me of the famous Kabyle smile. Indeed the Kabyle smile stretches from ear to ear, but it runs across the throat and it is made with a knife.

At the gates of the Marengo Gardens I buy a copy of the *Echo d'Alger*. There is nothing about Fort Tiberias, but of course after all this time it would not still be news, even if the press had been allowed by the military to learn something about that affair. There is nothing either about 'Atrocious Outrage at Laghouat', but doubtless that will rate a substantial little column tomorrow.

At length there is an enormous paw on my shoulder. Such a mass of flesh and bone I do not think I have seen before outside a butcher's shop.

Nounourse's voice is a terrible growl.

'Meet me again on the north side of the place du Lyre. Start walking now.'

Nounourse never meets me in the place du Lyre, but a match seller gives me the message: 'In fifteen minutes' time leave the place du Lyre, go up rue Randon and enter the kasbah at the Médée checkpoint. Then left, then up Affreville to the Zawiya of Sidi M'Haıned Cherif, then up the Barberousse steps to rue Abdallah and over to rue Nfissah and into the impasse de Ramadan. Do not take any short cuts. I will look after your bag.'

Of course, it is grief and anguish for me to surrender my bag. But I am schooled in discipline and the avoidance of needless risks. I surrender by bag to the comrade, only warning him not to let it be searched by the security forces. I can afford to be without my drug for a little while, for after all I hardly think that I am yet an addict.

The kasbah comes cascading down the hillside in flights of steps and narrow streets. Streets, houses and courtyards coil around one another. The Battle of Algiers was won for the French almost two years back. Massu's paras no longer guard the entrances to the kasbah. There are only bored gendarmes at the Médée checkpoint. There is no longer any curfew.

Nevertheless, as the darkness comes on, I hurry and those few people I meet in the kasbah are hurrying too, as if flames of fear were licking round their ankles. Even before the outbreak of this war, which is not a war, the kasbah was not safe by night and the markets closed before the evening prayer. In this close warren of little alleyways and covered passages, whose walls are broken only by heavy painted and studded doors which open to release or admit veiled and hooded figures, a fanciful man might dream that he stood or walked in the Cairo of the *Arabian Nights* and revel in its mysteries. I have no time for such rubbish. What savour can there be in the stink of poverty? And certainly the kasbah stinks – some of the stink is shit and rotting vegetables, some of it is the disinfectant which trickles out of great drums which are rolled down the alley by boys in blue overalls watched by steel-helmeted soldiers. What sort of a literary turd can take pleasure in the kasbah, a racial ghetto and a cheap labour camp? This is the charmed world of Harun al-Rashid! And who is it who contemplates those thickly studded doors and windows covered with closely worked mashrabiyya and seriously thinks that some sort of enchantment lies beyond them? What lies beyond the door is a man with too little work and too many children and an ignorant, illiterate wife who fears the beating her husband will infallibly give her tonight, before he ploughs her like a tilled field, and the hungry children cower in the corners hearing and seeing it all. These picturesque houses are structures of oppression, prisons for women, and the kasbah a place of incarceration for the people of Algeria. The kasbah is a good home for criminals and rats, a breeding ground for mental illness.

Close by the steps that go up to the Zawiya Ben M'Hamed, I am witness to a scene. An old woman, too old to need to veil her tattooed and warty face, is stopped by a gendarme. She is carrying a flaming torch and a bucket of water. Where is she going? What is she up to? She tried to push past, screeching in bad French, that she is in a hurry. The torch is for setting fire to Paradise and the water to extinguish the flames of hell, so that we should not live in expectation of one or fear of the other. The gendarme smiles and lets her by – and taps his head significantly. Then, catching sight of me, he shouts that I should hurry to get out of these parts and asks if I would like an escort. I shake my head vigorously and I too hurry on in the direction the old woman had taken, but she has vanished.

I am now, I guess, about ten minutes from the impasse de Ramadan, but I never reach it. Just short of the impasse de Grenade (where two years back Ali la Pointe made his last stand against the paras), a man shoulders me through an open doorway. Two others, waiting in its shadows, bring me to the ground and after a brief struggle bind my hands. A huge hand comes over my mouth. For a long time then nothing happens, the men in the dark are audibly recovering their breath. The hand is still on my mouth and I know it is Nounourse's. I fear I may suffocate.

Somebody on the roof whistles. A light across the court-yard comes on and Nounourse drags me into the now lit-up reception room. I am flung on to the sofa, the only bit of furniture in the room. Nounourse lowers himself carefully down beside me. I can smell the swimming pool's chlorine on his breath. Three other men come into the room. Two of them come up close and examine my face. At length one of them says, 'All right, it is him, with a beard. This is comrade "Yves", or rather since his cover has been blown, it can be Captain Philippe Roussel.'

I let out an enormous sigh of relief.

A second man smiling puts my bag on the floor.

'And this, comrade, is your bag?'

I am almost weeping with relief, but I nod.

'Thank God!' I say. 'Now you must arrange a meeting with Tughril for me. I have information from Fort Tiberias for him.'

'In time, comrade. That can be arranged perhaps. First there is something which should concern you more directly.'

The bag is opened for me and the chloride carefully placed to one side. A man takes a step towards the sofa with the sachets of morphine. Another has moved close to me, on the other side from Nounourse. He is fiddling with the button of my cuff.

'This is yours, comrade Captain?'

'Yes. That is – I stole it. I – '

'Is it for your own use? What do you want this stuff for?'

Before I can answer, Nounourse booms, 'Comrade Captain. By article five of the Tribune of the Federation for National Liberation, the following crimes against morality when discovered to have been committed by Party members or by soldiers serving in the Army of National Liberation are punishable by death – pederasty, the consumption of alcohol and the use of drugs. This article specifically was reaffirmed at the Summit of the Wilayas at Sounnam in 1956.'

'All right, but wait till I – '

'There can be no extenuating circumstances.'

The man in front of me has started to juggle with the sachets of morphine. I wonder why he is doing this, until I deduce from the direction of his eyes that he is trying to distract me from something. I twist my head to the left, but it is too late to prevent the descent of the hands of Nounourse and the wrapping of the cord around my neck.

Chapter Fourteen

'Do you like stamps, Captain?'

Chantal looked incongruously provocative as she leaned over the table and I presumed that 'stamps' was code for something else. That proved not to be the case.

'Postage stamps, I mean. Have you ever collected stamps?'

I shook my head and wondered as I did so, why Maurice at the head of the table was looking so apprehensive, but she went on excitedly, 'I have a magnificent stamp collection. Come upstairs and let me show you my stamp collection.'

What should I say about those wretched stamps? They were nicely set out on loose leaves of cartridge paper and written up in a copperplate hand. Chantal turned the pages – stodgy French dignitaries in miniature and uninspired allegories of France and her provinces were flipped over. Chantal paused for a moment over a mint set showing military scenes – vignettes of 'the grandeur and servitude of military life'. For example, the one franc stamp showed Napoleon's bear-skinned Imperial Guard trudging through the snow, while behind and to the right of them, youths in uniform gave the Sieg Heil salute. Each stamp had an heraldic label attached to it – a complex monogram dominated by a sword and a great V and crowned by a steel helmet. I leaned over to read the writing on the stamps, 'La Légion des Volontaires Français contre le Bolchévisme', and as I did so Chantal rested her hand on my shoulder.

'Fieldpost stamps from the Russian Front. Uncle Melikian

was with the French Legion when von Paulus surrendered at Stalingrad. He vanished after that. But come and look at this album – '

She sat cross-legged on the floor. Her long gown accommodated this unsuitable posture with extreme strain. I joined her there and, together on the floor, we looked at her collection of German stamps. I did not know Chantal then, and at that time this eminently innocent half-hour had the quality of a nightmare, where at any moment something just as strange, but much nastier might happen.

'A different style, you see.'

Race horses, opera houses, airships – what was I supposed to be looking at or for? Chantal watched my face anxiously and then as if she were engaged in trying to prompt, began to speak very slowly.

'There are no stamps like this any more . . . Quite a different style from today's stamps . . . It is a world we have lost . . . Look!' (A close-cropped youth sounding a herald's trumpet.) 'That boy has no doubts . . . And that stamp there!' (A modern building in Breslau in a series commemorating the games there in 1938.) 'The sweep of that line shows no doubts either . . . And that one.' (In the same set, an old building in Breslau.) 'Do you see? It is different and yet similar. Then, before the war, they built in a European tradition. Europe was not a colony of America . . . Isn't he lovely?' (A horse, the winner of the Vienna Cup in 1943.) 'Isn't he magnificent? We have had thoroughbred horses since the days of Charlemagne and his chivalry, now why not thoroughbred people? . . . See!' (Siegfried kneels over a steel-corseted Valkyrie.) 'Like Wagner himself, this stamp shows us that it is possible to be strong yet beautiful.'

I found it uncomfortable on the floor and stood up. Chantal fished about for her cigarette holder and then her cigarettes. I found her the ashtray.

'In France now, our France of the dirty rats, Mendès-France, Blum, Mitterrand, since the war, it is fashionable to mock "Strength through Joy". But, Captain – I'm sorry, Philippe – Philippe, do you think we shall find joy in those incomprehensible Left Bank films, the drugs and cocktails from America, the Negro music, and the lies put out by the RTF? Philippe, believe me, I speak from my own experience. It is possible even for a woman to know the joy that comes from strength – and the strength from joy.'

She flushed. Then she stretched out her hand and pulled me down to my knees on the floor once more. The cigarette was stubbed out. Doubtless the Legion and the officers' mess had coarsened my emotional reflexes but I was thinking, 'Is this my opportunity? Is this the moment to which "Come up and see my stamp collection" was leading?' In fact, no. The affair of the bed of gardenias was to take place a few days later in my flat. But on this first evening, Chantal composed herself to kneel facing the window and I knelt and listened in discomfort while she prayed.

'Oh God, almighty and eternal, who has established the Empire of the Franks to be the Instrument of Thy Holy Will in this world, fill with Thy celestial light always and everywhere the Sons of France, that they may know what they must do to extend Thy Kingdom.' The end of the prayer was marked with a clap of the hands and she was up and striding over to her jewellery box on the dresser. She wanted to show me a signet ring – a vast crude thing too large for her fingers. The signet was the complex monogram I had already seen, with its great sword and V.

All the Children of Vercingetorix possess such a ring. In 1948 a few of the surviving veterans of the Légion Française contre le Bolchévisme came together to form what was originally a social club and mutual aid group. But its membership was disappointingly small and gradually the membership was broadened to include all those who looked back with nostalgia to Fortress Europe holding out against the menace of Asiatic Zionist Bolshevism – elderly survivors of the pre-war Camelots du Roi and Action Française, some Belgian Rexists, disgraced Vichy functionaries and the like. After 1954 and the Philippeville massacre there was a small influx of Algerian *pieds noirs*. Bitter officers returning from defeat in Indochina added fresh blood and expertise to the group. The veterans' club reconstituted itself as a semi-secret elite dedicated to making a stand against the conspiracy by Jewry's Bolshevik International and its Anglo-American and Negro allies to overthrow civilization in Africa. The new league was known as the Children of Vercingetorix. The de Serkissians joined of course. The stamps were rubbish, but I had found Chantal at prayer very attractive. A glib intellectual might comment that this was an attraction of opposites, but I doubt if things were so simple.

Alas, it is of course impossible to explain the aesthetics of fascist philately to my captors. They are hardly the types to collect stamps – and, as for neo-Nazism, a common opinion among the Arabs in Algeria now is that Hitler's chief crime was that he concentrated on the Jews rather than the French. I am reminded of the frustrations I so regularly experienced lecturing on counter-insurgency to those dumb platoons of legionnaires in Fort Tiberias. I even have great difficulty in explaining to the men in the room why the Children of Vercingetorix pose such a danger to the liberation struggle in Algeria. Over the last year I have sent Tughril many reports on the subject of the Children of Vercingetorix and it is to him I should be talking now – not this gang of amateurs.

Once Nounourse had the garrotte round my neck, he had paused, enabling me to bark out in my best Saint-Cyr parade-ground voice, 'Stop this nonsense. I am a major in Wilaya Four of the Army of National Liberation. I was given this rank by the Command Council of the Army of Liberation in Tunis. I demand to be heard and tried by officers of my own rank or above. Where is Colonel Tughril? It is he who must decide whether I can best serve the revolution by living or dying.'

Nounourse listened, growled and then tightened the garrotte, so that I should never have managed another sentence. But a young man sitting on my other side, half shaven with steel-rimmed glasses, looks up appealingly at Nounourse.

'He should at least have the right to make a confession before we kill him.'

'What is there to confess?' growls Nounourse. 'I don't

tolerate addicts, winos or pimps in my cell. Oh, all right then, examine him, doctor, and tell us whether he is an addict or not.'

'I am not really a doctor, you know – just a student,' he tells me with a shy smile. He has the sleeve of my shirt up. He clicks his tongue.

'He is addict all right.'

'So I kill him,' growls Nounourse.

'The confession first,' says the 'doctor' and the others agree. 'It will be better that way.'

By now I am perfectly relaxed. The charade with the cord around my throat has only been staged to impress or to panic me. It has succeeded in neither. I make my report, somewhat edited, for I judge that some of the material is for Colonel Tughril's ears only. I wind up proposing that firm action be taken against the Children of Vercingetorix. I particularly urge that a squad be detailed to murder Chantal. Because of her position in both that neo-fascist league and in military intelligence, she poses a unique threat to the operations of the FLN in Algiers and the Sahara. Whether it is because of the compression of my narrative (which still takes over an hour) or because of my holding back some things which I judge to be for Tughril's ears only, I don't know, but the comrades are not happy with my report.

The 'doctor' starts. Having first saved me from Nounourse's noose, he now seems determined to play prosecuting council.

'So you shot your way out of a military security meeting?'

'Yes.'

'And then you shot your way out of Fort Tiberias?'

'Yes.'

'Well done,' but the doctor clicks his tongue.

Then Nounourse booms in my other ear. 'Did you kill this clever fellow, this . . . Raoul?'

'Yes, I think so . . . Yes – er that is I left him for dead.'

'You should be sure. Always finish them off.' And Nounourse takes his hands off the cords to make an interesting wrenching gesture.

'And Zora, you killed her?'

'Zora? Oh yes, I killed her.'

Why do I lie? I am far from sure that Raoul was dying when I left al-Hadi's flat, and, as for Zora, I certainly did not kill her. I remember thanking her for the clothes – an unnecessary piece of politeness – and I left her comforting her frightened infant. Come to that, why didn't I finish Raoul and Zora off? There is something about an interrogation . . . I have noticed it before, when I went through the charade of interrogating the fellagha at Fort Tiberias, something that makes the interrogatee want to rush into a panicky lying, pointless lies that will not cover his tracks or convince his captors . . . But why should I be lying? Perhaps it is that I do not think that my audience deserves the truth?

The inquisition goes on.

The doctor wants to know, 'And these people, this Eugene and Yvonne Dutoit, you killed them too?'

'Oh yes, I'm sure that will be in tomorrow's papers.'

There is a growl of satisfaction from Nounourse, but my difficulties continue. The other two in the room carry on the questioning. They are, I should judge, simple labourers, perhaps not even that, perhaps members of Algiers's vast legion of unemployed. Maybe they are simply trying to get the story straight in their heads. Nevertheless, they seem to intend some sort of threat with every question.

'You killed comrade al-Hadi?'

'Yes. I had no choice. It was necessary to preserve my cover.'

'And yet you also tell us that within twenty-four hours of this necessary killing, your cover was in fact blown?'

'Yes.'

'You agree that that was most unfortunate?'

'Of course.'

'Captain, you walked about in the Sahara for a week and you had no food and water?'

'Oh no, it wasn't as long as that. Three days, maybe four days. I can't be sure. I was delirious for part of the time and, towards the end, unconscious.'

'But you walked about in the desert with this bullet in your leg? You are a very strong man.'

'Ah no. You don't understand. That was at the end, when the Arabs picked me up.'

'Ah yes, that was what you said but, tell me, why did this bedu shoot you in the leg?'

'I don't know. Perhaps it was, as Zora said, an accident.'

'So you believe what this Zora said? You really remember nothing of what happened until you awoke at the flat belonging to al-Hadi? How long were you prisoner of that unusual woman?'

Nounourse says something about al-Hadi's wife, too fast for me to catch, and the others laugh. But I laugh too in order to express my solidarity with the group. In fact I am intensely irritated. They are getting nowhere with this rubbish. Certainly they are not impressing me.

The 'doctor' who is not really a doctor leans towards me.

'You laugh and yet you are dead man.'

'We have never seen a dead man laughing before,' affirms the juggler.

'You should know,' continues the 'doctor', 'that garrotting is a slower process than hanging on a drop scaffold. Normally death in a garrotting comes from asphyxiation. Though it is possible that in Nounourse's hands your neck might snap – if the cords don't break first. I keep telling Nounourse that he should use piano wire, but he won't have it. I believe that I am right in saying that even after your neck has snapped, you will retain consciousness for between a minute and a minute and a half. And then everything in your bowels will come bucketing out.'

The 'doctor' turns to address the others on the floor.

'And yet here he is laughing and not bothering to convince us about anything.'

'I am, damn it. It is you who are not wishing to be convinced.'

'Well, we shall try again. Forgive so many questions. You forgive us, please?'

'We have to be clear.'

'Yes. This Zora woman was holding you for these friends of yours, this Raoul and Chantal, and they are Children of Vercingetorix?'

'I don't know about Raoul. He was – is – was Chantal's friend. Chantal certainly belongs to the Children.'

'When Raoul came to the flat of Zora, you engaged him in a long debate about communism?'

'Yes, or rather he engaged me in it. As I said, he was trying to turn me from Marxism. Of course, he failed.'

'Mmmm. You should know, comrade, that all of us here in the room are socialists, but we are Algerian Nationalists first. We are not Marxists and we are not going to take orders from Moscow or Peking.'

'Thank you, comrade, for this important clarification. I hope – I am sure that nevertheless we share a common struggle against the hegemony of French monopoly capitalism in Algeria.'

'Mmmmm.'

No one in the room looks very satisfied, and the questioning is resumed.

'How long were you the prisoner of the woman, Zora, and her dog?'

'Christ, I don't know! I was drugged. A week at least. It could have been much longer.'

I allow a certain degree of panic to appear in my voice. I have their number now. This little gang of street-corner freedom fighters, they want to get the feeling that I am cracking, that I acknowledge their ascendancy. This is the crude emotional trade off that they are demanding. I'll make them pay for it later.

The 'doctor' clicks his tongue.

'You have not told us as much as you might. The implication is that Chantal and her ally, this Lieutenant Schwab, intercepted the bedu before other army search parties could, paid the bedu to pick you up, contacted this woman Zora and, having told her how you tortured and murdered her husband, found it easy to persuade her to keep you in her custody until Chantal and Raoul could meet at Laghouat and decide what should be done with you, but it happened that you escaped before Chantal could arrive.'

The 'doctor' has counted the argument off on his fingers. He is the only bright one here, perhaps even a little cleverer than I am. His view of the events is clearer than mine. But Nounourse is scratching his head. Which fool was it who said, 'The unexamined life is not worth living'? For it is a terrible thing to fall into the hands of stupid examiners. The group's interrogation techniques are amateurish beyond belief. If this cell is to stay in existence, it will need licking into shape.

'Yes, I suppose that must be it.' I agree with calculated feebleness.

But the 'doctor' scrapes his nails against his half-shaven chin.

'Well, there are many mysteries in this story.'

The juggler with the packets of morphine picks up the questioning.

'You tell us that, for six years now, you have been a double agent, making a mess of the intelligence records of the French military and sending invaluable information to the FLN here in Algiers?'

'Yes, I have.'

'What a hero!' But there is a distinct lack of enthusiasm in this commendation.

'Colonel Tughril can corroborate what I say.'

The 'doctor' leans over to smile at me.

'It's a pity there is no Colonel Tughril in this room. Indeed we have never heard of Colonel Tughril.'

'And we live here,' affirms the juggler, but then he looks round the room (which is so sparsely furnished that it might be a dentist's waiting room) as if he had never seen it before.

Nounourse lets out a terrible rumbling laugh and the cords round my neck tighten a little. (So who have I been sending reports to?)

My voice comes out rather wheezy.

'Listen, for that matter what evidence have I that you really are an FLN cell? It is all trust, isn't it? Reflect a little.'

'You came to us, not we to you.'

'You shot your way out of a legionnaire fort and walked across the Sahara and killed I don't know how many people to come to us.'

'And now you don't like us.'

And Nounourse wants to know, 'Did you kill the child?'

'The child? What child?'

'The woman Zora's child.'

'Ah. Oh yes, I killed him too.' (We are making such a melodrama of this that I can hardly stop myself from laughing.) 'God help me, I killed the child.'

'You are a fine fellow,' says Nounourse thoughtfully.

The juggler resumes his performance with the little sacks of morphine. It is as if the weights of guilt and innocence, of truth and lies, were coming to rest and being weighed, first on one palm and then on the other. We all watch him. Then, abruptly, the cord hangs loose around my neck and Nounourse stretches and makes himself more comfortable.

'I take the sofa.'

He looks around challengingly.

'We are going to sleep now,' the 'doctor' tells me helpfully. 'It is six hours to daylight.'

'What has been decided?'

'Nothing has been decided. But first I should look at that leg of yours. Lie down over there.' And he points to a corner of the room beside an inner door.

And so he does. The comrades even allow me another shot. I get the impression that Nounourse might have vetoed this gesture of mercy, but, once assured of sole possession of the sofa, Nounourse is extravagantly sprawled in sleep, snoring heavily and with arms and legs projecting at all angles over the sides of the sofa. The 'doctor' is even kind enough to administer my shot. He tells me that one should always squirt a drop out of the needle before inserting it. It prevents air bubbles getting into the veins.

'Thank you, doctor.'

'I am not really a doctor, you know,' he tells me again. 'Just a student.' And he gives me another of his charming shy smiles. 'I am Mr Jalloud.'

135

The comrades dispose themselves to sleep on the dusty carpet. I lie awake for a little while. As the 'doctor' says, nothing has been decided. It has all been an infuriating waste of time, their self-important examination of my credentials. That is the trouble with amateur revolutionaries, this business with the noose around the neck and the solemn questions, as if they were inducting me into some seedy Masonic lodge. This sort of thing is not, or at least should not be, what revolutionary activity should be about. They have failed to take any decisions, either with regard to the implications of my cover having been blown, or with regard to the now very imminent putsch of the paras and the *pieds noirs* in Algiers. But I am alive, and as long as I live I can do great things even with such a third-rate cadre as this one. Nounourse's snoring is so stentorian that it is hard to be sure, but I am almost certain that there are noises coming from behind the door by which I lie. I think that I hear a prolonged wailing. But it is hard to be sure. Then I too plunge into a deep and mysterious sleep.

In the morning I am woken by the juggler flinging open the shutters and the comrades move about the room in the grey light before the sunrise collecting their things. The juggler unties my hands. The call for the *fajr* prayer comes from a nearby mosque. Just as I think we are about to leave, Nounourse goes to the door in front of which I had been lying and unlocks it. A family emerges, a man, a woman and three children. They look frightened and grey in the grey light. Nounourse starts shouting at them. I gather that they have been our unwilling hosts all this time. The comrades commandeered their house for the night. Nounourse gets the man to bring us bread and stands over him while he makes coffee. Nounourse continues shouting and waving his garrotting cord at the man. Then, once we have finished breakfast, Nounourse has smiles for everyone, especially the children. We all shake hands with the terrified family, before issuing out into the kasbah.

The juggler and the other anonymous fellow swiftly disappear. While I am wondering what I should do now and how I may take the initiative, another part of my mind is off in a fantastic fugue, imagining what would happen to the kasbah if the Children of Vercingetorix took over this quarter. Once the old tenements had been dynamited, preferably with their inhabitants still inside them, I imagine that we might see a colossal structure with a podium and arena for mass rallies crowned by a shrine of honour to the fallen Sons of France and then an avenue of pseudo-classical colonnades sweeping down the hill. Away with the Arab mess! All the buildings will have strong crisp lines, in a harmonious blend of the old and the new traditions of Europe.

I barely hear Nounourse booming out behind me. 'We have a mission for you. You can go with Jalloud. You will help him. You will do exactly as he tells you. Remember I am never very far away and remember also that I do not like you, Captain Addict.'

Chapter Fifteen

Why did I tell such terrible lies? It is as if Koot Hoomi – some great astral spirit – was dictating nonsense to me. I think that Raoul is not dead. I am sure that Zora is not. I am bound to be found out sooner or later. As we pick our way out of the kasbah, I am possessed by the fear that at its exit we shall encounter, by chance, Raoul with a bandage round his head or Zora flanked by infant and alsatian. But this is only a passing flicker. I have no time for pessimism – or fantasy. They are both alike products of a bourgeois individualist liberalism. Precisely the products of a historical moment, they are poses adopted in bad faith as a reaction to the strains of industrial capitalism. As Lenin says, 'We can (and must) begin to build up socialism, not with fantastic material especially created by our imagination, but with the material bequeathed us by capitalism.'

'Where are we going?'

'We need more morphine,' Jalloud tells me.

'What?'

'And some other things as well.' But he will tell me nothing more.

We are not going out by the Médée checkpoint, but we walk west in the general direction of the Bab al-Oued and exit by the rue des Zouaves. Jalloud's case is checked, but of course there is nothing incriminating in it. As we head up the boulevard de Verdun, Jalloud becomes talkative once more. He tells me that we are going to his hospital. He is attached to its staff while he is doing his doctorate. He is doing a thesis on cenesopathy, but there are problems with it.

The Verdun Hospital for Nervous Diseases is situated just a little way short of the big Muslim cemetery, beyond the civil prison. Set a little way back from the boulevard behind pleasant rows of trees, the place nevertheless resembles the prison. And this is not by chance for, like a prison or a barracks, the hospital is an instrument of social control. At the gate of the hospital there is a massive queue of hopeless Arabs, so hopeless and unexpectant that perhaps they are not a queue. Several groups are brewing tea on the flagstones and one family has a goat with them. Jalloud produces a white coat from the bag and makes me put it on.

'If anyone asks, you are Major Beaufré from the Army Medical Service and you have to sort out some queries on your supply roster. There will be no problem.'

But Jalloud does look a little nervous. However there is no problem. The uniformed guard at the gate is arguing with a ferocious old Kabyle woman whose streakily dyed hair and patchwork dress make her look like a gypsy queen. She lunges up at him and, though I do not understand Kabyle, I guess that she is heaping the curses of her ancestors on him. The guard's mouth is screwed up in distaste.

'You cannot see Dr Fanon. We have no Dr Fanon here.'

Jalloud flashes his identity pass at the guard and he waves us through. Once we are inside the hospital and pacing down the corridor, Jalloud starts speaking in an urgent low voice.

'Well, we have some time before the ward visits. I can show you round and you can see some of our patients. But first I should like to show you how to do a blood transfusion.'

And this is what he does. He takes me into a sort of glorified store cupboard, where there is a row of transfusion trolleys and other apparatus closely crammed together. Jalloud talks at a tremendous manic pace and tubes, needles, plastic bags and anti-coagulant are brandished before my face and then whipped away.

'Pay attention please. This is important.'

Then he goes through it again at twice the pace.

'Well, I'm sure you will manage,' he says finally. 'We'd better not be caught in here. I'll take you round a ward or two.'

He takes me into a sunny airy ward. A few of the patients are in dressing-gowns and Jalloud's 'special' patient is one of them. He is clearly pleased to see Jalloud, but rather apprehensive of me, even though I am Jalloud's friend. The patient conforms perfectly to the classic symptoms of cenesopathy. He has difficulty in speaking, for he is in constant terror that he is about to swallow his tongue, but haltingly he describes for my benefit how his body is perpetually alive with electric shocks, like continuous pins and needles, but much more painful. For the last two years he has hardly been able to sleep. Also he is terrified of touching light switches. His case is an important part of Jalloud's thesis, but the problem with the thesis is the aetiological aspect of the case. These symptoms first appeared after he was taken in for a week's questioning by the gendarmerie.

'Of course, my professor and I are agreed that there is no connection,' says Jalloud.

On the next bed is the cenesopath's best friend.

'This one has to be watched,' says Jalloud, gesturing towards the watcher, a nun who surveys the patients from the end of the ward, while her hands work away at a piece of tacking. 'This man has only been in a few months and he has tried to commit suicide, I think, five times now. His wife was raped during a *ratonade* in the *bled*. He hallucinates too. On Friday the patients had couscous with mutton. But this poor man thought that the mutton was a bird resting on the couscous – a maggoty bird – and as he continued to look he thought he saw that the couscous grains were really maggots too. Hospital food is like that for him. However what we are treating him for is internal lesions. We cannot understand how he got them . . . Out in the *bled* they blow us to pieces and here we try to patch them up again.' And Jalloud gives me one of his funny smiles.

'But that one over there will interest you, I think.'

The man whom Jalloud surreptitiously points to is at the

end of the ward. He is a European and we do not approach him, for fear of being overheard by the nun.

'The case is a little obscure. I believe that he nailed a dog to some sort of electric wheel and got the wheel to spin so fast that the brains flew out of the dog. There were fears for the safety of his family . . . He had good prospects too . . . He was a gendarme assigned to traffic control, but his superiors thought so highly of him that they assigned him to interrogation duties.'

An unfortunate European victim of this terrible war, but really the French should build bigger hospitals and put all the Arabs in them, for, from the perspective of the colonist, what is revolution but a criminal psychopathic reaction against a stable and ordered society? The psychotic, the amnesiac, the lethargic, the insomniac, the abouliac, the paranoid, the deviant and the paraesthetic drift in and out of the wards and down the corridors. It is not so very different from the streets of Algiers – only the pretence has been removed. We are drifting with them. We pass a fat man sitting up in bed in a private room chanting happily to himself.

'Kill. Kill. Kill the blacks. Kill. Kill the Arabs. Kill the Jews. Kill. Kill the *pieds-noirs*. Kill. Kill the flics. Kill – Good morning, doctor,' he shouts cheerily as we pass, and as we move on we can hear him continuing to chant, 'Kill the doctors. Kill. Kill the sisters . . .'

Jalloud and I dart into another of the hospital's glory holes. This one is locked, but Jalloud has the key. He produces two Monoprix carrier bags from his case and takes a few handfuls of stuff from the shelves – morphine and other drugs – and puts them in one of the bags.

'The comrades in the *bled* need these things very badly. Maybe they need the morphine even more than you do. What do you think? You can take it out for us. They will not search you with your lovely white skin. Right now, you stay here. I will lock you in. I am just going to see if your patient is ready for you.'

I stand in the dark and wait and I wonder if he is really going to come back or whether this is not some grotesque practical joke. It is possible that Jalloud will come back with the security guards. It is possible that he will not come back at all. It seems a very long time, waiting. Thinking about the gendarme, here is evidence, if evidence were needed, that it is hard to be a torturer. It takes skill, intelligence and often considerable physical strength to achieve successful results. And, naturally, the greatest challenge is to stay human at the end of it all without degenerating into a psychopath.

But Jalloud comes back in a state of high excitement.

'It is all ready. The patient is under heavy sedation and the apparatus is lined up right along beside the bed. Perhaps I should tell you about this patient too. You will be interested in him. He is an officer in the Territorial Reserve. He had the misfortune to be captured by the fellagha in the Aures mountains. I fear that he suffered many hardships at their hands before making his escape. Now he is prone to paroxysmal tachycardia, but there are psychosomatic complications. He told me that every night he dreams that pale fellagha in white robes congregate around his bed to drink from his wounds. Well this morning we – no, you – are going to make his nightmare come true.'

'What!'

'You are going to drain his blood. The comrades in the *bled* have need of blood too. I have shown you how to do it. There should be no problem. You have enough sacs for maybe three litres of blood. That should finish him off. But if you think you cannot get it all in the carrier bags maybe a little less will do. You can find your own way out of the hospital, I think. You should not be stopped getting out, as I say. I can meet you and collect the stuff by the obelisk in the parc Jaubert at twelve thirty.'

'What about you now? Why do I have to do this on my own?'

'Oh, I am going on a ward round with the consultant. It will be my alibi.'

Before we exit from the cupboard, Jalloud gives me a shot of morphine to set me up. Then we march smartly down the corridor. Jalloud points me to my patient who lies, apparently asleep, in a private room. Jalloud gives me an encouraging squeeze on the shoulder and then hurries off for his ward round. In my time I have done parachute drops, flown a helicopter, blown up bridges, repaired the sump of a lorry, cooked soup made of snake's flesh, cut off the gangrenous leg of a wounded man and put another out of his misery. I am hardly going to flinch from this. The needle goes into the jugular. Though one of the rubber tubes is badly frayed and some blood goes over the sheets, in fact I am rather pleased with myself. Perhaps I should have been a doctor? But then, in a sense, I rather fancy that I am a doctor of sorts – diagnosing the sickness of society and then to work cutting out the cancerous growths at the heart of that society. My 'brother' officer in this bed is one of those cancers. At one point the patient opens his eyes and rather feebly tries to say something. I pay no attention. Three litres will kill him of course. I can imagine that one day there might be another better world in which one would have the right to say that what I am doing is 'atrocious, disgusting'. But that world has not been achieved yet and it will be achieved only by continuous struggle. In that struggle there can be no half-measures. There is no nice way of accomplishing a revolution – or of resisting one.

With the blood in the bag, I walk out of the hospital. It is very simple. I have some hours to kill and I stroll over to the place du Lyre. I note that the opera house, in an unusual gesture of extravagant confidence, will shortly be presenting all four parts of the *Ring* cycle. Its more usual fare I believe is operetta – or at its most ambitious Gounod. The beginnings of an idea form in my mind. Then I buy a paper and take it with me to the parc Jaubert. Yes, my little horror is in on the second page. 'Ghastly Crime at Laghouat'. I bless the *Echo d'Alger*, and the RTF, and *Time* magazine and the BBC World Service. Without them it would not have been worth my while stuffing plastic explosive up that woman's skirt. But as it is, I can imagine that this evening or some time soon in London on the BBC Radio there may be a discussion programme about politics, and there may be some discussion of FLN atrocities and everyone will agree that atrocities are atrocious, but then some liberal intellectual – and England is full of such people – will come on and say, 'While in no way condoning such atrocities, nevertheless they have to be understood in the context of the continuing oppression which is a feature of . . .' and so and so and so on. It is for that beautiful liberal intellectual, and so that everyone may hear what he has to say about the injustices of French colonialism, that I killed Eugene and Yvonne – and, of course, I shall kill again.

It does not surprise me that Jalloud never turns up. That would not be this cell's style of operation. Instead a boy comes up and tugs at my sleeve and tries to take the bags away from me. He points to the park gates where Nounourse is standing and Nounourse indicates that I should give the bags to the boy. The boy darts off with the bags, and then Nounourse gestures that I am to follow him, Nounourse. We set off at a smart pace. It is fifteen minutes before he allows me to catch him up.

'So there you are, Captain Addict!'

'Where are we going?'

'You are coming to stay with me. My home shall be your home.'

I have never heard the traditional Arab formula of hospitality pronounced in such a surly voice. Nounourse goes on.

'You did what Jalloud said? And everything that we need is in those bags?'

'Yes.'

'Good. But remember, Captain Addict, I am always watching you and I do not like you.'

'I don't care who likes me.'

'Did you kill a French officer in the hospital?'

'Yes. That was a test, wasn't it?'

'The comrades in the field really needed the blood.'

Nounourse's flat is in the Bab el-Oued. The Bab el-Oued is a mixed quarter of poor whites and Arabs, living shoulder by shoulder and competing with one another for the same miserable jobs and services. Much of the area is occupied by large modern apartment blocks and Nounourse's flat is in one of these blocks. As we go up the stairs, his neighbours call out salutations to him and ask after his day. In every sense Nounourse is a big man in this neighbourhood.

I am formally and surlily presented to Nounourse's wife, Saphia. Saphia wears traditional Arab dress, but no veil. She receives my respects without rising from her chair and when she does get up and moves to the kitchen, the exertion makes her pant. I imagine that I can hear the insides of her thighs rubbing together as she walks. Saphia is very plump. She cannot weigh so very much less than Nounourse, but she has the eyes of a doe set in a moistly lustrous moon face. Having fetched some Cokes from the kitchen, she sits listening to what goes on, expressionless, with her eyes never leaving my face. It would be unwise for me to return her gaze. Nounourse asks about cakes and she lazily tells him that food will have to be later. I expect Nounourse to start shouting, but nothing happens.

'My wife is a great trial to me,' Nounourse says. 'She has been sent from heaven as a trial for me.'

Saphia continues to look on placidly. Nounourse sets to, opening the Coca-Cola bottles. He has his own technique. He just squeezes the glass and the top pops off. Catching my expression, he tells me, 'I used to be a great sportsman – not just the swimming, but also the wrestling and the boxing. I was Algiers boxing champion. Watch this!'

He gets up from his chair and hoists it up and puts one of the chair legs in his teeth. Then he walks round the small room holding the chair up by his clenched teeth, looking a little like a performing seal. Then he puts the chair down and thrusts his fists in my face. He lowers down at me.

'With this fists, I can smash a man's head like a coconut. So watch it, Captain Addict!'

Sitting down and now in a sudden good humour, he tells me, 'Also I used to be the biggest bandit in all Algiers! I used to be chief bouncer at the Dolly Night-club. All the other bandits walked in fear of me. You know the Dolly Night-club? I used to protect the drug sellers and the tarts. I made lots of money, and I killed men who did not respect my boss.'

So ho! It is much the sort of background that I should have

guessed. Nounourse is one of 'the dangerous class', the social scum, that passively rotting mass thrown out by the lowest layers of an old society. He belongs to the class that Marx calls 'the lumpenproletariat'. As Marx describes it in *The Eighteenth Brumaire of Napoleon Bonaparte*, the lumpenproletariat consists of 'vagabonds, discharged soldiers, discharged gaolbirds, escaped galley slaves, swindlers, mountebanks, lazzaroni, pickpockets, tricksters, gamblers, maquereaus, brothel-keepers, porters, literate organ grinders, rag-pickers, knife grinders, tinkers, beggars', a 'whole indefinite disintegrated mass'. According to Marx this lumpenproletariat has very little revolutionary potential and the criminal as revolutionary hero is a romantic aberration of little significance.

This is not quite Nounourse's view of the matter.

'I was the biggest bandit in Algiers, but the comrades showed me the error of my ways. They came to me and said, "Listen, Nounourse, can't you see how bad it is what you are doing? You are serving up whores to the filthy French and you are killing your Arab brothers with those dirty drugs." That was in 1954. And I said to myself, "Nounourse, you could smash their heads like coconuts. You can get a lot of respect for that, but first you should think about what these good men have to say." So I reflected a little and I looked at the whores in the streets and the houses – not all the whores are in brothels – you understand me? – and I looked at the lipstick on their mouths like red wounds and the short skirts inviting a man's hand to be stuck up inside them, and I saw the men being sick in the streets from too much alcohol. And I thought to myself, "It is true what they say. We are being used. But you, Nounourse, can change things." So I killed my boss. He was a dirty Spaniard, and now I who used to be the biggest bandit in all Algiers have my own revolutionary cell. We cleared the pimps and drug pedlars off the streets and dropped them in the sea. Now everyone fears me and I can respect myself. And I am in charge of my own cell and I run it very well!'

Saphia sighs heavily.

The afternoon goes by slowly. Nounourse has taken the

afternoon off from the Hydra Sports Club and Saphia has nothing to do. We share silences and desultory conversations. Nounourse wants to know about my experience of life in the Foreign Legion. The Legion fascinates him. He really admires the Legion.

'They are really tough men. They are the professionals in this business. Not like us. Of course they have all the right equipment.'

I describe my experiences in the hospital and Nounourse says, 'Jalloud is a good man. Even his professor thinks well of him.'

On the walls of the flat there are Sellotaped pictures of Elizabeth II and of Johnny Weissmuller as Tarzan. Saphia likes Johnny Weissmuller. Saphia is proud to have this acknowledged. Elizabeth is Nounourse's enthusiasm.

'If the French had a queen like that, we should not be having this war. I would die for that woman!'

Nounourse is a mine of inaccurate information on Her Majesty and her unhappy life and the wicked doings of the Queen's relatives, all of this he has culled from French scandal sheets. I gather from Nounourse that the House of Windsor is the number one bandit family in England. The Royal Family is fair, but tough when it comes to managing their multifarious rackets.

'I am like the English. This I can respect.'

And it is not just the Royal Family that Nounourse is keen on. The English are the number one footballers. Everyone knows that. Nounourse's strength lies in his simple beliefs. In that alone he resembles a member of the true proletariat. He is sturdy in his simple beliefs. I find Nounourse's Anglophilia refreshing. It is not shared by the French in Algeria. Many of the *pieds noirs* believe that the English are working to destabilize the French in Algeria and that the English secret service is supplying arms to the FLN. Listening to the World Service is like listening to the Voice of Cairo. Chantal's hatred of the English takes an extreme form. To tease Nounourse, I give him a dose of Chantal's opinions. 'England is the headquarters of the Masons and the refuge of the Jews. It is the centre of a network of plots. The senior Masons in the English army, the banks and the Church meet to plot the seduction of children, the corruption of the family and the creation of a socialistic society modelled on the anthill. British secret-service men kiss each others' arses. It is part of their initiation ritual. There is no cruelty of which the English are not capable. Homosexuals and sadists to a man – if you can call them men.

'Ah no, these are not my opinions.' (For Nounourse has risen wrathfully to his feet and I instinctively put my hands up before my face.) 'I am just telling you what this woman Chantal goes about saying. According to her, the English invented the concentration camp during the Boer War. According to her, they also invented terrorism. Before the Second World War, terrorism was only a matter of deranged individuals, like the anarchists with their infernal machines. But the English taught the world how to organize terrorism. They sent their secret-service men to murder Heydrich in Czechoslovakia. She believes it was they who murdered Darlan, Pétain's governor here in Algiers, and it was certainly they who paid the communists in the French Resistance to murder Germans and commit random outrages in the streets of France. And Malaya, Cyprus, Kenya, Egypt – there is hardly one of their colonies where they have not practised torture, not because they needed to, but really to satisfy their perverted lusts.'

Nounourse sighs heavily.

'This woman should surely die,' he says.

But the atmosphere remains uneasy. It is as if he still suspects me of sharing Chantal's opinions. But Nounourse is very naïve and it is boring talking to a man with whom I have so little in common. It is boring just sitting here, chatting away, just killing time. I long to be up and out of this pokey little flat and involved in some action.

At last, some time after the desultory conversation has declined to dismal silence, Jalloud comes in. He is in a high good humour and immediately Nounourse and he start horsing about around the room. Jalloud puts up the ludicrous pretence that he too is a boxing champ, and they move about parrying, lunging and whooping. Saphia hardly bothers to open her eyes and I am also bored by this childishness. I no longer have a sense of humour. It is something that I have put behind me. Who can laugh in this land of death and torture? Eventually Jalloud comes staggering up to me, gasping for breath and makes an attempt to slap me on the back which goes rather wide of its mark.

'Hey! Hey! So this morning, you murdered a fellow officer! Bravo! You should chalk your murder score up on a wall somewhere.'

'That was not murder,' I tell him. 'That was the necessary elimination of an enemy of the people.'

'Oh, tra–la! What nonsense! The man was lying peacefully in his bed and you killed him. The nurses are running about screaming and the whole hospital is in a total rumpus. That has to be a murder.'

'Murder is not the word for it. You are a bright student, Jalloud. You should be able to understand what I am about to tell you. Listen to me, will you? For us the difficulty is to find a language whose vocabulary and indeed whose very grammatical structure has not been appropriated by the oppressive power. We need a language in which the words are not inevitably channelled towards the conclusions of the imperialists and the liberals. For this reason, we have given new meanings to such words as "Democracy", "Peace", "Violence" and "A Necessary Execution of the People's Will". These words do not belong to the *pieds noirs*, or de Gaulle, or the United States or the Zionists. They belong to the people. Today in the hospital I have executed the will of the people. I murdered no one.'

'Doubtless you have given new meanings to "Lies" and "Stupidity" as well.'

But Jalloud giggles nervously. He really does not want to quarrel with me. Jalloud is a bright young man – perhaps an intellectual even – but, as with Raoul, I am not impressed. I am not an intellectual, but I am a Marxist and Marxism is a powerful engine for the production of thought. On a very wide range of issues it does my thinking for me, so that I can talk with a Jalloud or a Raoul on more or less the same level, confident that my ideology has the answers.

'Killing that officer was a test that I am who I say I am?' I venture.

'Of course, but we really needed the blood, and they are not going to give it to us. We have to take it.' Then Jalloud continues, 'Well, now it is time for us to decide what we are going to do about you and this young lady of yours.'

Chapter Sixteen

I pace around the room taking nervous drags through my preposterous cigarette holder. I have been kneeling at prayer, seeking guidance from the God of the Franks, but no guidance has come. I am filled with excitement and apprehension. Something terrible is brewing. If only I could lay my hands on Philippe, many of my fears would be laid to rest. I know, having beaten it out of Zora, that Philippe must have made contact with Tughril now. Unfortunately it is not possible to guess from Philippe's skilfully botched intelligence records who Tughril is. When I catch up with Philippe, I will make him pay for the dance he has led us across Algeria. I shall make him kneel before me and beg for mercy. When I think how I deceived him in bed, I laugh ruthlessly.

Ah, it is no good. It has turned into unintentional parody. My attempts to enter the mind of Chantal strike me as pitiful, childlike fantasy, and, as Lenin says, 'You must dream, but only on condition that it is permitted to you to believe in your dreams.' 'Know the mind of the enemy' has always been my watchword, but I have no idea at all what goes on in the mind of Chantal, and, as is plain from the Security Panel incident, I never have had. Part of my trouble is that I have never been up against a woman before. From Saint-Cyr to Indochina to Algeria, I have lived in a world of men. It is not just Chantal, but all women. I have no idea how their minds work. It would be hard enough for me to enter the mind of any woman, but there are additional problems. Chantal is not of my class. The de Serkissians are *haute bourgeoisie*, plutocrats even I suppose. It is never really possible to transcend the bound of class consciousness. Saint-Cyr graduate I may be, but this does not furnish a simple *laissez-passer* to the upper-class mentality. Not only is she not of my sex or class (and she is younger than me too), but she is a fascist. How does a fascist think?

I pace round the room watched by the placid Saphia. Try again.

I am Chantal. I am back in Algiers now. I am pretty sure that Philippe is in Algiers too. As I step in circles round the room, I wonder if I have any clues as to where Philippe will be and what he will do next, and I try to guess what my reactions will be to what he does next – or do I mean his to mine? It is a fair bet that Philippe has been successful in getting information about the planned co-operation between right-wing *pied-noir* groups and the paras into the hands of the FLN by now. That particular trick has been lost by us. My guess is that he will feel peculiarly bitter towards me for having unmasked him at the Security Panel. He will certainly have more respect for my abilities, and my elimination will be one of his priorities. I should take care to vary the times and the itineraries of my trips from the villa to the office, and I should always travel armed. Security at the villa should be stepped up. I will get Daddy to put more men on the wall. I will have a description of Philippe circulated to our men throughout the city. But I am aware that by now he will not look much like old photographs of him.

Ah, it really is no good. Yet it is vital that I should be prepared for Chantal's next move. I have seen so many military strategies and intelligence plots come to grief on the assumption that, while one's own men are on the move, the enemy is standing stock-still just waiting to be hit.

Plod. Plod. Of course she is looking for me and guarding herself. That is ploddingly obvious, but I want to know how she thinks as well as what she thinks – I want to enter the fascist romantic style of thought. Maurice is an old-fashioned ultra and Vichy collaborator and of course there was Uncle Melikian, but Chantal's own brand of wolves-at-the-door fascism began, I should guess, as dinner-party chit-chat kind of thing – opinions produced at table and frivolously defended in the interests of *épater* one's elders, but, in time, such opinions harden and in defending them one becomes strongly attached to them. Slowly the shocking romantic frivolity hardens into a total delusional system. In the system, her daddy, her villa and Western Civilization, as she imagines it, are all under threat from the fanatical devotees of a German Jew who lived in London in the nineteenth century. *Das Kapital* is the cabbala of a thieves' kitchen of psychopathic terrorists, venereal free-lovers, death-camp commissars and well-poisoners. The real danger to her gilded existence is boredom and futility, but she fears what she wants to fear in life. It is the same with her enthusiasms – they are her own delusional projections.

This passion for D'Artagnan for example. It is plain to me that she has read the book with her eyes shut. Armed with the analysis provided by correct ideology, I recognize D'Artagnan for what he is – an *arriviste* of near plebeian origins, at best a lukewarm defender of the King and quite indifferent to the Church, rather sympathetic to Cromwell's republicanism in fact. Does D'Artagnan not tell the King of France, 'The voice of the people is the voice of God'? The man was a social-climbing snob. Why else sleep with Milady de Winter? A glorified grocer with interests in the wine trade and in property. But with the book on her lap and her eyes shut, Chantal sits in the torrid over-scented garden and dreams and sighs over a D'Artagnan who is as much an hallucination as the appearance of a four-foot-high purple spider in her garden would be. D'Artagnan is her hero and Captain Philippe Roussel, late of the Foreign Legion, her master villain, but this does not prevent a love –

The return of Jalloud brings a welcome end to my fruitless pacing. He and Nounourse went out over an hour ago for a walk around the block. Jalloud is very cheerful. He tells Saphia to leave us alone. He has to chivvy her into the bedroom, for she is reluctant to leave her chair, but off she goes sighing, bulging and swaying to collapse on to her bed. Jalloud produces an envelope from his pocket.

'I had forgotten. We found these photographs in your bag and I had them developed by one of the comrades.'

Yes, there she is, Yvonne sprawled like a discarded rag doll with the black stuffing coming out of her head. It is a good photo. I do not trouble to conceal my satisfaction, but Jalloud says, 'She could have been your mother.'

'That my fellow Frenchman should prefer their mothers and France to social justice, I can understand that. These things are not abstractions. France is family and people that one loves, houses we have built, fields that are cultivated. The pull is strong. Of course it is. But understanding is not the same as agreeing. Social justice comes first. And no half-measures. As Lenin says, "One should always try to be as radical as reality itself." '

'Talking to you is like pressing the button on a tape recorder,' says Jalloud and he gives me another of those disarming smiles.

I do not reply, but what I think is that I do not care if I am predictable, so long as I am right.

Jalloud puts the photos back in his pocket and continues, 'Nounourse will be back soon. We have been talking – about you of course and your information. Comrade, I am happy to be able to tell you that our cell is prepared to take part in the sabotage of the Vercingetorix plot and the "elimination" –' (he pronounces this word with ironical relish) '– of Chantal. We would like very much for you to help us. And we will be asking neighbouring cells in Algiers for their help too.'

'Thank you, Jalloud. I don't want to seem ungracious, but shouldn't all this be cleared with your commanding officer first? I don't know what you call him or who he is, but he is at present the only FLN colonel in Algiers. The codename he used when I sent my reports to him was "Tughril". If we act without clearance from above, I fear that we might all end up smiling the Kabyle smile.'

'Oh, don't worry about that,' says Jalloud. 'I am "Tughril".' And he giggles in nervous self-deprecation.

'You can't be "Tughril". Nounourse runs the cell.'

'Nounourse runs the cell and I run Nounourse, and all the other cells in Algiers too, for that matter. Fortunately, not all the cells are in the charge of men like Nounourse, or the job really would be too much for me.'

Jalloud is very young. I don't know whether to believe him or not. However, I suppose I shall have to act as if he really is who he says he is. There can be no proof. But Jalloud claims to have read all my reports and found them very useful.

'Nounourse really wanted you dead, you know,' says Jalloud. 'We have been walking and talking, and now I have sent him on a longer walk to cool off.'

I decide to risk it.

'People like that, ex-petty criminals –'

'Nounourse's crimes are not so petty.'

'– ex-criminals are not to be relied upon, at least not as the leaders of revolutionary cadres. Listen to what Engels says, "Every leader of the workers who uses these scoundrels as guards or relies on them for support proves himself by this action to be a traitor to the movement." For your own good, I suggest that you get rid of him.'

Jalloud smiles gently.

'Well, I can see that you two have not hit it off. But you listen, Engels is not in charge of the Algiers wilaya. I am and I say Muhammad before Engels or before Marx. Muslim does not murder Muslim. Social justice is not going to be achieved that way. I have told Nounourse all your good points and told him to like you. Now I am ordering you to do the same. Nounourse is a fine fellow.'

'The man is a clown! A buffoon! At best a circus strong man!'

Jalloud laughs delightedly.

'Well yes. He has a big mouth, no? I can tell you a story about that. This was two years back, when I was not yet colonel, but only a major. Nounourse was in the group of cells I had been put in charge of. My orders were to form them into a commando platoon and to use this platoon to give the French a very big fright. Our plan was to blow up the big gasworks down by the docks. That really would have been an explosion – had it come off. You must remember the incident? It was an obvious target and naturally the French were not fools about it. There was always a very heavy guard of armed gendarmes around the gasometer. My plan was to send a platoon in with a time-bomb on a short fuse. They were to fight their way up to the steel casing of the gasometer itself, plant the bomb, then scatter, but not scatter so far that they could not hold off the gendarmes and the fire-brigade with their sniper fire. Then, if possible, my men should make their separate ways back to headquarters. However, when I briefed the men, I made no attempt to conceal from them the probability that they were members of a suicide squad. They listened to me very carefully. Then, as soon as I had finished, Nounourse was up on his feet, demanding that he lead the section that actually carried the bomb. He said that he was going to stand over it with his sten gun, until the device actually went off and if it did not go off then he could make it go off with his teeth. He beat on his chest just like Tarzan. Yes he actually did! (It is Saphia who encourages him in this. She has a thing about Tarzan. She is always reading the comics.) So he was banging on his chest and telling us at the top of his voice that he was the greatest bandit in all Algiers, and how many gendarmes he was going to kill and lots more noise. Everyone was looking up to him. But I had my eye on another man in the group, not noisy like Nounourse. A dyer from the tanneries. This dyer said quietly that of course the mission made him afraid, but he was just going to do his duty. He hadn't much experience, but he was going to do his duty.

'So, well, there is not much more to tell. On the day of the mission I put Nounourse in charge of the section of the platoon that was carrying the bomb. He would have broken my head like a coconut if I hadn't, but in the same squad I put that modest young dyer who was not afraid to admit that he was afraid. When night fell the comrades went off down to the docks. I wept as I kissed them all goodbye. Everything went wrong. The details are of no interest. Down by the docks the comrades took a wrong turning on the way to the gasworks, and blundered into a cul-de-sac. They were spotted by a gendarme. Also perhaps there was a leak in our security, for that night the docks were crawling with regular troops as well as gendarmes. The comrades find themselves trapped in this little road without an exit. And what happens? Nounourse sets the bomb against the wall at the end of the road and starts its fuse, and they shoot away at the police and soldiers. The bomb goes off. A couple of the comrades are injured in the blast and one is killed. But those who can go through the wall, while Nounourse holds the troops off, making his Tarzan cry all the time. At the end he runs out of ammunition and has to bludgeon a soldier down with the butt of his gun. Then Nounourse makes off. It was amazing he escaped, for he was carrying another man, that young dyer who was too frightened to walk and the load was not very pleasant, for the dyer has shitted in his pants. Later that night we executed the dyer for cowardice in the field.'

Jalloud scrapes his chin and gives me a very direct look.

'I tell you all this to show you that things are not always what they seem. Or rather they are precisely what they seem. That is the paradox.'

Again I am not sure whether I believe Jalloud, but there is no point in saying so.

'I had better give you another shot before Nounourse comes back. He does not like to see drugs being taken in his flat.'

While Jalloud busies himself with the solution and the injection, he continues to talk.

'Nounourse is OK. You will see. He obeys me. They all obey me. I bet anything that you think I am too young to be in charge of a whole wilaya. It is not so. Some months back this summer I and some of the comrades had to go to Arzew to meet a Bulgarian who was saying that maybe there might be arms from Russia for us, maybe not. You know Arzew? This meeting was on the cliffs by the sea where we could see that we were not being watched. We had look-outs in all directions. The Bulgarian was thinking maybe what you are thinking, that I was not really in charge of my men. So I told him to be a witness to what was going to happen and I made a signal to one of my watchers on the cliff and he threw himself off the cliff down on to the rocks below, dead, just like that, and the Bulgarian's doubts were at an end. It is true. Nounourse was there.'

Jalloud sighs heavily.

'So now, I and my men are at your disposal. You can snap your fingers at them, like me. What is your plan?'

It will not do to show any hesitation.

'The demonstration and putsch are still more than a fortnight off. I have ideas about that, but first I propose that we put a spoke in their wheels by eliminating Chantal. That woman is dangerous.'

'Murder Chantal? Why not?' says Jalloud indifferently. It does indeed seem that he will go along with anything I say. 'Why not? But how? and where?'

'Just this morning I noticed that the opera house is mounting the *Ring* cycle. The first night of *Rheingold* is the day after tomorrow, and –'

'And she will be there.'

'All the old Pétainist scum will be there, come to celebrate the Aryan Artist as Superman. In any case, it is the event of the season. The de Serkissians will have a box for the first night. That is a certainty.'

'The opera –' Jalloud hesitates. 'That will be difficult. To get in will be possible for you, perhaps for several of us. But what about weapons? Will we not be frisked and searched at the doors? Will it be the gun or the bomb? And how are we going to escape? None of us knows the opera house. Does it have to be the opera?'

'The opera will be best. The de Serkissian villa and the SDECE building where she works are both heavily guarded. Besides, action like speech has its rhetoric. An outrage at the opera will have a definite effect – and it will prove to the world that there is nowhere that these people can be safe.'

Jalloud deliberates.

'OK. I can see that, but the details will be difficult. We will need to know more about the layout of the place and the location of the de Serkissian box. That is important. We will need time maybe to "persuade" some of the stagehands or other backstage people to co-operate. It could be done perhaps . . . but we can't just charge into it.'

'True. I have thought about that. *Rheingold* is on Monday. Three days after that is the first night of *Die Walküre*. Later come *Siegfried* and *Götterdämmerung*. So I will go to the first night of *Rheingold*, reconnoitre and report back. Then later we make the attempt on one of the other first nights.'

Jalloud thinks hard. Then he seems to see a possibility.

'Yes. Good. It would be best if we murdered that woman during *Götterdämmerung*. That is *Twilight of the Gods*, is it not? It will have a good effect, as you say.'

He stands up and walks about, waving the now empty syringe in an excited fashion.

'But I am coming to the opera too! I have never been to an opera before! Let us take a box, if we can . . . We will need proper dress, but I can fix that. Our expenses can all come out of the FLN funds.' He giggles a little hysterically. 'But what Nounourse will make of it, I do not know.'

At that moment the door opens.

'Ah, there you are, Nounourse! We were just talking about you.'

Chapter Seventeen

Jalloud looks elegant and excited. From time to time he self-consciously runs his fingers down his jacket. He has provided me not only with a dinner-jacket, but also a hat, white scarf and gloves and a gardenia in my button-hole – and dark glasses. I am to wear the hat tipped over my eyes and the scarf wrapped round my mouth, for fear lest any of my former comrades-in-arms recognize me. I look like Rudolph, Prince of Geroldstein – as impersonated by a grocer in a small-town amateur dramatics society. I am only thankful that Jalloud's mates in the kasbah have failed to produce the sash of the Légion d'honneur. When Nounourse sees me, he roars with delight and throws a punch at my stomach. It is true that I have a paunch, but it is a muscular paunch. It can take the kick of a mule. I don't even grunt. Nounourse gives me a funny look.

Jalloud is frantically hunting for his binoculars and he asks me if we should take money for ice-creams. Saphia in her chair gets irritated by Jalloud's jokes and nervous gestures. I am irritable and I sweat profusely, for, over the last two days, Jalloud has been watering down the doses of morphine.

In the foyer, I thrust past the fat white women with gold on their bosoms and the men with shiny faces. The men bow to hear their partners' words, then bob away as I thrust past. Ah, the charm of the upper classes! Well, I am determined not to be charmed by them. These people have come together in the evening's stifling heat in a sort of demonstration to the world outside. For, after all, in one thousand three hundred years of history, the Arabs have produced nothing that remotely compares with Wagner's *Ring* cycle. Squeezing their bums into their seats is, then, a political act for these idlers. Certainly I hate opera. What is remarkable is that they do too and that they are so bad at disguising it. They will talk about anything except the music that they are here for and they will shift restlessly on their seats. Even so, it is a price they are ready to pay, if only to have something to talk about at the dinner parties which form the life-in-death of the dull winter season in Algiers. If a socialist revolution in Algeria succeeded only in closing the opera house and putting an end to those dinner parties, it would already be something. Personally, I used to enjoy the dirty stuff we sang in the barracks on Camerone Night. I am also fond of the songs of Edith Piaf. She sings for the little people.

The audience is stacked and raked in the confined space, like so many birds of prey nesting on a cliff face, squawking and extending their jewelled talons. We have a box. Jalloud's French army issue binoculars sweep the balcony, the grand tier, the circle and the stalls. There is no sign of Chantal or of her family. General Challe is here though. Jalloud has spotted him in a front stalls seat. If only we had managed to smuggle weapons in tonight . . . I, too, scan the house obsessively. Since I have returned to Algiers, I have been conscious of Chantal as an unseen presence. Wherever I go, she walks with me, a ghost who walks hip to hip with me and who matches her steps precisely to mine and at night I have lain awake wondering if my ghost also walks with her and when she lies with another man is my ghost also present as the third one in the bed, unconsenting but repeatedly violated? I find the strength of this romantic and certainly neurotic fantasy somewhat eerie and Marx's guidance on these matters is enigmatic. What he says in *The German Ideology* is that 'The phantoms formed in the human brain are also, necessarily, sublimates of their material life-processes, which is empirically verifiable and bound to material premises.'

Chantal must be here tonight. Certainly, there is a lot at

stake. If Chantal fails to appear, then my stock with Jalloud and the comrades will fall. The opera house is, I suppose, small by comparison with those to be found in the cities of mainland France, but it makes an attempt at grandeur in miniature. The gold and red striped wallpaper, the red velvet coverings on the balconies, the cream-coloured imperial eagles in stucco alternating with bizarre human-headed, butterfly-winged caryatids – it seems that operatic culture came to an end in the Napoleonic era. With so much cream and gold, the general effect is of sitting inside a rather sickly multi-tiered wedding cake.

I lean over to Jalloud and whisper, 'One day, my colonel, all this will be yours.'

He laughs but I continue.

'No, I am serious. Shall I tell you when I was last in an opera house?'

'Yes. Tell me when you were last in an opera house,' says Jalloud indifferently. He continues to look around him.

'It was in Hanoi in 1955. We were all brought together in the Hanoi opera house. I was among the last batch of those to be repatriated – the survivors of Dien Bien Phu and the death march into captivity. There were some hundreds of us brought in from Lang Trang. What strikes me now is that the Hanoi opera house had the same tatty colonial pretensions as this place. Its balconies were decorated with stucco and gold palmettes, fringed by swords, lances and tropical foliage. The stalls seats had all been ripped out and those of us who could still walk milled about in that area. On the stage the little yellow men in black cotton uniforms yelled out orders and tried to organize us into proper groups. (But that is how I might have described it before Dien Bien Phu. Since Lang Trang I had learned to see them as us and us as them.) There was no usherette, but a man from the Red Cross walked around distributing cigarettes. That was the first as well as the last time I ever set foot in an opera house and it was a terrible moment for me. For the first time in many months I was re-encountering the men I had learned to hate and now, they told me, I was about to be shipped back to the country that had betrayed me.'

'It must have been awful.'

'You musn't be impressed by all this.'

But Jalloud is not really responding. I wonder if it is conceivable that I am becoming a veteran revolutionary bore? I begin to study the programme notes and, despite myself, I become interested. I hate opera. Opera is reactionary, of course. It shows a flattering mirror to the upper classes. The message is that, whether exchanged as babies by gypsies, disguised as troubadours or on the tumbril to the scaffold, true nobility will out and the assembled spear-carriers in the end have nothing to do but acknowledge that nobility. But, now as I begin to study the programme notes, I begin to sense that Wagner's *Ring* may be different. My only previous acquaintance with this man's music I owe to Chantal. The vilest night we spent together was the night she put a record on the gramophone and challenged me to make love to her in time to the rhythms of the *Liebestod* from *Tristan und Isolde*. No two orgasms are ever the same. Every orgasm is a new discovery, but something that was so slow and as painful as the *Liebestod* orgasm was an unwelcome discovery.

Jalloud is a bright student. He has his 'bac' and he knows the plot of *Carmen*, but, as far as opera goes, that is it. I have a lot of problems explaining the plot of *Rheingold* to him. But in a box I have the luxury of continuing to whisper once the performance has started. The brooding notes of the 'ring' motif inaugurate the primal fantasy, that is the awakening of consciousness, which spirals and rises through the murky waters – yes, I should say it is even the awakening of class consciousness in a world of primitive communism, before man learned to value gold more than love.

Ideology is the key which unlocks all art, so, while Chantal may listen to the horns give voice to a hopeless yearning for the lost citadels of Europe, I hear something different, a lament for the way in which human beings have been sacrificed for gold. Alberic cheats the Rhinemaidens. He is robbed by Wotan who in turn cheats the giants. Fasolt kills Fafner.

They all want that ring of power which is profit, this golden ring which turns the wheels of the dynamos and sends the dwarfish proletariat underground to work for their subsistence . . . There is a price for everything. That is Wagner's message. And the gods are doomed. The fortifications of Valhalla are no stronger than those of Sidi Bel Abbès. That is why Wagner is great. He has got the enemy's number.

Act One ends. Freia (Christa Mannerling) is cheered to the rafters. Her presence on the stage reassures the matrons in the stalls. It is possible to be very fat with streaky mascara and still be a goddess. There is no interval but Jalloud, bored, goes for a walk round the balcony corridor. I stay in the box. It is not safe for me to leave the box. When he returns, he tells me to relax (but it is he who is so nervous!). He has spotted a group of people who are obviously the de Serkissians. They are on the same side of the house, two boxes away from us. He says that Chantal looks very pretty. He is even more flushed and excited than before. And I too feel something of his excitement. Revenge! Soon, I shall be revenged! Already to be in the same building as her and she not knowing that I am here, and for me to be closing in for the kill, there is something sexual in this.

Wotan and Loge are reascending from Nibelheim and I am concentrating on the hammering of the dwarfs on their anvils when I am nudged in the ribs. I do not immediately respond, but eventually I turn to see if Jalloud is enjoying this. My stomach does a queer lurch. In the murk it is hard to be sure but it seems to me that Jalloud's face has turned black and that his head is at a queer angle. I stop breathing for a while and then slowly I turn. Now I see that the door to our box is open. In the shadows at the back of the box stands Nounourse. His finger is on his lips signalling me to silence. Then the same finger crooks and beckons me to join him at the back of the box. Nounourse looks resplendent in white dinner-jacket and cummerbund. He seems to creak a little as he leans to whisper in my ear.

'Get ready to run, Captain Addict, when I say so. We are going left down the corridor. Stick close to me.'

He slips me a weapon. It is my familiar old Tokarev. Nou-nourse tiptoes to the edge of the box. Wotan and Loge are preparing to haggle with the giants. Then Nounourse gets a grip on the corpse of Jalloud and hoists it on to the red velvet parapet. He gives voice to a great wordless bellow forcing the orchestra to falter and then to stop altogether. Then with the cry of 'Algeria shall be free!' he tips the body of Jalloud down into the darkness of the stalls. Shrieks rise from all parts of the opera house, like birds taking to air. A shot is fired.

'Run, Captain Addict!'

Out in the corridor of the grand tier, Nounourse has turned not towards the main staircase, but in the other direction towards what I fear may be a cul-de-sac. It is a struggle for me to keep up with him. In fact there is a door marked private at the end of the curving corridor and we charge through it to find ourselves on the fly floor. A stagehand who has been fiddling with the ropes and counterweights flattens himself to let Nounourse pass along the bridge. But I am smaller fry and moving more slowly and he is brave enough to take me by the lapels. I break his fingers for him and follow Nounourse down the ladder. There are three more stagehands at the foot of the ladder apparently prepared to tackle us. Perhaps they are under the impression that we are only rowdy first-nighters? Nounourse and I drop from the ladder screaming at the tops of our voices and they back away, all save one who catches the hard edge of Nounourse's hand on the edge of his nose. Blood sprays over his overalls. I move in to stomp on his instep and, as he totters, I am about to bring my gun down on his collar bone, but Nounourse pulls me away. We run down a short flight of steps and issue out through the stage door.

Chapter Eighteen

As we hurry along to the bus stop on rue Michelet, Nounourse explains.

'Jalloud bought me a ticket. He told me that you had to
be killed tonight at the opera.'

But that is all that Nounourse is prepared to explain.

'Later, later.'

We attract queer looks on the bus because of our formal
attire and because we are an Arab and a European travelling
together, but Nounourse is in a hurry to reach his flat,
though afraid to take a taxi. It is difficult for me to sit still
and impassive in the bus. As the adrenalin drains away, it
seems to me that my bad leg has been replaced by a ball of
fire.

Once inside the flat, he starts yelling at Saphia to get her
out of bed and they set to, throwing things in suitcases and
tying up bundles of luggage in sheets. Nounourse is sending
Saphia to Mtidja where she has relatives. Saphia gives Nounourse one final look of languid reproach. What has her
Tarzan done now? We are in the flat for less than fifteen
minutes. What takes more time that anything else is that
Nounourse decides to hack his beard off, making use of
only a dry cut-throat razor.

'Come on, Captain Addict,' shouts Nounourse. 'Or
would you rather wait here to see who comes for us first,
the flics or the FLN execution squad?'

So we set off into the night walking towards the suburb

of Belleville and, as we walk, Nounourse begins the difficult work of explanation.

'It was Jalloud's idea that I throw the body down from the box, but when he had that idea he thought the body was going to be yours. That first afternoon when Jalloud and I went for a walk round the block, you remember it? That was when Jalloud was giving me the orders to kill you. Then he was thinking that he would have me arrange an accident in a swimming pool for you, but then when you have your ideas about going to the opera, Jalloud thinks that it will have more effect if you, an unidentified European, are killed during the performance. So there was Jalloud sitting and pretending to listen to the music and look for this Chantal woman, but really he was sitting there waiting for me to slip into the back of the box and then come quietly towards you with my strangling cord.'

Nounourse cracks his knuckles with glee.

'He certainly got a surprise! I will tell you what he was thinking about you. This is what he was thinking about you, not what I was thinking about you. No offence? You understand? We were walking around the block then and he was saying to me, "Nounourse, this Captain Philippe Roussel, he is a mad dog, one hell of a mad dog. And what do we do with mad dogs? That is right. Nounourse, we put them down. This Roussel is a psychopath. You know what is a psychopath, don't you? This man is more interested in killing people than in anything else. The revolution does not need his sort. You know, Nounourse, you and me and Ait Ahmed, Abou Missoum, Khadir and the others, we are not Marxists, we are Muslims and of course we fight against the French, but we do not love murder like this man. Besides, I do not believe that this Philippe is a proper Marxist. He only likes adventures and violence, and he knows nothing about ordinary people. This Philippe has ideas in his head, but where do they come from? They are not CP policy in Algeria, nor are they Moscow policy either. They are bugs in his brain," and Jalloud said that you were dangerous, because you had a will to death – your own death.

'Of course I am very surprised by what Jalloud is saying, but I am not going to argue with him, for he is my superior officer. Then Jalloud says, "What did you think, my good Nounourse, of what he is telling us about this Mademoiselle Chantal de Serkissian? You thought nothing about it? I tell you what I think. I think that this woman is the biggest bug in the mad dog's brain. Of course, he is bitter because she denounced him as a traitor in front of his officers, but I do not think that this makes her a fascist. I have never thought it fascist to collect stamps – even German stamps. I am not going to let the resources of our organization be wasted by pursuing all the mad-dog ideas that this adventurist renegade has. Besides, as you can see, he has a drug problem. He is not reliable. Get rid of him for me, Nounourse."

'I am saying nothing, just nodding as if I were agreeing with Jalloud. In fact, though, I am a crafty man and I have thoughts of my own. You know I think it is a good thing to kill the French until they get out of my country. So I have decided that I admire what you have done for us. I like you, Captain Addict, that is what I decided then. If you are a mad dog, then I think we need lots of mad dogs to be our comrades. "Do you know what a psychopath is, my good Nounourse?" he is saying, but what does he know about it? He is only a student, not a proper doctor.'

Nothing more is said until we reach Jalloud's flat in Belleville. I keep my thoughts to myself. Now that I have thought about it, I am not surprised by Jalloud's actions. I might have given the same order myself, if I had been in his shoes. I respect his ruthlessness. After all he had my ruthlessness, but he lacked my luck – or what the Arabs call *baraka*. And in an odd sort of way, if I had been killed, I do not think that my ghost would have resented it. I have never served the revolution for personal reward. Quite the contrary. And, when the revolution is successful in Algeria, it will not surprise me if, instead of being thanked, I am swiftly purged. History shows us that after the triumph of communism in any country, members of the vanguard party are among the first to be purged. Such people, because of their work in the vanguard, often have an exalted idea of their status and refuse to accept proper party discipline. They are the products of a particular historical moment. Once that moment has passed they may well be of no further service to the proletariat. If one day my comrades decide that I should be eliminated, I think that I shall accept this quietly. But as for Jalloud's idea that I have a will to die, the simple fact is I am alive and he is not, and Jalloud was not right about Chantal either . . .

When we arrive at Jalloud's flat, Nounourse kicks the door in and he takes money and weapons out of their places of concealment. Nounourse wants to get this stuff out before Jalloud's body is identified and other interested parties come to search the place. I am mortified that I can find no morphine in the room. But with our loot wrapped up in cardigans in paperbags, we go off to one of the two big hammams in Belleville. It is past midnight, but Nounourse still manages to find someone to give him a proper shave in the foyer of the hammam. The hammam is closing down for regular business, but this is where we shall sleep, on the still warm tiles of the steam room. As I compose myself for sleep I see advancing upon us through the thinning steam a procession of emaciated wraiths in ragged white robes. Silently they move around us and find places to lay themselves down. It is the charitable practice of this and other hammams to allow the beggars of the quarter a floor to sleep on during the cold winter nights.

Nounourse is not quite ready for sleep. He rolls over to whisper in my ear.

' "Do you know what a psychopath is, my good Nounourse?" ' and here Nounourse attempts to imitate Jalloud's nervous giggle. 'Jalloud used to talk to me as if I were the chump with the muscles. I heard it in his voice. The oaf who does the heavy lifting jobs, good old Nounourse! But I am not simple at all. I am a crafty man. Together, you and I will do great things, Captain Addict. We will shake this city by its throat!'

Nounourse's whisper has built up into the familiar boom, and some of the beggars are making timid complaining noises, but Nounourse has not quite finished yet.

'And you should have heard the vile things that Jalloud was saying about Margaret, Princess of England!'

Minutes later, the snoring begins. I pity the beggars, but I too am very tired and fall swiftly asleep myself. In the morning Nounourse is up first and bellowing for the barber. This business of shaving is quite a trial for him. His honour was closely entwined with all that hair on his face. No longer the Barbary corsair, he more closely resembles the man he actually is – mentally weak and the victim of circumstance. There is, of course, a certain irony in the fact that he has been obliged to lose his beard for the purpose of disguise, while I have been obliged to grow one. My beard makes me look a little like Landru, the sinister lady-killer of the 1920s, but I am not unhappy with it. I enjoy the luxury of not shaving, and, as the growth proliferates, in some strange way I feel myself to be returning to the origins of communism – that is, away from that *kulak* turned *apparatchik*, the clean-shaven Khrushchev, with his vile denunciations of Stalin, beyond Lenin, with his thin little beard, back to Marx and the florid profusion of genius itself.

Later in the day, Nounourse finds us lodgings in the quarter, making use of a criminal acquaintance from his pre-FLN days and paying him off with FLN funds from Jalloud's flat. We do not go out for a couple of days. After a couple of days, we estimate that the police will lose interest in the incident of the murder at the opera. After all, at the moment there are twenty murders a day in the Belleville quarter alone. The FLN are a different matter. It is hard to guess how long it will take them to work out that Jalloud has been murdered and by whom. Fortunately, only three other cell members besides Nounourse have seen my face. None of the other cells know anything at all about me. Nounourse and I agree that it is best that, whenever possible, it is I who go out to do the shopping and to reconnoitre for our next outrages. Nounourse entertains himself by doing press-ups, a hundred at a time, and by running on the spot in the tiny little room. Then he sits and broods, hunched over himself like a great djinn trapped in a little bottle. I am his master now, but, for the time being, I have no orders to give him.

We are not good company. I am as restless as he is, since I am at last undergoing the 'cold turkey'. I get aches and popping flashes in the head and I sweat a lot, cold and hot. Everything looks very grey and dusty. Even when I am out in the streets and am looking up at what I know is a blue sky, I see it as grey and dusty. The food tastes like that too. It is difficult for me to move about very much, for I keep getting the shits in the most agonizing way. I have to talk my way through the stomach pains, and it seems that everyone in the streets is looking at me talking to myself about the pain in my stomach. Plans have to be made, but it is hard for me at the moment to think clearly. My thoughts keep slipping sideways and besides I can muster no enthusiasm for my ideas. It will pass. I know it will, but I can't imagine it.

Nounourse asks me lots of questions about Chantal.

'That woman sounds like a whore and a bitch. You tell me when and I will kill her for you.'

Myself I do not think that she will live to see *The Twilight of the Gods*, nevertheless the day of the barricades and the putsch plot is coming closer and that must be my first priority. In the days that follow I walk backwards and forwards across Algiers. It is not just a matter of supplies or of spying out the land. It is a matter of clearing my head, and of something else perhaps. The mornings are thick with white mist. Sometimes it is midday before the sun breaks through. Still, it is remarkably clement for January. Although two days pass before I dare venture out of our refuge, I manage to find an old copy of the *Messager d'Alger* with a report on the outrage at the Algiers opera house.

The story is that a medical student, Jalloud bin M'hami, was collaborating with the police in Algiers and providing them with invaluable intelligence. He was however brutally murdered by an FLN assassin in the opera house as a warning to other collaborators. The assassin was seen by a number of the people in the audience and the orchestra and he is described as thin, tall and wiry, possibly with red hair. None of it is true of course – at least I don't think it is, but it is no more a lie than anything else that is supposed to have happened in this city of Algiers.

Nothing is explicit but everyone knows that something will happen soon in this city. Few of the Arabs dare venture out of their quarters – Belleville, certain sections of the Bab el-Oued and, of course, the kasbah, a rotting piece of gruyère sliding down the hill (as General Massu put it). The fat white ladies no longer find it easy to hire agreeable Arab boys to carry their heavy loads of shopping home. *Pied-noir* men gather at street corners and talk. The men on the streets with machines for making *citron pressé* or *orange pressée* are distributing leaflets. I walk about and observe. The writing is, as they say, on the wall. 'Death to de Gaulle'. 'Victory to the FLN', 'Massu to Power', 'Long live death. Down with Intelligence'. Several times I spot painted eyes on the walls with great Vs underneath, like insomniac bags – the emblems of the Children of Vercingetorix. I walk about and I suppose that I am saying goodbye to the city. I could never have believed it, but it is a sad moment for me. I look in the windows of the shoe-shops, the shops selling sportswear, the pâtisseries that sell brioches and *pains au chocolat*. I see the Arab women in their gondourahs filling the European milliners like vengeful ghosts and the pretty young Algerian women in the hairdressers. I note the style of the buildings, the neatly trimmed hedges, even the little beer mats on the café tables and I am filled with sadness. As Marx says, 'All the houses, in our times, are marked with a mysterious red cross. The judge is history, the executioner is the proletariat.' I do not dispute that. Still it seems incredible to me that this French city, so very French, shall just perish and its former existence become no more credible than that of Atlantis. I am not without sentiment. I understand the point of view of the poor white inhabitants of this city. Only I reject it.

I spend a lot of time at the docks. When my mission shall have been accomplished I plan to leave this country. One misty morning when I am walking along the quay towards the offices of the Compagnia Transatlantique, the thing I have been expecting and yet was not expecting happens. An arresting hand falls on my shoulder. I spin round fast and the Tokarev in my pocket is out and pressed against the man's heart. The man wears a long heavy overcoat of the sort that is worn only by tramps and by members of the Anglophile upper class. On his head he wears an old-fashioned trilby and his face is covered right up to his eyes by a scarf. There is something very odd about the face. Perhaps it is those liquid gleaming eyes. The hands rise in deprecating response to my gun.

'Philippe, don't you recognize me?' The voice is muffled, but there is a weedling pleading tone to it. 'Don't shoot, my old friend, my old sparring partner. Don't you recognize me?'

'How can I recognize you with that fucking scarf around your face?' And I reach up to strip it from him.

I wish that I had left the scarf where it was. What I see is hard to describe. It takes me a while to puzzle it out – those big eyes full of a pleading and a pitiful good will, much lower down a mouth with a couple of broken teeth and, between the eyes and the mouth, two big slits like a dog's muzzle. There is something of a *memento mori* in this apparition, as if death had come down to the docks today to detain me with his hand. It is only when the head turns in shame to help my understanding that I realize what it is I am seeing. The man's nose has been cut off.

'Philippe, I am Raoul.'

If this were not Algiers, one might think the man to be the victim of advanced syphilis, but I have seen the victims of such operations before walking the streets of Algiers. In

1955 the FLN ordered all Muslims to abstain from smoking. They said that smoking only filled the coffers of the *grand-colon* tobacco companies. Some Arabs ignored the FLN's command and kept on smoking. They were taken by the FLN and they had their noses removed. I believe that secateurs were used, of the sort that are normally used for heavy-duty gardening. Posters of the victims were circulated in France by General Massu's propaganda department. I had seen such faces before, but, of course, it is worse when it happens to a European.

'It is all up with me. I cannot dream any longer of practising at the bar. Obviously. After you left, Zora left with her children – I don't know where – but I managed to get the rest of the needle out of my ear. Then Chantal arrived at last with Lieutenant Schwab. I tried to explain to him how it was that you escaped, but they would not believe me, or perhaps they did believe me, but they did not find it satisfactory. I don't know. Anyway they did this to me. An accident in a way . . .'

Raoul goes maundering on. All the time I keep looking over my shoulder. It might be that Raoul is being shadowed by Vercingetorix ultras. It might be that Nounourse has come out this morning and is tailing me. I shudder to think how he might react if he discovers that Raoul is still alive. In any case I do not want to keep looking at Raoul's face.

'No, I'm not bitter. That is strange, isn't it? The conclusion she came to was logical, logical but wrong. But no bitterness. I think it is time for the killings and the mutilations to stop. I'm glad I've found you, my friend. I enjoyed our debates. They gave me much to think about. Indeed, I think that they were the last moments of real happiness in my life. I knew you would come to Algiers in the end. I hoped we would meet again. I have been looking for you. Since that day, I've often wondered why didn't you kill me?'

I have nothing to say to Raoul. It is Chantal I should be talking to. I am amazed by her guts. Did she really order this? The ferocity is really admirable. Admirable but at the same time animal, for, since right-wing atrocities do nothing to advance the cause of humanity, they can only be viewed as ugly historical freaks going nowhere – the two-headed calves of politics. But I wish I had my camera with me. What a woman! Raoul is still talking and now there is a note of bitterness in the shaky voice.

'I have wished it too, that you had killed me, many times. But life must continue, eh? Would you like a cigarette?'

I shake my head. He fishes out a Bastos from his overcoat and gets it alight and, soon, ghastly smoke issues from the two holes in his face.

'Afterwards, I had difficulty at the hospital. I had to tell them that it was the work of FLN terrorists. If I had breathed a word about the Children of Vercingetorix, I think it would have been the end of me and of my parents. I have been reading *The Diary of Anne Frank*. I recommend it to you. It is something better than either your Karl Marx or anything Chantal has to offer.'

He is fishing about in the pockets of his overcoat for something.

'I pity Chantal and I fear for her sanity. Look at this.'

He thrusts an embossed card into my hand. It reads: *Mlle Chantal de Serkissian has much pleasure in requesting the attendance of M. Raoul Demeulze at a party to celebrate the staging of the Ring Cycle at the Algiers Opera House and to meet the cast.* R.S.V.P. It is dated four days on.

'Bad taste, I think. It arrived in the post last week. I suppose it satisfies something in her . . . For a time I thought of actually appearing at her party and causing a . . . Well, never mind. What is the phrase that is so popular nowadays? "The suitcase or the coffin." It's the suitcase for me. In fact I am leaving Algiers. That's why I'm down here today – to go to the shipping office. I think I may take up painting. Well, goodbye, old fellow. Look after yourself, won't you? And do keep thinking about the labour theory of value. You weren't very logical you know.'

A final inspiration comes to me.

'Give me that card, Raoul.'

He does so and I watch him shuffle off down the quay. I think that what interests me about Chantal is that she does not share that exaggerated fear of violence which is so common among the bourgeois. The working class are different. They are capable of understanding that violence can be a liberating force and therefore enjoyable. Chantal is different too. I rest, pressed against the harbour wall, watching to see if Raoul is being shadowed.

Chapter Nineteen

Rather than go back to the flat where I will only have to face more of the childish interrogations of Nounourse, when I have climbed out of the dock area, I plunge into a Moorish bar. It is a place I have never set foot in before. I should like a drink – several drinks – to fortify myself against Nounourse's rumbling attacks against alcohol and drugs and to help me sleep against his snores. It is a matter of waiting. Of passing time, before we strike again. The place is full of lonely men. A Kabyle in a postman's uniform and gauntlets looks up as I enter and his gaze follows me to the bar. I buy a glass of red wine and move over to the pinball machine. I hope that my absorption will protect me against any conversational overtures. It is an American machine, the jaunty 'Swing Time' model. 'IT'S MORE FUN TO COMPETE!' A crew-cut little urchin sticks his head out from behind one of the buffers and a balloon issues out of his mouth, 'HOW YA DOIN'?' and on the other side of the field of play another's balloon reads, 'TOO BAD! TRY AGAIN!' The whole thing is styled for the sixties – the decade into which, against all the odds, I have survived two weeks. The styling of this awful machine is surely the harbinger of the next ten years – slick, smart, materialistic, well behaved – a dream of life for the no-hopers in this bar. The first game was just to get the feel of the machine and see how the roll-overs worked. I put some more centimes in. The first ball is the crucial one. It builds a foundation for a cumulatively growing score by lighting up a chain of lights for bonus points, but though I try to concentrate, I am all the time aware of the watching Kabyle as a ghostly image on the glass panel of 'Swing Time'.

I am on the third ball and building up a killer score when a swinging blow to my back makes me lose control of the game and the ball drops between the flippers. Tilt. My hand goes into my pocket and I spin round.

'Hey! Hey! How goes it?'

Who is this man? Heavy set, big ears, hooked nose and a depressed-looking face on which a smile sits awkwardly. A soldier of France.

'No, it's not a ghost! Don't worry about the game. I'll buy us another. After all, "It's more fun to compete!" And let me freshen your glass. You look as though you need it. Wonderful seeing you again!'

He strolls over to the bar. The Kabyle never moves his eyes from me. Who the fuck is the man at the bar? Perhaps I should leave now before he returns with the drink? I don't remember him, but that proves nothing. You never know in this life who you are going to see again – and who you aren't. You can be like as one with someone for years and then they vanish completely and forever, or maybe forever. You won't know until you are dead. Others keep cropping up again and again in your life in a hundred different contexts and coincidences. From the window of our little hideout I saw Zora in the street two days ago, a child holding her hand and a baby in her arms, just as I had imagined she would reappear. Two men in trenchcoats marched along behind her. For a long time after this woman had vanished into the distance I played round with the idea that this was Zora leading the flics towards some place where she thought they might find her husband's old contact, Tughril. Then I played around with the idea that she wasn't Zora at all, for if I am honest with myself the angle of vision was difficult and the woman didn't look very like Zora. And maybe the trenchcoated men had nothing to do with her. Or maybe, very likely indeed, they were taking this anonymous woman to identify her slaughtered husband's body in the morgue. It is hardly likely that I shall ever know the truth.

'You don't remember me, do you?'

He is back with a cognac for me and a beer for himself. I grunt in a friendly yet noncommittal way.

'You always used to drink cognac. That I do remember. You said it stopped dysentery. Complete rubbish, of course.'

Rubbish indeed and I don't remember saying that, but he punches me on the arm encouragingly.

'Hey! Hey! Red River Delta! Haiphong! Tonkin! Taking the Shan tribesmen on the trail! Remember now? Great times!'

He wags his head from side to side and mugs friendliness. Even so, his face is pretty grim and I have the impression that if I say that they were not great times or that I cannot quite place him, he will take a swing at me. So I just smile. He tries to smile back, but it's more like a rictus.

'The name is Edmond Durtal. I'm buying, so I'll take the first game.'

And he sets the machine for two. As he positions himself over the flippers, I casually rest my elbows on the edge of the frame, so that he cannot jiggle the machine about as he would like, to pay him back for that slap on the back. He soon loses his first ball.

He looks at me closely.

'Mind you, I would have had difficulty in recognizing you with that beard. You remind me of the artist . . . that artist with the prostitutes . . .'

'Toulouse-Lautrec.'

'That's the man. And you are in civvies now! I don't believe it. How's life treating you? What are you doing? Tell all.'

I say nothing, but tap my nose.

'Oh, I see. Undercover stuff. Lots of bad hats in this bar, are there?'

He doesn't quite take it seriously, but, still, he believes me. Now it's my ball, but he is leaning against the machine.

'I'm sorry. Would you mind taking your elbows off while I'm shooting?'

He steps away reluctantly. I am clocking up a satisfactorily high score, but all the time I am thinking. I still cannot remember this Edmond. It could all be a fraud. Maybe the Kabyle is with him? Maybe this Edmond's job is to detain me in footling conversation while his sergeant goes to fetch reinforcements? Despite all my precautions this morning, I could have been followed, or there could have a tail on Raoul down at the quay. He could be SDECE or he could be from Vercingetorix. He could be a fellow-traveller working for the FLN. But, on the whole, I think it is probable that he is the fool he looks.

As he is firing off his second shot, I ask him. 'And you? What are you doing now?'

He attempts a sort of shrug to the table behind us where he has left his *képi*.

'Sections administratives des Services specialisées. Still only a captain, but what the hell!'

So he is with the *képis bleus*, Soustelles's social workers in uniform.

He lets the ball get lost while he tells me more.

'It's very rewarding work. I'm with the big regroupment camp outside Blida. Every day it's something different. Jack of all trades and master of none! One day it's getting the men organized to dig ditches, the next it's the clinic and getting a cyst on some old Fatima's scalp treated, the next it's telling them how to deal with potato blight and the next it's teaching the kids how to play football. It's building bridges. I couldn't have believed I could be so happy. And those kids, once you've got their trust, the smiles you get from them . . .'

If it's an act, it's a very convincing one. I grunt as I too lose my ball. He moves closer and gives my beard a tug as if to reassure himself that it is genuine. His eyes bore into mine. Then he squares himself up to me challengingly.

'You think that I have gone soft, don't you?'

'It's your go. No, I don't. I think your lot do a great job getting the old men to paint the gates of their regroupment camp and getting the fatmas to arrange flowers in tin cans, while our lot go out into the *bled* and knock the hell out of their husbands.'

He manages to laugh.

'Well, I suppose there's something in that. Still the same

old comrade in arms! Ever the cynic. That's how you were in Indochina, always one of the awkward squad.'

'I'm not cynical, Edmond. I certainly admire what you do. You take risks like the rest of us. At any time you could get blown up in the field or knifed in your tent. It takes courage to turn your back on an Arab – or for that matter to shake hands with one. And yes, you could win the war for us.'

'That's right. It's an adventure of the heart. There are risks, but the troubles will die down if and only if we can establish some sort of basis of mutual trust. And – it shouldn't be me telling you this – but in that camp I'm like father to them. They bring their problems to me and we talk things through. There is nothing soft in listening to what the Arab has to say. He often has a point. What we need in Algeria now is the faith of a child and the hands of a warrior . . .'

'Faith of a child, hands of a warrior.' I nod thoughtfully, but I am not thinking about that. I wonder if it can be possible that he does not know what I have become, what I have done? It is in fact now well advertised. There are fly-posters on buildings and lamp-posts everywhere and I find it hard to take a piss in a public *urinoir* without facing my image pasted on the wall in front of me. I appear in batches of nine or twelve photos of wanted men – the only European in the batch – every one a killer on the run. Families have been set alight in their farm houses, a priest has been executed by progressive mutilation, a pregnant woman has been eviscerated and the foetus ripped from her womb, and yet, eerily, almost every grainy snapshot shows a smiling face. But, of course, most of these photos date from the times when there was still hope for these men, before the oppressive structures of the colonialist apparatus had been fully exposed, before these men had to take to the cellars and the hills. Some of the photos show signs of retouching and were, I guess, made to be used by marriage brokers or given to fiancées. Mouloud Besmuti, the one who cut the woman open, has the biggest grin of all and it looks to me as though his snapshot may have been taken in one of those fairground booths. I am the only one in this gallery who is not smiling – a boot-face, crew-cut officer's military passcard photo.

Edmond has turned back to the machine.

'I like pinball. It's not a snob's game. I'd really like to get some of these machines in our camp. They would love it, flashing lights, bright colours and all, but I doubt if the general would wear it.'

'He'd be right too. Machines like this would encourage unhealthy expectations in our Arabs.'

'What the hell do you mean, old fellow?'

'Just look at it.'

I point to the design on the backglass. On a podium there stands a blonde with cupid lips. She has been poured into a skimpy little black cocktail dress whose unrealistic curves are brought out by the glossy highlights and she is being seren-aded by young men in white tuxedos with slicked back hair and knowing grins. The ambience is something between a high school prom and a brothel. Here is a scene from the dream life of capitalism. As Marx puts it in *The German Ideology*, 'The phantoms formed in the human brain are also, necessarily, sublimates of their material life processes, which is empirically verifiable and bound to material premises.'

'That's what the West is to the Arabs. They will think that everyone who steps off the boat at Marseilles is given a white tuxedo and . . .'

'You are a devil for cynicism, my dear fellow!'

'I'm not cynical. A cynic, looking at your *képi-bleu* type work, would say that by giving to the Arabs, you prevent them from taking and what the Arabs need to be taught is how to take. But you will never hear me say that.'

'I have heard you say that.'

A look of fixed dislike has settled on his face. It's got a bit awkward for him now and he is wondering what to say next. Perhaps he will walk away and leave me in peace. Damn the man, let him leave in peace. But, no . . .

'It's not a matter of being lovey-dovey with the Arabs: it's a matter of being able to heal wounds as well as inflict them. Simply, if we are not human –' He breaks off. 'You do think

I have gone soft, don't you?' He rests his clenched fists on the machine. 'You little arsehole! You don't remember anything, do you? How about that time, in Hoa Binh, at the Bishop's Palace in the Garden of Supplications after the chaplain and I found you with that little Chinese tart? I beat you to pulp. I could do it again now for old time's sake.'

I raise my hands deprecatingly.

'Yes, yes, that was quite a thrashing, but it's your go. Let me get the drinks this time.'

I walk away, thinking, and I think that I have nothing to fear. Indochina was a long time ago and I was a different man before Dien Bien Phu. That's true. But I'm not sure that I was ever in Hoa Binh. Certainly I never went to the Bishop's Palace and I don't think I can remember being in any fight over a Chinese tart. What the hell was or is the Garden of Supplications? Now that I think about our little chat as it has run so far – 'old comrade in arms', 'old fellow', 'little arsehole' – not once has he called me by my name. It is certainly quite likely that we met on one or other of the Red River operations, but I am pretty sure that he has got me mixed up with someone else. In which case, it is now time to throw him off the scent completely. The Kabyle's glazed eyes follow me as I return with the mollifying glass of beer.

And then I casually try it out.

'I shouldn't like us to quarrel and, by the way, Edmond, I think that you have forgotten my name. It's Antoine – Antoine Galland.'

'Antoine! That's fine! Let's shake on – ' But his hand never reaches mine. He wrinkles his nose.

'No, wait a minute, surely . . . have I been muddling you? . . . Surely . . . Philippe. Sorry. I thought you were Philippe Roussel. Surely, you were one of Joinville's team . . .'

It is very quiet between us. Then he tries a short laugh.

'No. It's Antoine. That's right. I had forgotten . . .'

'No, Edmond. Now, you remember. Yes, it's Philippe Roussel. Keep that hand away from your holster. I have killed and I will kill again.'

And I ease the handle of my Tokarev out from my pocket far enough for him to see it.

'I want you to go and sit over there. I want you to sit on your hands.'

'What?'

'Sit on your hands. You liberal colonialists have had plenty of practice at that.'

He shakes his head, but he does as I tell him. I give him a fraternal hug round the shoulder, leaning low over him to prevent others in the bar from seeing what I am doing, and I get the gun from his holster and slip it inside my jacket. It is time for another gamble. I speak very low and he has to incline his head to hear it all.

'Now, don't turn round straight away, but there is a man sitting behind us, the one in the postman's uniform with the gauntlets. You must have noticed him. He's been keeping you under observation all the time we talked. He's one of my men. In a minute I am going to walk out of this place. OK, you can turn your head now and look at him.'

The Kabyle's regard which had dropped for a moment is fixed on us. It's an unnervingly impassive stare.

'What I want, Edmond, is for you to just sit and reflect for a while. You are going to stay here, until ten minutes after my man has left. Then, of course, you can raise the alarm, but on the whole I think it would be better if you managed to forget we have ever met. Don't you? We have our men in your filthy regroupment camp at Blida. They can take your head off your shoulders any time. It's been nice talking to you, Edmond. I only wish I could remember you as well as you remember me.'

Once more, I stroll over to the bar. It is important that I do not look back. I buy a beer. Then I walk over to the postman and hand him the beer.

'It's a grand job you postmen are doing in these dangerous times. This beer comes with the compliments of that officer over there.'

Close up, it is clear that I have guessed right. The postman is almost completely blotto. He has difficulty in raising the glass in his gauntleted hands, but he raises it in a sort of half-toast to Edmond and looks at him in bleary puzzlement. I slip Edmond's gun on to his lap. The postman is so past it that he does not seem to register this.

Then I walk out. Never run. It is for my enemies to run. But I admit I am somewhat shaken. I have been walking around this city in a sort of fantasy, for it is as if I imagined that I were Fantômas, the master criminal whose disguise the police and the authorities are incapable of penetrating. Yet twice in one day I have been recognized. These are risks which are not worth running. It is quiet in the foggy street outside. Then I hear the matchstick crackle of gunfire. It is impossible to tell in which direction. Hardly an hour passes in this city without the sound of shooting. I do not think that Nounourse and I can exist in that confined room for much longer without trying to kill each other. I am getting out of control and dangerous to myself. It is plain that our final strike in Algiers must be soon.

Chapter Twenty

The barricades are going up. On the Saturday the shopkeepers and workers come out with picks and shovels and start hacking at the surfaces of the roads and levering great lumps up to form barriers across those roads. These new walls are crowned by wood and barbed wire. The militias are out in the streets too, sporting their arms and standing guard rather self-consciously over the barricades that are going up. Occasionally a police officer or a para will stroll up and they and the militia men and shopkeepers chat casually. But most of the time the police are happy to keep to themselves, playing cards in the shade of their armoured black marias. The leaders of the demonstration and the strike walk about having oblique conversations and shifting their gaze to see what their comrades are doing. People everywhere are waiting for people somewhere else to do something. As I do the shopping, I hear the phrases which are the small change in this season's currency of conversation. 'The suitcase or the coffin', 'It's now or never', 'We are at the last quarter-hour', 'The days of hope, like Hungary in '56.'

It is midwinter, but the temperature is spring-like and the girls who bring picnic baskets to the men on the barricades are in their summer dresses. The young men slick back their hair and joke with the girls. In the evenings, in place of the traditional *paseo* up the boulevard Guillemin and round to Trois Horloges, there are street parties where the young dance the rumba and the cha-cha-cha and the old look on, for once, indulgently. Where cars can still drive, convoys of cars drive around aimlessly sounding their horns to the rhythm of *Al–gér–ie fran–çaise*.

The last time they played this game, the *pieds noirs* took Government House and brought Generals Salan and Massu to the balcony. They put an end to concessions to the Arabs, forced the fall of the government in France and brought de Gaulle to power. This time it is again no concessions to the Arabs and they plan to remove de Gaulle from power. There is a lot of swagger and hard talk in the streets, but Marx's phrase keeps running in my head, 'the first time as tragedy, the second time as farce'. The putschists will form a Committee of Public Safety and will demand that Jacques Massu, the torturer of the kasbah, be brought back to Algiers. They are reckoning without Captain Philippe Roussel.

The day of the strike comes, 24 January, 1960. In the heart of the city and in the white suburbs the shutters come down. The clusters of men on street corners are getting larger. Every cluster has its transistor radio blaring. They talk casually and eye other groups up and down the road as they talk. At last, from the higher reaches of the city, small bands begin to move off down the ravine roads and flights of steps in rivulets, then in great streams of humanity, heading towards Government Square. The strategy worked out by the Children of Vercingetorix and other ultra groups is that their militias and the vast mass of the white population of Algiers will descend on Government House in such numbers that the gendarmes guarding the place will be forced to withdraw and the commissioner of police will call in the paras and the Foreign Legion. Key officers in these regiments will then declare themselves in sympathy with the aims of the demonstrators and from that moment on the coup will be properly launched. In order for the army to declare itself in this way, it is crucial that the gendarmes are forced out of the way as peacefully as possible, so, although the militias march under their banners with their antiquated Lebel rifles sloped over their shoulders, the rifles are for show, not use.

Everything is ready for the demonstrators in Government

Square. A triple line of steel-helmeted and gauntleted gendarmes is drawn up in front of the floral clock. They have their truncheons out and look tough, but they must know that they will have to withdraw in the face of a demonstration of this size. Behind the floral clock, the French and foreign camera crews have got their cameras up on platforms. Nounourse and I lie pressed very low on the roof of one of the administrative buildings on the side of the square.

The crowd floods across the square. A man in the striped uniform of a former Belsen inmate, flanked by two veterans of the First World War, leads its advance under a banner which bears the motto 'ALGERIA IS OUR MOTHER. ONE DOES NOT ABANDON ONE'S MOTHER'.

They carry wreaths for the French Algerians who died for France in two world wars. Prominent behind them is Lagaillarde, the ex-para whom they are calling 'the D'Artagnan of the barricades'. The leaders are all trying to smile for the cameramen. In twenty years' time, or sooner I estimate, those anxious smiles will come to resemble deathmasks. The crowd's shouts come up to us on the roof like the sound of the sea drawing back on gravel. We look down on a thousand snaking lines of tricolours, placards, *képis*, headscarves, berets and steel helmets and on the clenched fists which dance up and down above the heads. What a tremendous sight! Just the sort of mass demonstration of spurious comradeship and high-minded emotion to give Chantal one of her shivers up the spine.

The crowd advances to within a few feet of the first line of gendarmes and stops. It shuffles and looks at itself and its front line ripples uncertainly. There is a lot of taunting, as each man dares his neighbour to go a little further than he has done and to risk coming within range of a truncheon. Of course people further back in the crowd are impatient and trying to push ahead, but still the mood on both sides is fairly good-humoured, taunting rather than genuinely threatening. There are a few flurries and flailing blows. Rather than really lash out and provoke serious trouble, the police keep taking steps backwards. I am reminded of a comic newsreel being run in reverse. Even now as the police keep withdrawing in good order, both sides take care not to trample over the floral clock – the famous floral clock in Government Square which has marked the hour for so many demonstrations. But the hands on this clock show that we are indeed at the last quarter-hour.

It is time for the Bad Fairy Carabosse to put an end to the mob's honeymoon. The distance is formidable. Nounourse and I have only our pistols, but the lines of gendarmes are closely packed, and we do not even have to hit them. We only have to make them realize that they are being fired upon. We take aim and fire. One of the gendarmes does indeed fall. A couple of police officers fire over the heads of the crowd. The militia men at the front kneel to return their fire, but the militia fire into the ranks of the police. Nounourse and I fire again. More gendarmes fall. This was not expected and it seems that, apart from the officers, the police were not issued with ammunition.

The crowd in movement has its choreography. It splits apart like an exploding star. It shoots flares of humanity up the streets that lead out of the square. I note with interest that though almost everyone is running, no one is running very fast. I come to the conclusion that there are two reasons for this. Firstly, the crowd in flight runs with its head hunched low in expectation of a bullet in the back and it is difficult to run fast in that position. Second, the crowd cannot run fast for fear of trampling over itself. The mob in flight travels at a half-trot.

Within a few minutes the square that was packed is almost empty. There are militia men firing from the stairs and from behind the camera platforms. The police have got tear-gas grenades out and are lobbing them into the centre of the square. Already I can see a dozen of their number lying motionless, pressed to the ground as if they were seeking warmth from its flagstones. The square is littered with abandoned placards, picnic food for the outing and high-heeled shoes. A pair of deserted children look on bewildered with their thumbs in their mouths. Ever since the firing started, there have been cries from both sides of 'Cease firing!', 'Cease your fire!', but sporadic firing continues. There is not a soldier in sight.

I find the whole business utterly fascinating and for a long time I lie there peering over the edge of the roof. It is the living and dying proof of what I have always known, that one can understand violent revolutionary change only by actually participating in it. The right man at the right time, I have put history in motion. Pointing to the bloody city below us, I quote Lenin to Nounourse, 'And when, on an earth which has finally been subdued and purged of enemies, the final iniquity shall have been drowned in the blood of the just and the unjust, then the State which has reached the limit of all power, a monstrous idol covering the entire earth will be discreetly absorbed into the silent city of Justice.' Eventually, when it is clear that the action has moved away from Government Square, I roll over and bask in this beautiful Algerian sun of ours. Nounourse and I chat idly. I find his company more tiresome than ever. This simple soul thinks that I support the Arabs. He is, of course, in error. What is going on in Algiers and throughout the world is not a football match, where everyone, playing or watching, is either for the French or for the Arabs and one cheers and waves the rattle without thinking. History is not a football match and it is history alone that I support. However, Nounourse and I agree that it has been a very good morning's piece of work, and already I am thinking about how to deal with Chantal and the brood of Vercingetorix.

It is dusk before we come off the roof. It is 'like Hungary in '56', but, like Hungary in '56 it is moving into a darker phase. Barricades of tyres are being set alight, sending filthy black smoke up into the ink-blue sky. Grim-looking shopkeepers are assembling collections of bottles filled with petrol behind the barricades. There is still no sign of the army. On the one hand, too many French policemen have been killed for the paras to declare themselves to be on the side of the rioters. On the other hand, there are too many rioters about for the troops to attempt to regain control of the city yet. No one knows what will happen next. The Great Fear has come upon the people.

As we pick our way towards Belleville, I marvel once more at the capacity of revolution to generate mess. Shredded banners, pools of blood and petrol, corpses covered with newspapers – Arab victims of random lynchings. And there is all the normal refuse that has not been collected since the strike began, spilling out of bins and bags. Already the rats are out in the streets here – and in Constantine, Philippeville and Oran.

Chapter Twenty-one

Götterdämmerung has been postponed. A curfew has been imposed by the Governor of Algiers. De Gaulle has broadcast on radio and television telling the army and the people to stand firm. When Frenchman fires on Frenchman, then 'France has been stabbed in the back before all the world', but 'nothing is lost for a Frenchman when he rejoins his mother', and in fact the army's coup fails to materialize. The beautiful weather breaks and people drift away from the barricades. Thunder clouds roll over the city and the steep and badly guttered roads become dangerous sluices. The army makes its appearance at last to help the shopkeepers in demolishing the barricades. The curfew is lifted, but too late for the staging of the last episode of the *Ring* cycle. All the same, the de Serkissian party for the visiting cast is announced in the *Gazette d'Algérie*.

On the morning of the party I wake from a curious dream. I dreamt that Chantal and I were twins entwined in each other's arms in a cocoon which has been laid by a human-headed creature with wings and left to float on the tides of the Bay of Algiers. Then thick red curtains sweep down and nothing more can be seen. That was the dream. If, in fact, I were living inside a melodramatic opera, then, yes, when I go to the villa tonight I would discover that Chantal and I were twins. I was the one stolen at birth by a wandering bedouin. Inside the villa Chantal's old nurse would identify me by my birthmark. She would tell the story to Maurice and the chorus of assembled guests and I would renounce my murderous ambitions, but it will be too late, for Chantal will have drunk the poison. Though the dream fills me with foreboding, I have no time for dreams and in fact I am heading for an end which is more squalid than that.

Nounourse and I are getting on one another's nerves and, now the weather has turned, it is bitterly cold in the flat and there is no heating. We can find nothing to do but clean our guns. I am still hanging on to my faithful old Tokarev, but I only have three more shots left in the magazine. I am full of doubts. I am unable to imagine how it will be when I come face to face with Chantal once more and aim this gun at her. It is not just that either. I am beginning to distrust my motives in heading for the villa tonight. Not that I believe that I am a prey to murky subconscious forces. There is not evidence at all there is such a thing as a subconscious. It is the invention of nineteenth-century bourgeois thought. It makes the doctors rich and the bourgeois believe that there is more of interest in themselves than they could ever have guessed. No, no subconscious. But, looking at my problem with materialist objectivity, there is the matter of simple sexual desire. According to Arab folklore, there is such a thing as magnetic meat. There is a fish which swims in the sea which lures its victims to it by virtue of its magnetic flesh. It may be like that with Chantal and me. Never mind what goes on in the head: meat calls to meat. This is morbidity . . .

At last it is time, if we agree to walk to the villa slowly, for us to get ready. We still have our opera gear, though both suits are very crumpled and, in Nounourse's case, slightly soiled. Nounourse has stolen an umbrella and, pressed together under it, we make our way up the hill of the corniche and past the casino and on towards the Villa Serkissian. There is a police van parked outside the gate, but the gendarmes are not going to challenge people in dinner-jackets, no matter how sodden and crumpled they may look. The drive is lined by sullen Corsicans with guns. I wave Raoul's invitation in the face of the guard at the door and jerk my thumb at Nounourse behind me.

'My bodyguard.'

The man at the door does not bother to examine the card carefully and we are through. Paoli, Maurice's major-domo, is just inside the door waiting to shake the hands of new arrivals and guide them to the drinks.

'Monsieur Rouge,' I say and stroke my beard complacently. Paoli looks puzzled. Perhaps I am familiar to him, but he cannot quite place me. Finally, doubtfully, 'Of course. How good of you to come.'

'I shouldn't shake hands with my bodyguard if I were you. He has a rather strong grip.'

Paoli eyes Nounourse admiringly. I'm sure Nounourse could get a job with Maurice's establishment. Nounourse grins savagely down on him.

'Well, no then, but let me find you both a drink.'

'I'll have gin and he'll have fruit juice.'

We are guided to the bar behind which a black waiter is at work mixing fancy cocktails. We get our drinks and Paoli is called back to the door. I am both excited and apprehensive. I pat my hip to reassure myself that my gun is still there and in doing so, I notice that I have an erection. I turn to face the guests. This is not supposed to be a fancy-dress party, but I see plenty of clowns here. Distinctly elderly members of the *jeunesse dorée*, alcoholic landowners, public servants who retired after Vichy, officers who have resigned from the army to find new careers as mercenaries and the mafia of *grandes dames* who run the big charities in this part of the world. A few of them sport Vercingetorix tie-pins or brooches. Generally, decorations and bosoms are much in evidence. I can't actually see anyone sporting the iron cross, but there is a man with a monocle and duelling scars. I can't see Chantal.

When the major-domo comes back to the bar with two new arrivals, I call out to him.

'Hey, Paoli! Where is the lovely daughter of the house, Chantal? Was that her name? I so much enjoyed meeting her last time.'

'Chantal has a headache and is lying down upstairs, but she

has promised to come down later.' Paoli looks rather pained himself. I am certain that he is lying, I don't know why.

'And where is our host, Maurice?'

'He is attending to Chantal.'

He continues, 'But let me introduce you to some of the other guests.'

'No need. Isn't that Christa Mannerling over there? I'll go and introduce myself.'

Nounourse positions himself against one of the walls and I move off towards Christa Mannerling. Christa (Freia in *Rheingold* and Brünnhilde in *Die Walküre*) has breasts like great sweating cheeses. Only a rich society could have produced all the fine quality meat that has been pumped into this lady's corset. I insert myself into the group of attentive listeners who have clustered round her. I have nothing to say to her. I just want to be quiet and inconspicuous in a group while I work out what my next move should be. I knew that getting in would be easy. Getting out will be difficult and has not been planned for. One shot fired inside the villa and the grounds will be alive with police and Maurice's gunmen. It may be a heaven-sent opportunity that Chantal lies on her bed upstairs where I may kill her silently.

In a moment then, when I see that Maurice is back down-stairs, I should slip away from this group of bores and make my way quietly up the stairs and then I should . . . and then . . . and then I will ease the door handle round and step silently into the room. Chantal will be lying on the bed in a long evening gown. On the bedside table will be the familiar crucifix and much-thumbed copy of *Le Hobbit*. Her eyes will widen when she sees me. I will show her the gun and tell her to strip. As soon as she has stepped out of her panties, she covers her breasts with her arms. An appealing gesture. Meat calls to meat. The gun falls disregarded from my hand on to the bedside table, but as I move forward to embrace her, she snatches up the pistol and points it triumphantly at me. I tell her to fire away. 'It's not loaded.'

'And what do you do. Monsieur . . . er . . .?' inquires Christa breaking into my reverie.

'Madame? I? I er . . . am in pharmaceuticals in Grenoble.'

'How interesting.'

'Well, it is kind of you to say so, Christa, but you don't look as though you mean it. Actually, it is interesting. I am the biggest man in pharmaceuticals in Grenoble. Remember the name – Rouge. And when I say I am the biggest in Grenoble, we are talking about big money here, a pre-tax turnover of around 2 billion francs. Have you ever heard of phylodoxidrine?'

She shakes her head.

'Very few of your sort of people ever have. But it is a very big seller, especially in Africa, very big in Africa, and it is the taxes on the growing sales of companies like mine which keep the opera and the army going in this part of the world.'

As I keep talking, I notice that Paoli and one of his henchmen have come over to join our group.

'I have to say though that I'm not sure that we really need an army out here. Speaking as a major tax-payer, I can tell you that it seems a disproportionate fiscal burden and, speaking as a big exporter to Africa, I can tell you that we have been pleasantly surprised how much our sales have shot up in our former colonies since independence. Under the old regime there were a lot of restrictive regulations that really were getting in the way of efficient pricing and distribution of our drugs. So the message is – the colonists can go and we can still clean up on the profits.'

Paoli looks murderous. I turn to face him directly.

'We see very good prospects in the Congo, now that the Belgians are pulling out. Generally, we see a lot of possibilities in the newly emergent nations of Africa . . . If my company's experience in Senegal is anything to go by, one can get away with murder in these People's Cannibal Republics. Well, not murder, but marketing contraceptives as virility pills and . . .'

Someone has started to play the 'Tarnhelm' motif from *Rheingold* on the piano and Christa drifts off in that direction. Paoli is whispering to his side-kick. The man has a vaguely military appearance. I prod the side-kick in the chest with my finger.

'One does not find the real buccaneers of our time in the ranks of the Foreign Legion or the Paratroops, for all their smartly tailored uniforms. No, indeed. Today's adventurers are going into the front line of the developing new technologies. Pharmaceuticals is one of them and I'm proud of my role in that industry.'

I am talking more and more loudly. But it is no use. They are not listening to me. I am effectively talking to myself. I return to my gin and to contemplation of the staircase – the murky ascent to the scaffold of a death-in-love summation – killed by the woman I love – effectively the auto-execution of the terrorist. Crap, all crap. I don't want to die. I am too useful to the revolution. If I do have a death wish, it takes the form of wishing all oppressors and collaborators were dead. But now, as I look around the room, it strikes me that these people had their chance with Hitler and Mussolini and they muffed it. As for neo-fascism, 'the first time as tragedy, the second time as farce'. Looking at the Children of Vercingetorix scattered round the room, I am struck more powerfully than before by their preposterous appearance. They are the amateurs of revolution. History is not travelling in their direction and in the deepest recesses of their shrivelled hearts they know it.

Atrocity is no longer the monopoly of the Junker and the Nazi and the owner of slaves and plantations. For, in my time, the politically mobilized working class and the freedom fighters of Africa and Asia have learned to make much more effective use of terrorism and torture than these played-out reactionaries ever could. And indeed the jokers in this room are not the real enemy. The real enemy is Monsieur Rouge, who is so big in pharmaceuticals in Grenoble, and his friend Monsieur Jaune, the technocrat in one of the Paris ministries, and Monsieur Bleu, the leader of the Farmer's Union, and Monsieur Vert, the Left Bank novelist they all read, and the vast mass of busy lawyers, doctors, publishers, journalists, librarians and undertakers who toil for the repressive democracies of the Western world. The structures of oppression are indeed diffuse and subtle.

It follows that Chantal is a glamorous irrelevance. I am getting out of here. I am not going to be redeemed by the love of a bad woman after all. I signal Nounourse over and together we confront Paoli.

'It has been wonderful talking to your guests. So sorry not to be able to thank our host, but we must be going now.'

'But you have only just arrived. I hope you are feeling all right?'

'I'm feeling fine – only just a little bored that's all. But thank you for having done me the honour of receiving me in the de Serkissian home.'

If Nounourse had not been standing beside me, I think Paoli might have declined to shake my proferred hand. I walk over to Christa Mannerling to say goodbye to her too. I offer to send her a free sample of my company's slimming pills. Then, 'Come on, Nounourse. Let's go.'

This winter the French lost the game in Algeria. In two years, three years at the most, they will be ceding independence and pulling out. I think that tomorrow I shall go down to the office of the Compagnie Transatlantique . . . I think we may go to Cuba – or perhaps the Congo.

'Find the umbrella, Nounourse.'

But Nounourse is blocking my way. I should have realized that he was going to be more trouble than he was worth.

'Captain Addict, I did not come here to drink fruit juice or to listen to your joking with your white friends.' Nounourse is whispering, but his thunderous whispering can surely be heard by Paoli and half the people in the room behind us. 'Are you a legionnaire or are you chicken? What is with you? Your Chantal must die and I came here to fix it for her. Now I am going to do it and you are going to help me do it. We go upstairs together now, or I shoot you dead here on the spot.'

There is no time and this is not the place for me to argue with Nounourse. I have only just understood myself how irrelevant killing her will be.

'Enough. Let's get out of here, Nounourse. Something is wrong. Where is Chantal? Where is Maurice? It all feels wrong.'

'We will find her upstairs and then we will kill her.'

So we stand, glaring at one another, when I hear a shout from behind me.

'Captain Roussel – that is you with the beard, isn't it? – it is I who ask you to stay.'

The shout has come from halfway across the room and the voice is that of Maurice. Paoli who had been standing with the door open for our exit now closes it again. The guests part between us and Maurice crooks his finger summoning us to him. We go towards him, but, before we are close, he gestures with his head towards the stair.

'You are needed up there. My daughter needs you now. Please, now go up.'

There is something in his voice I can't quite make out. Menacing, of course, but perhaps wheedling too?

'Go up. It seems that you are expected. In the name of God, hurry!'

I look at Nounourse. Is he in on this too? But he looks baffled and terrified. We ascend the staircase. Maurice and Paoli watch us from the foot of the stairs. Why don't they shoot us now? Or must it be done upstairs, out of sight of the guests? Indeed, there is a Corsican with a rifle at the head of the stairs and I see another, similarly armed, at the far end of the corridor. The nearer of the two guards inclines his head to us.

'Her bedroom is over there, but you must knock before you enter.' And he motions us past.

Clearly everything is wrong, but I see no way of walking out of this trap. Nounourse has lost his confidence and he makes me knock upon the door while he flattens himself against the wall and his head turns from one Corsican to the other. A strange mewing sound comes from beyond the door. I take it that we are to enter. The bedroom is mostly in darkness, but a table lamp illuminates something shaking under the blankets on the bed. Nounourse covers me with his gun while I walk over to strip the blanket away. The mewing noise redoubles in volume. It is made by the bloody thing on the bed, a body that is swathed in silk streaked in red. I cannot understand it. Raoul comes in from the bathroom and he says something to us, but I am not taking it in, for I am slowly coming to interpret and to understand what it is that I am looking at. Chantal's eyelids are fluttering up and down at a fantastic rate. I am looking at Chantal, but she does not look like Chantal.

'. . . and there is no point in talking to her. She can't talk back.' Raoul is in a sports jacket and he carries a gun, but he regards Nounourse with a friendly eye and it is clear that there will be no shoot-out in this room.

'Are those gumen still posted on the corridor? Is that really the party I hear downstairs? Incredible. You took your time. Who is this gorilla? I take it that he is your man? I've been here over three hours now, but I waited, certain that you would be coming. I told Maurice that I was sure that you would be coming and I told him – yes, I ordered him – to send you up when you came.'

Despite his casual dress, Raoul himself is far from casual. He is sweaty and he gabbles. The holes in his face seem to dilate. Nothing makes any sense to me. I go and sit down with my back against the wall. Then I ask him to explain himself.

'When we met on the quayside and you took my invitation card from me, it was not difficult for me to work out what you wanted it for and what you were going to do to Chantal. Then I began to reflect on Chantal and her values and then I thought about Anne Frank and her values. (I told you that I had been reading her *Diary*, didn't I?) Then I thought about your values and what you are trying to do in the world. Everything passed in a dream, as I came to examine my own values – prejudices, as I now regard them – and I realized that I had only been using sophistry to defend the interests of my class formation. Then I went back over the arguments we had at Laghouat and I realized that you were right about the labour theory of value! It was a wonderful moment for me. I now understand that labour cannot have two values, one for the labourer and one for the capitalist who employs him. (We are talking about the capitalist's margin of profit here, are we not?) As Engels says, "Turn and twist as we will, we cannot get out of this contradiction, as long as we speak of the purchase and sale of labour and the value of labour." No, what we should be talking about is the sale and purchase of labour *power*. Labour *power* –'

'Shut up, Raoul. Never mind all that. Tell me what you are doing here.'

Now Nounourse, who has been paying no attention to us but has been standing over the bed, looking down saucer-eyed at Chantal, raises his head, curious to see how this mad-man will explain himself. Raoul smiles at Nounourse and me, seeming to wish to offer us some faint reassurance.

'You are right, of course. However, the point is that every-thing follows from the labour theory of value. It is the lynch-pin of Marxist theory. Everything follows from that, as in a very beautifully constructed piece of –'

'Enough of that, Raoul.'

'I am simply trying to tell you that I am on your side. "Things are as they are and their consequences will be what they will be. Why then should we wish to be deceived?" Marxism is true and, as you should know, for me, if a thing is true, it is true to the limit. I now saw that forgiveness for Chantal was out of the question. She is the enemy and I also realized that I wanted to make contact with you again. There was only one place I could be sure that I would find you at. So I came here at the beginning of the evening and I brought a gun and a cut-throat razor with me. I have not killed her, for I thought we might need her to get out of this place. So here I have been these last three hours. We have been arguing, but I always had the gun on her. A bit like Laghouat really, but different.'

He laughs reminiscently.

'Occasionally I have had a little chat with Maurice and his men. As I say, I told him to expect you and let you through.'

Here Nounourse interrupts. Nounourse is having difficulty with all this.

'You have cut out her tongue?'

Raoul is looking at me for approval.

'She was talking that old fascist propaganda. She will never change. So just now I cut it out. I find that I no longer have my old nose for political debate. The tongue is a slippery thing to get hold of and it was a messier business than I expected. As you see, there is a lot of blood, but she is in no danger of dying. Anyway. I didn't want to hear more of her. I have long thought that there is such a thing as repressive tolerance and, as I see it now, freedom for her and her father and her father's friends to talk is freedom to talk their way into doing other people down. I don't want to hear any of the old siren songs. Imperialist and racist ideas do not deserve a voice. The time for debate is over. It is time to act!'

Nounourse's face lights up and, catching Nounourse's expression of approval, Raoul gestures grandly with the razor.

'Now, shall we make Cleopatra's nose shorter and change the face of the world?'

Nounourse has never heard of Cleopatra. As for me, I am not sure that I do approve. The ruthlessness, yes. But this melodramatic private vengeance, this posturing and all this over-excitement on the part of a new convert . . . His nervy jokes . . . I am not sure. But it hardly matters now. Raoul is right when he says that it is time to act.

'Forget it. How do we get out of here?'

'My car is outside. We walk out with Chantal. Very difficult for them with all these people around. I told Maurice not to cancel his little soirée. They will not dare touch us as long as we have her. We drive around until we have shaken any tail they put on us. After that I am not sure.'

'So let's get moving then.'

Raoul and I help Chantal get dressed, while Nounourse prudishly turns his back to us. She is shivering, very cold, but with a high feverish pulse. I kiss her firmly compressed lips. Raoul looks at me strangely, but there is nothing sexual in this kiss. I was never really in love with Chantal. That was not possible for me. Engels was right when he said, 'Sexual love in a man's relation to woman becomes and can become the rule among the oppressed class alone, among the proletarians.' I work for the love of the proletariat, but I know that I shall

202

never experience that love myself. I see things as they are. I kiss with my eyes open. I am kissing not a woman, but a mutilated figure, the embodiment of all the casualties that have happened and that will happen in this war in Algeria. Her eyes are wonderful nightmare eyes.

Raoul gets a cigarette out and alight in his lips. Nounourse is as amazed as I was by the effect of the smoke issuing out of Raoul's face. Then we hoist Chantal up. She will have to be helped to walk. Raoul and I each take an arm and, as we come out into the corridor, Nounourse brings up the rear, covering us with his gun. The Corsicans lay down their rifles and watch us walk by. One of them looks as though he is about to be sick. Down below I can hear someone playing 'The Cake Walk' on the piano. Normally, Maurice would not tolerate that 'black boogy-woogy, jigger-jigger music' in his house, but obviously he has other things on his mind now. I think that we shall go to the Congo. This moment has the quality of a dark dream, but I recognize our behaviour, the behaviour of all of us in this house, as a manifestation, one manifestation among many, of the bizarre and decadent features of the capitalist world in its dying throes. Surely Marx was right when he wrote that capitalism 'can just as easily turn the real, natural and essential powers of man into abstract ideas, as it can turn real imperfections and phantoms of the mind into essential powers and capacities'? As we descend the staircase the music stops.

FOR THE BEST IN PAPERBACKS, LOOK FOR THE

In every corner of the world, on every subject under the sun, Penguin represents quality and variety—the very best in publishing today.

For complete information about books available from Penguin—including Pelicans, Puffins, Peregrines, and Penguin Classics—and how to order them, write to us at the appropriate address below. Please note that for copyright reasons the selection of books varies from country to country.

In the United Kingdom: For a complete list of books available from Penguin in the U.K., please write to *Dept E.P., Penguin Books Ltd, Harmondsworth, Middlesex, UB7 0DA.*

In the United States: For a complete list of books available from Penguin in the U.S., please write to *Dept BA, Penguin, Box 120, Bergenfield, New Jersey 07621-0120.*

In Canada: For a complete list of books available from Penguin in Canada, please write to *Penguin Books Ltd, 2801 John Street, Markham, Ontario L3R 1B4.*

In Australia: For a complete list of books available from Penguin in Australia, please write to the *Marketing Department, Penguin Books Ltd, P.O. Box 257, Ringwood, Victoria 3134.*

In New Zealand: For a complete list of books available from Penguin in New Zealand, please write to the *Marketing Department, Penguin Books (NZ) Ltd, Private Bag, Takapuna, Auckland 9.*

In India: For a complete list of books available from Penguin, please write to *Penguin Overseas Ltd, 706 Eros Apartments, 56 Nehru Place, New Delhi, 110019.*

In Holland: For a complete list of books available from Penguin in Holland, please write to *Penguin Books Nederland B.V., Postbus 195, NL-1380AD Weesp, Netherlands.*

In Germany: For a complete list of books available from Penguin, please write to *Penguin Books Ltd, Friedrichstrasse 10-12, D-6000 Frankfurt Main 1, Federal Republic of Germany.*

In Spain: For a complete list of books available from Penguin in Spain, please write to *Longman, Penguin España, Calle San Nicolas 15, E-28013 Madrid, Spain.*

In Japan: For a complete list of books available from Penguin in Japan, please write to *Longman Penguin Japan Co Ltd, Yamaguchi Building, 2-12-9 Kanda Jimbocho, Chiyoda-Ku, Tokyo 101, Japan.*

FOR THE BEST IN PAPERBACKS, LOOK FOR THE

☐ **THE ELIZABETH STORIES**
   Isabel Huggan

Smart, stubborn, shy, and giving, Elizabeth discovers all the miseries, and some of the wonders, of childhood. These delightful stories, showing her steely determination throughout a series of disasters and misunderstandings, remind us that if growing up is hard, it can also be hilarious.

"Twists and rings in the mind like a particularly satisfying and disruptive novel"
— *The New York Times Book Review*
                    184 pages   *ISBN: 0-14-010199-3*   **$6.95**

☐ **FOE**
   J. M. Coetzee

In this brilliant reshaping of Defoe's classic tale of Robinson Crusoe and his mute slave Friday, J. M. Coetzee explores the relationships between speech and silence, master and slave, sanity and madness.

"Marvelous intricacy and almost overwhelming power . . . *Foe* is a small miracle of a book." — *Washington Post Book World*
                    158 pages   *ISBN: 0-14-009623-X*   **$6.95**

☐ **1982 JANINE**
   Alasdair Gray

Set inside the head of an aging, divorced, insomniac supervisor of security installations who hits the bottle in the bedroom of a small Scottish hotel, *1982 Janine* is a sadomasochistic, fetishistic fantasy.

"*1982 Janine* has a verbal energy, an intensity of vision that has mostly been missing from the English novel since D. H. Lawrence."
— *The New York Times*
                    346 pages   *ISBN: 0-14-007110-5*   **$6.95**

☐ **THE BAY OF NOON**
   Shirley Hazzard

An Englishwoman working in Naples, young Jenny has no friends, only a letter of introduction—a letter that leads her to a beautiful writer, a famous Roman film director, a Scottish marine biologist, and ultimately to a new life.

"Drawn so perfectly that it seems to breathe"
— *The New York Times Book Review*
                    154 pages   *ISBN: 0-14-010450-X*   **$6.95**

☐ **THE WELL**
   Elizabeth Jolley

Against the stark beauty of the Australian farmlands, Elizabeth Jolley paints the portrait of an eccentric, affectionate relationship between two women—Hester, a lonely spinster, and Katherine, a young orphan. Their simple, satisfyingly pleasant life is nearly perfect until a dark stranger invades their world in a most horrifying way.

"An exquisite story . . . Jolley [has] a wonderful ear, [and] an elegant and compassionate voice." — *The New York Times Book Review*
                    176 pages   *ISBN: 0-14-008901-2*   **$6.95**

FOR THE BEST IN PAPERBACKS, LOOK FOR THE

FOR THE BEST IN ·PAPERBACKS, LOOK FOR THE

☐ **THE NEWS FROM IRELAND**
William Trevor

This major collection of short stories once again shows Trevor's extraordinary power. In the title story, his evocation of the anguished relations of an Anglo-Irish family through several generations approaches the dramatic and forceful effect of a full novel.

"Trevor is perhaps the finest short story writer in the English language." — *Vanity Fair*   *286 pages*   *ISBN: 0-14-008857-1*   **$6.95**

☐ **THE SHRAPNEL ACADEMY**
Fay Weldon

At a military school named for the inventor of the exploding cannonball, perhaps it should come as no surprise when the annual Eve-of-Waterloo dinner, for which the guest list includes a young weapons salesman and a reporter for a feminist newspaper, hilariously and spontaneously combusts.

"This is Fay Weldon's funniest novel . . . an original, unconventional comedy." — *San Francisco Chronicle*
           186 pages   *ISBN: 0-14-009746-5*   **$6.95**

☐ **SAINTS AND STRANGERS**
Angela Carter

In eight dazzling, spellbinding stories, Angela Carter draws on familiar themes and tales—Peter and the Wolf, Lizzie Borden, *A Midsummer Night's Dream*—and transforms them into enchanting, sophisticated, and often erotic reading for modern adults.

"Whimsical, mischievous, and able to work magic . . . Carter's stories disorient and delight." — *Philadelphia Inquirer*
           126 pages   *ISBN: 0-14-008973-X*   **$5.95**

☐ **IN THE SKIN OF A LION**
Michael Ondaatje

Through intensely visual images and surreal, dreamlike episodes, Michael Ondaatje spins a powerful tale of fabulous adventure and exquisite sensuality set against the bridges, waterways, and tunnels of 1920s Toronto.

"A brilliantly imaginative blend of history, lore, passion, and poetry" — Russell Banks   *244 pages*   *ISBN: 0-14-011309-6*   **$7.95**

☐ **THE GUIDE: A NOVEL**
R. K. Narayan

Raju was once India's most corrupt tourist guide; now, after a peasant mistakes him for a holy man, he gradually begins to play the part. He succeeds so well that God himself intervenes to put Raju's new holiness to the test.

"A brilliant accomplishment" — *The New York Times Book Review*
           220 pages   *ISBN: 0-14-009657-4*   **$5.95**